THE SWORD AND THE CROSS CHRONICLES

DEVOTION

OLIVIA RAE

DEVOTION

Please Note
This is a work of fiction. Names, characters, places and incidents
are either the product of the author's imagination or are used
fictitiously, and any resemblance to any actual persons living or
dead, business establishments, events or locales is entirely
coincidental.

For information, please contact:
oliviarae.books@gmail.com

Cover Design by Kim Killion, The Killion Group, Inc.
Interior Formatting by Author E.M.S.

Bible Passages are from the King James Version

Published in the United States of America.

Books by Olivia Rae

The Sword and the Cross Chronicles

SALVATION

REVELATION

REDEMPTION

RESURRECTION

ADORATION

DEVOTION

Contemporary Inspirational

JOSHUA'S PRAYER

Coming Soon!

A LIFE NOT TAKEN
(Secrets of the Queens, Book 1)

Contact Olivia at
Oliviarae.books@gmail.com

For news and sneak peeks of upcoming novels visit:

Oliviaraebooks.com

Facebook.com/oliviaraeauthor

For my sister, Mary,
Always seek the good even in the bad times.

And to the glory of God

Prologue

But they hearkened not, nor inclined their ear,
but walked in the counsels and in the imagination
of their evil heart, and went backward, and not forward.
Jeremiah 7:24

England, Near the Southern Coast,
Rockbridge Castle, June 1199

THE HARD CLUNK OF A STONE AGAINST THE CASTLE wall just below Rose's window signaled the time had come. Finally. Freedom. She threw a cloak around her shoulders and gazed about her childhood room one more time. This had been her sanctuary, and now her prison. No woman should live under a man's control for seventeen summers, but her father couldn't let her go. She should have been wed years ago, so now she would take matters into her own hands.

Another stone hit the sill and bounced into the middle of her room. She took a deep breath. A warm breeze swirled around her face when she poked her head out of the window. There below she could see Conrad's golden head glistening like a bright star in the moonlight. Her savior had come.

"Let's go," he said, flashing a bright smile. "We must hurry. We have to make it to the coast within the hour."

"One moment, Conrad."

She cast one more glance around her room and at her tattered rag bunny sitting on her pallet. Her father had made

1

Bit the day after her mother had died. The worn rabbit had been her companion through most of the trials and storms of her life, but that was the past. Conrad would laugh at her if she brought the ragtag animal. Besides, she was a woman now, and women didn't need toys to soothe their woes. They had their husbands' strong and muscular arms to keep away the night terrors. She gave up a simple prayer. *Heavenly Father, Bless my dear Conrad and make our journey swift and safe.* She then tossed the long rope out the window.

Conrad's calm and confident words coached her down the castle wall and into his arms. He pressed a hard kiss to her lips that tripled the speed of her heart. Soon. Oh, so very soon she would be Lady Rose de Laval. Conrad's wife. He grabbed the satchel from her hands and secured it to the back of his mount before he lifted her to a grey mare.

"We must make haste. The ship will not wait for us, and I fear your father suspects something is amiss. His eyes were ever on me at dinner." Conrad hoisted himself onto the large destrier and glanced back at the dark castle.

"Nay, that is not the case. He had quite a bit to drink this eve. I am sure he suspects nothing and is fast asleep." Rose flashed a warm smile at her beloved.

But the wary look on Conrad's face spoke his doubt. He kicked his mount in the sides and took off toward the sea. She did the same, for freedom was but an hour away.

They rode in silence, and only the hard pounding of the horses' hooves on the rigid earth could be heard. The sharp salt air teased her nostrils and warmed her blood. A crash of waves against the shoreline told her they were close. She tossed a glance at her love, but he did not send a reassuring look her way; his eyes were fixed on the single lantern that swayed on the distant ship's bow.

At the rocky cliff, Conrad jumped from his horse and lifted her off the mare's back. "Not long now, my love," Conrad cooed. "Soon we will be together forever."

They grabbed their few belongings before heading down the stony path to the waiting rowboat below. They were almost there. Rose closed her eyes and sent up another prayer. *Thank you, Lord. Thank you for answering my prayer by giving me my beloved.*

She opened her eyes too late and stubbed her toe on a protruding rock. Rose stumbled down the treacherous path, yet Conrad wouldn't pause. "Careful," he warned. "Or all this will be for naught."

She tried to adjust her steps to the steep path as it switched back and forth until, by the grace of God, they made it to the beach. They ran to the rowboat, the soft sand seeping into her slippers.

"Where ya been?" a gruff sailor asked Conrad before flipping a blurry eye her way.

"My lady was a bit timid. But all is well now."

A pang of hurt skipped over her heart at Conrad's terse and degrading comment, but the hurt disappeared when he flashed her another breathtaking smile. She took his offered hand and stepped into the rowboat before the sailor and Conrad pushed it into the sea. As they moved closer to the larger ship, the warm summer air turned cool and brisk. Rose shifted her gaze back to the shoreline, back to her home. Someday she would return when her father's anger had subsided. When he would finally accept Conrad as his son-in-law. Her father couldn't stay angry at her forever. He never could.

The rowboat bumped against the hull of the ship, and Rose was guided to a rope ladder where she made her way onto the English cog. Soon she and Conrad would be in Normandy, far from her father's grasp. The moment her feet hit the deck, she wondered if she had made the right decision. A foul stench drifted up from the hold, making her gag. In the moonlight, Rose could feel the sailors' hungry gazes upon her. She clutched the front of her cloak and edged back toward the rail.

From behind, Conrad placed his hands on her shoulders and whispered in her ear, "We've made it, Rose. Is that not wonderful?"

Wonderful? Aye, it should be. She had dreamed of this moment for so long, but now that it was here, no joy infused her body. Instead, twinges of regret began to seep into every crevice, every organ, and every bone. What would her father do when he found out she had left? Conrad believed her father would forgive her as he always had when she would stretch her boundaries. But standing on this swaying deck amidst a group of unsavory sailors, Rose began to doubt her rash decision. She turned her head away when Conrad tried to kiss her cheek.

He slowly turned her around. 'Twas then she saw a fleeting hardness in his gaze. A shiver went through her body, and his features softened. He raised a hand and let his fingers trail gently down her cheek. "You're frightened, aren't you? Don't worry. I won't let anything happen to you." He placed a protective arm around her shoulders. "Come. I have arranged for us to have the captain's quarters on this journey. It isn't as nice as your chamber at Rockbridge Castle"—he gave her shoulder a squeeze—"but we will have each other to keep away the drafty sea air."

His lewd remark sent a chill cascading down her spine. Surely he didn't think they would…before they were wed? But before she could give word to her thoughts, he led her to the captain's door.

Conrad gave a swift knock before lifting the latch. "We made it, Augustus."

But Augustus was not sitting in the captain's chair, no, not at all. There sat the man she had known all her life. The man she had loved and at times hated.

"Hello, Rosemond. Did you enjoy your little excursion?" A wide grin split his lips. "Sir Conrad should have paid Augustus a few more coins to keep his loyalty. The man and I go way back. Besides, my purse is larger."

Her throat became as dry as a rotting fish on a bleached beach. How could he humiliate Conrad so? Tears of anger welled up in her eyes and spilled over her cheeks, yet her words wouldn't come.

"Lord de Payne, your daughter and I—"

In a flash, her father flew out of the chair and held his sword to Conrad's throat. "Speak not to me, boy. For I know what plan you whittled in that wooden head of yours. We shall discuss this later, at the castle." Her father motioned with his chin to his guards. "Take my daughter home."

The stiffness in her throat fled, and her screams filled the air. "Conrad... Conrad..." Not once did he even look her way, his hard gaze remained on the devil. Her father.

The edge of the sun peeked out over the horizon, and the birds chirped loudly in yonder trees; however, the beauty of the early day was lost on Rose as she sat on her pallet hugging Bit close to her. Two guards stood outside her door. Now, in truth, she was a prisoner. She thought to escape through the window again, but the long rope had disappeared and a few knights stood below her window. Indeed, her father had taken every precaution to ensure she would stay put.

All night long voices rang out in the hall below, yet she could not make out a single word. Surely Conrad would not leave until he had gained her father's approval. Finally, the door scraped open, and Rose flew through the entry before the guards could draw another breath. She flew down the stairs and raced into the hall only to come to an abrupt halt when she saw her father and Conrad standing by the hearth.

"Ah, there she is. Come, come, my dear. Take a seat." Her father motioned to a stiff-back chair near the hearth where a few embers glowed.

Rose turned an askance eye toward her beloved, but Conrad quickly looked away. With slow cautious steps, she walked to the offered chair.

"Why do you look so glum, Rosemond? Sir Conrad and I have come to an agreement."

Rose's pulse quickened and heart began to blossom with hope. She looked to Conrad, but he kept his gaze fixed on the wall over her head. Could he not give her a hint as to what was decided?

With a clearing of the throat, her father drew her attention. A small curl of his lips sent Rose's heart to the dungeons. Nay, Conrad would fight for her. He loved her. A glance in his direction did not give Rose the assurance she desired. He still held his gaze on the blasted wall.

Her father clasped his hands behind his back and shifted his gaze back and forth like a preying beast deciding if she or Conrad would be the next to be devoured. "Sir Conrad, don't you have something to say to my daughter?"

In that moment, Conrad turned white and his jaw clenched. His golden gaze finally rested on her. However, it did not hold the warmth and desire that had captured her heart last fall. These topaz eyes were filled with anger, disgust, and, worst of all, defeat. "Lady Rosemond, I withdraw any claims I have made to you. They were foolishly spoken." He dipped his head. "Forgive me."

"Nay." She shot to her feet. "Do not let him do this to us." She waved a hand to her father.

But Conrad did naught but shake his head.

She rushed over and grabbed his hands in hers. "Conrad, I love you. I will always love you. Do not listen to him. I will go anywhere with you. I do not care if he disowns me."

Conrad patted her hand and then gently pulled his hand away. "Forgive me for hurting you so, but I have no desire to wed you." With that, Conrad threw back his shoulders, gave her his back, and strode from the hall, ignoring her anguishing pleas and cries.

The slam of the large wooden door reverberated through her chest and shattered her heart. Nothing. There was nothing left. All that she was, and all that she would ever be, went with Conrad.

"Rosemond," her father said softly. "I am very sorry. In time, you will see God has been merciful to you."

Dazed, Rose turned to her father. His features wobbled, and she struggled to maintain focus. He gave her a tender smile as if that would fix all. A heat burned through the darkness in her chest and infused the shards that used to be her heart. White-hot anger coursed through her veins and exploded from her body in a violent shake.

She gritted her teeth and raised a fist to her father. "Don't you dare talk to me about God's mercy. For neither you nor He cares what happens to me or cared what happened to Mother. As far as I am concerned, you both can go to the devil!"

One

"For a friend of mine in his journey is come to me, and I have nothing to set before him?"
Luke 11:6

England, Crosswind Keep, September 1202

"MAKE HA...HASTE, O GOD, TO DE...DE...LIV...ER, deliver me, O Lord." Theo de Born let out a heavy breath and sighed. Only four more verses to go.

"That is wonderful. Your reading is getting better and better. I can tell you have been practicing," Lady Catherine encouraged as she pointed to the next verse on the parchment.

Theo rolled his shoulders and took another deep breath. "Let them be a...ash...am...ed, ashamed and con...con... founded that seek after my soul: let them be turned back... ward, and put to con...con...fu, confu, confu..." He pulled a hand through his long hair and slammed his fist on the table. "Ah, it is no use. I shall never be able to master these words. Why could not the monks have developed a language where one symbol meant one word? These words are all a confusion."

"Ah, that's the word." Lady Catherine smiled, and her deep blue eyes grew merry.

"What?"

Again, she looked down at the parchment and pointed to the frustrating word. "Confusion. That is what this word is. 'And put to confusion, that desire my hurt.'"

The words just rolled from her mouth, while he stumbled and tripped over every letter.

Lady Catherine reached out and squeezed his hand. "And the monks did not write these words. They are God's words that our monks have translated from Latin just for you and me. Though if the Church knew these were given to us, there would be hell to pay. For sacred words were not meant to be given to knights and certainly not to women."

How true. Even the great Lady Catherine de Maury would be scorned by the Church for such a practice. Crosswind Keep had been in the de Maury family for many years until the eldest son, Julian, gave all to the Knights Templar when he joined their order. The only stipulation, that his mother, Lady Catherine de Maury, could live out her life at Crosswind. Julian went crusading, and when he returned, he gave up the order and traveled north with his wife, Ariane.

But Lady Catherine remained and made her home with a handful of the more scholarly Templars. An oddity, indeed, since most of the order were warrior monks. Even though these monks owned Crosswind, Lady Catherine was still clearly in charge. She cajoled the monks into translating parts of scripture so she could learn to read and write better. And it was these skills she now tried to teach to Theo.

"Aye, well, I know. I should be grateful. Oh how I wish I had taken the Church as my profession instead of the sword. If I had, I would know these words and not be the broken mess you see before you." Theo carefully pulled his hair over the right side of his face, covering his scars.

Gently, Lady Catherine brushed back his locks and gazed at his full face. "You are a beautiful man. Your heart is strong and filled with loyalty and love. I fear Hugh would still be a shell of a man had you not challenged him for Lady Eleanor's hand."

She spoke of her second son. But Theo did not ask Lady Eleanor to marry him because he wanted to save Hugh de Maury from his mundane life. Theo wanted the woman for himself...and the land that came with her. Truly God did have a sense of humor for, in a twist of fate, he had gotten the small manor anyway, minus the woman.

"Aye. Hugh and Eleanor are a good match. I am also grateful they have given me Taine Manor, but none of these things I have earned. I intend to pay them back, if they want the coin or not. If only I could make Taine Manor viable again, but the land is sparse and the manor is in need of so many repairs."

"Hugh and Eleanor would be happy to help."

Theo's gut rolled. "Nay. I have taken enough from them. I'll not take more. Surely I am capable of doing something."

Her eyes filled with the pity he loathed. He did not want her or anyone else to feel sorry for him. Falling off the battlement at Château du Vent Doux had maimed his body, but it did not destroy his soul or his spirit. He wanted to do something with his life, and since the sword was no longer an option, he had to use his smarts or, in this case, the lack thereof.

"Do not be so hard on yourself. You have only been at this for a short time. Plus, I only see you but once a month. Most who learn this skill practice daily." Lady Catherine turned her gaze back to the parchment. "Now then, should we continue?"

Ah, he truly was dense. She did not pity him because of his disfigurement. She pitied him because he was thick in the head. He took a heavy swallow, wet his lips, and continued, "Let them be turned back for a re…reward of their shame that say, Aha, aha." Theo paused and wrinkled his brow. "I care not what my enemies say. Nor what they think."

Lady Catherine leaned back in her chair. "Do you have a lot of enemies, Theo?"

Not anymore. No one considered a lame man an enemy. He shook his head.

"Then quit stalling and finish your reading."

He squinted and leaned over the parchment again. "Let all those who seek thee rejoice and be glad in thee: and let such as love thy sal…salva…salva…"

"*Shen*. The end of the word is *shen*. Salvation. You are doing well, finish up the rest."

Theo glanced back at the words but shook his head and pointed. "I have not a clue what that says."

With a bend of the head, Lady Catherine peered down at the words. "Thy salvation say continually, Let God be magnified."

"Why do they not just say, God be praised? Must they always use different words? What is wrong with these monks?"

Lady Catherine folded her hands in her lap and tapped her thumbs together. She tilted her head; a sharp smile creased her lips. "I believe this was written by King David. He loved the Lord so much he found many ways to praise Him."

"Nonetheless, I believe shorter is better."

"Shorter. What do you mean?"

Theo cleared his throat and let his gaze settle on the parchment. "Shorter words. These are so long," he said quietly.

The fall winds battered the wooden roof, causing the beams to creak. The chill in the air intensified when Lady Catherine said naught but stared at him as if he were a branchless tree. Suddenly her laughter filled the hall and echoed off the rafters.

"Oh, Theo. I do so miss your humor when you are not here."

He could feel his cheeks warm like a young lad after his first kiss. "My lady, I do not jest. It is the long words I trip and stumble over."

She placed her delicate fingers on his hand once more. "Indeed. They are many, but you will improve. Just keep practicing. Here, we shall read this last verse together."

Lady Catherine placed a finger below the words, and together they began to read. "But I am poor and needy." He stumbled, but she pushed on. "Make haste unto me, O God: thou art my help and my deliverer; O Lord, make no tarrying."

"Thank goodness that is done." Theo beamed.

With deft fingers, Lady Catherine rolled up the parchment and handed it to him. "Practice this." She then reached over and pulled out another. "And Psalm fifty-eight too."

A loud groan floated from Theo's lips. "Not that one again. It is so long."

"Do you wish to master this skill or not, Sir Theodore?" Her tone and her formality signaled that she had had enough of his complaining.

"Aye, I do. I am sorry. It is just very tedious work for me."

She handed him the parchments, then pursed her lips. Theo squirmed under her intense gaze.

"We may only be able to have one more lesson before winter is upon us," she said, leaning back in her chair.

How well he knew it. Given the severity of his injuries, traveling here each month was difficult enough in the summer months, but when winter set in, coming here by cart could be treacherous. Not to mention how the simple aches of his body would deepen when the winter winds grew bitter.

Lady Catherine held her penetrating stare as she began to drum her fingers on the arms of her chair. "And sometimes the spring rains keep you away also."

Why would she speak of what he already knew? "If you tire of teaching me—"

"Nay, that is not it at all. I am just wondering"—she paused and narrowed her gaze—"how much faster you would progress in your studies if you could be taught daily?"

What was she trying to say? His spirit sank. He knew the answer. It would take him years before he mastered the art of reading. By then he could be an old man...an old crippled man. Perhaps there was no point to his life after all. Slowly, he placed the parchments on the table. "Mayhap there is no need for me to take these."

Lady Catherine slapped the arms of her chair and rolled her eyes. "Oh, do stop with the tragedy. I am not suggesting that you stop learning altogether. I am suggesting that you get instruction all year long."

Surely she didn't expect him to stay here permanently. To give up Taine Manor. Nay. The place wasn't much, but it was his home. He pressed his lips together and straightened in his chair. "I cannot move here. I have a manor to run."

With a huff, Lady Catherine let her gaze roam around the hall as if she were looking for another parchment of words to recite. "That is not what I am saying. I think we should find someone to stay with you at Taine Manor."

She jested. Yet she did not smile. "What scholar or monk would give up their comforts here to come and live at a drafty old manor in need of much repair?" Theo shook his head. "Nay. You cannot force one of these men to do so, for in their bitterness they will become a poor teacher."

"I am not talking about one of the monks. I am speaking of someone else."

Discomfort rested between his shoulder blades. Certainly she knew he was a man of modest means. He could not afford to hire a teacher. Why, 'tis the very conversation they had when she had offered her services in the first place. Unless she meant to take the burden of payment on herself.

A flush of humiliation burned and shook his insides. He looked to the floor and took a deep breath before meeting her gaze. "My lady. You know this is not possible. The expense would be a great burden. I'll not take a single coin which should go to the upkeep of Taine Manor. Nor will I take anything from yo—"

"Again, you misunderstand. I have an idea that will cost you or me nothing." Her eyes glowed and sparkled.

Suspicion grew in his gut. What cost nothing usually came at a heavy price. "What do you mean?" he asked cautiously.

"A fortnight ago, I was visiting the Benedictine Nuns in Godstow."

Did she not have enough religion among these walls that she desired to seek out more? "Do you visit there often?"

13

She paused briefly as if the question were a deep puzzlement. "I was there because a friend asked me to visit."

Who stuck in his throat, but she carried on.

"There is a young lady there. Not a novice. But she is living there all the same."

Not unusual. Many wives were sent away to convents, not all were expected to become a bride of Christ if the husband might want them back. But none of this had anything to do with his education. However, Lady Catherine continued her tale.

"This woman has been there for almost three years, and well...she is not happy at all."

The twisted muscles in Theo's right thigh began to ache. He really needed to stand, but he didn't want to be rude and disrupt Lady Catherine's story. "Perhaps you should tell her husband," Theo said briskly.

Perplexity blinked in Lady Catherine's eyes. "Nay. She is not married. Just very strong-willed."

Now he understood. "Ah, she is a termagant, and her father hopes the nuns will be able to teach her discipline and humility."

Lady Catherine slowly nodded her head. "Aye, but it has been difficult."

Theo chuckled. "The lady will not be gelded." He realized his error, for a woman wasn't a horse or a male. "I mean—"

"I know what you mean," Lady Catherine rushed on. "She is quite bright and quite intelligent."

The uneasiness crept back into his body.

"Her father was very diligent, and especially so after the girl lost her mother."

"He spoiled her."

"She was his only child."

Theo shrugged.

"He taught her many things. Things only a man usually knows."

The discomfort in his leg disappeared as it shifted upward

and expanded in his chest. "Lady, what are you trying to tell me?"

Lady Catherine cleared her throat and looked down at her lap. "She knows how to read and write."

His chair clattered backward and hit the floor as Theo struggled to his feet. "You cannot mean—"

"She has better skills than I." Lady Catherine stood and lifted her chin. "She could teach you much."

Theo raised his shaking hands as if they were a shield from her words. "Nay. I'll not take on some other man's burden."

"The nuns cannot handle her, and her father will not take her back until she has learned her place."

"Nay. I will not."

"She will die there. She needs hope."

"Nay," he roared.

"God has taught us to take on each other's burdens. You of all people should know this." Lady Catherine took a step forward, and he could feel his defenses begin to crack.

He tried to mortar up his resistance. "She may not want to come. I'll not force her."

"Of course, she won't want to come. She wants to be free to live her own life. To do as she pleases. But we all know this is not a woman's world and may never be. She must learn to be more subtle in her desires."

The cryptic words that Lady Catherine uttered made Theo wonder if they were discussing the same thing. "If she is strong-willed, she will not be a good teacher."

"Mayhap not. But you will not know unless you give her a try."

Theo bent over and picked the chair off the floor and used it to brace his stance. "Her father will never approve."

"He already has." Lady Catherine's words were soft and almost inaudible. Her gaze pinned on Theo.

He tightened his grip on the back of the chair, feeling a few splinters of wood pierce his palms. "This is why you went to the abbey? To find me a teacher?"

"Nay. Baron Walter de Payne asked me to check on the girl, so I did. The idea didn't come to me until afterward. I sent my thoughts with what I saw at the abbey. We both believe a change of scenery might improve her attitude."

Baron Walter de Payne was one of the richest and most influential men in England. Some even believed he could be more powerful than King John. Theo gritted his teeth. All the more reason for him to bow out of this disastrous scheme. "Does not the baron worry about his daughter's reputation? I am a single man."

Lady Catherine's eyes softened, and without a single word, she had answered his question.

Theo rubbed the back of his neck with his left hand. "Aye, no one would believe the lady's reputation would be tarnished by the likes of me. Still. This will not work."

"Do not be so hasty on your decision." Lady Catherine picked up the parchments in one hand and then looped her other arm through his as they walked to the hall entry. "If given a choice between the abbey and your home, she is open to your offer."

Theo stopped and could sense the snare before him. "Offer? I made no such offer."

At least Lady Catherine had the decency to blush. "Our offer. She was open to our offer."

A slow burn began in Theo's gut and slithered to his spinning head. In the name of the Almighty, what was going on here?

"Baron de Payne has already spoken to his daughter, and she has willfully accepted. Surely you do not wish to turn her down now?"

Without a step, he had walked right into the trap. Who in their right mind would turn down Baron Walter de Payne? Theo took a hard swallow. "When? When will she arrive?" he croaked.

"Why, I imagine within a fortnight. I do hope that is not too soon." Lady Catherine continued to guide him to the door.

A fortnight of freedom. He squeezed the parchments in his left hand.

"Now, promise me this year you will come to the fall festival. It is such fun. I do believe Lady Rosemond would enjoy it."

"Who?" Theo squeaked.

"Lady Rosemond de Payne, the baron's daughter."

"Ah, but—"

"Do try to make this work, Theo." Lady Catherine opened the door and gave him a hug before passing him off to his traveling companion, Daniel.

The lad helped him down the stone steps to the bailey. Theo opened his mouth in one last effort to change the outcome of this conversation. "Still, I—"

"Godspeed," Lady Catherine called from the hall entry. She waved and then promptly closed the hall door.

Somewhat dazed, Theo turned and fixed his gaze past Crosswind's gate at the road ahead of him. *Godspeed. Just what type of journey did Lady Catherine place him on?*

Two

God setteth the solitary in families:
he bringeth out those which are bound with chains:
but the rebellious dwell in dry land.
Psalm 68:6

"HEAVENS," ROSE GASPED AS SHE TOOK IN THE dilapidated manor house before her. The journey had been long and arduous. This is what she had earned for every bump and bruise she received while traveling to this desolate place. The manor, if it could be called such, was the most pathetic keep she had ever seen. Well, not quite. It was a mite better than Godstow. Anything was better than Godstow. At least here a bunch of nuns wouldn't be chanting and praying, and she wouldn't have to scrub the floors all day.

However, Rose couldn't help being disheartened by the dreary scene before her. A few wattle-and-daub huts stood outside a crumbling stone and wooden wall that circled the manor. The wooden gate had gaping holes large enough for a small lad to fit through. She cringed just thinking about what she might find within these walls.

"Are you sure this is the right manor?" Rose asked.

Percival, the nuns' mute servant, nodded his head.

"Aye, this is it. Not much to look at, but I am sure they have a warm fire and that is all my old bones need." Sister Mary Ella shifted in the back of the cart, pulling a coverlet tight about her. "Consider yourself fortunate. You do not have to journey back with us."

True, but still… The nuns tried to hide their exuberance when word had come that Rose had been offered another place to live. Her father's terms had been clear: go to Taine Manor or rot at the abbey. Well, he did not quite use those words, but that was the implication. As assurance, Percival was sent along to make sure she would arrive safely. In truth, he was to make sure she didn't run away. Sister Mary Ella came along as chaperone. Though she rarely opened her eyes to keep watch as she slept most of the way in the back of the cart.

Percival slapped the donkey's back, and the cart jerked forward. Rose winced as he managed to hit every rut from here to the entry. The ancient gate creaked open and offered a dismal view of her new residence. The manor was the oddest thing she had ever seen. A square stone structure covered in moss loomed in the middle of the courtyard. A makeshift wooden tower with exposed stairs was attached to its side. To the left was a rickety stable where the nicker of horses drifted on the cool fall breeze. There were few servants and even less knights. The whole place seemed so eerie that Rose expected ghosts to float out of the tower arrow slits.

Percival lifted her from the cart and then went to help Sister Mary Ella. A chorus of bleating drew Rose's attention to a well-groomed shed where a secure wooden fence housed what had to be at least ten goats. What madness was this that the goats held the best place in the manor?

Rose had not taken a step when the manor house door burst open and a spry middle-aged woman with a round jolly face rushed forward. "Welcome. Welcome to Taine Manor. We have been happily waiting for you." She came up to Rose and gave her a hug as if she were a long-lost relative. The woman turned her merry green eyes to a lad who could not be more than fifteen summers. "Daniel, do help that man with Lady Rosemond's things."

Things? She had next to nothing. The nuns had confiscated most of her gowns and all of her fine jewels.

They even took her mother's small silver cross. Nonetheless, Rose held her tongue and followed the woman up the worn stone steps into a very dark and dank hall.

Near the right wall stood a simple stone hearth where Sister Mary Ella quickly commandeered the only close stool. Snug against the left wall sat a few worn trestle tables and several benches. By the hearth, behind a long wooden screen, was the kitchen in need of major repairs. A number of broken stools were scattered about, and a few worn tapestries covered the walls. The place may have been sparsely furnished, but clean rushes covered the floor. The manor wasn't dirty, just old.

"I know it is not much, but we aim to make it as cheery as possible." Agatha beamed.

Rose glanced around the hall again, noting the lack of servants. "I have learned to make do with less, Mistress…"

"Gracious me. I forgot to introduce myself. I am Agatha Howard. The boy you saw outside is my son, Daniel. You will find there are few who still reside at Taine Manor. Most left after Lady Eleanor de Taine married Sir Hugh de Maury. Lord Leonard de Taine, Eleanor's uncle, God rest his soul, lost interest in the place as he got older. Everything, except for his goats." Agatha shrugged. "But I am sure in time Sir Theodore will return this place to the fine home it used to be." The wrinkles in Mistress Agatha's forehead bespoke her doubts.

Rose had her misgivings as well. The manor stood very close to a vast swampy wetland and was sparse of fine fields to farm. Clearly this place was built by a lesser lord who yearned for any land to call his own. Some said it was the same for the present owner. As if the thought would conjure up the man himself, Rose's gaze slid to the back of the hall where a wooden door led to another chamber.

"What lies back there?" Rose asked.

Agatha's smile faltered, and she clasped her hands in front of her. "That is Sir Theodore's solar."

"Of course." Again, Rose scanned the hall; there was not another door about. A warm heat spread through the pit of her stomach when she saw the pallets spread out in the corners. Surely they did not expect her to…

Agatha cleared her throat. "Your room is in the tower, my lady. Outside the hall."

Rose chuckled. A jest. Yet the paleness of Agatha's features held no merriment. "You are serious?" An evident pause followed by a quick nod gave Rose her answer.

"You will be pleasantly surprised once you see it. You have a nice view of the fen, and though the walls are wood, Sir Theodore has placed a heavy layer of mud between the planks to keep out the cool night air." Agatha gestured to the hall entry. "Come, let us take a look."

Marvelous. She would spend the winter in a drafty old tower overlooking a swamp. Mayhap this was worse than her cell at Godstow. Rose let her gaze slip back to the solar once again. Why would he not give her his cozy chamber? An honorable man would. "Where is Sir Theodore de Born?"

Agatha's gaze darted to the solar. "You will meet him later." She gestured to the hall entry. "Come. Let me show you your new chamber."

With every step Rose took upon the creaky, wooden stairs, the fall winds seemed to grow stronger. "Why were these stairs not placed inside the tower? Enemies from afar could easily kill any defending knights this way."

Agatha chuckled. "In all my years, I have never seen anyone attack Taine Manor. Lord Leonard de Taine used to say, 'The land is not worth the fight.'"

The former owner was indeed correct. Not even the Church would want this piece of Godforsaken land. And the Church seemed to want everything. Rose gripped the railing. At least, new planks replaced old weathered boards, and the railing had been reinforced. If she ever fell to her death, it would not be through a piece of cracked wood.

At the top, Agatha fumbled with the lock before she pushed open the door. She stepped in and motioned with her hand. "Come in. See, it is very delightful."

Rose crossed the threshold and was greeted by Daniel attempting to build a fire in a tall iron brazier, which resembled those in ancient Roman homes. Her gaze darted to a raised pallet piled with coverlets, then traveled to an arrow slit where light filtered in and rested on a narrow table with one lone chair. She had been wrong. Her cell in Godstow had been better.

Agatha fluffed up the coverlets. "I know it is not much, especially for a fine lady as yourself, but it can be quite cozy. Lady Eleanor spent many a happy hour in here."

A great fire began to roar in the brazier, filling the room with smoke. Daniel shoveled in more peat and began fanning the flames. All this did naught but make the situation worse. "Mayhap I should have moved this closer to the slit," he said, blushing.

Rose coughed as the smoke filled her lungs and smarted her eyes. She raised the hem of her cloak to cover her nose. "I cannot stay here," she cried and flew down the stairs. At the bottom, she coughed and gagged until her lungs were clear.

Agatha followed, calling to an aged knight, who took his good-natured time crossing the courtyard and climbing up the stairs.

"Dang fool boy," he muttered. "I should have done it myself."

A loud sneeze pierced the air. Agatha fixed a tight smile on her face. "Mayhap we should wait in the hall until Sir Rupert has taken care of the situation."

"You can tell Sir Theodore I'll not stay in there." On that, Rose raised her chin and the hem of her gown and strolled past the gaping Agatha. Better they all learn now she was not Lady Eleanor, who sheepishly accepted whatever she was given.

In the hall, Rose pulled out a bench, folded her hands in her lap, and sat. Her back ramrod straight.

Agatha entered, twisting her hands in her bliaut, her face almost translucent. From the hearth, Sister Mary Ella cackled, which quickly turned into a raspy cough. The old nun cleared her throat and turned her watery eyes to Agatha. "May God give you His strength, for you will need it now that Lady Rosemond is here."

And there Rose sat and sat while Agatha and a few other servants went about their duties. Oh, she was offered a cool drink and a bit of cheese, but naught else. She might as well have been a block of hard wood. After all, she did smell like a burnt timber. Sister Mary Ella's chest rose and fell as loud snores bounced off the hall walls. Since God had deserted her the day her father forced Conrad to leave, Rose no longer believed in heaven or hell, but if she did, this would be the latter. Even Percival had vanished. No doubt preferring the broken-down stable to this sad setting.

Daniel ran to-and-fro on Agatha's orders. Truly the woman had not lied; there were few here. Agatha helped out with the cooking while the boy seemed to do all the other chores. He disappeared often out into the courtyard, and then he would reappear. The smell of farm animals followed in his wake. Once or twice Rose thought to get up and help the lad, but her days of doing chores were over. If they perceived her as a weak soul, she would be scrubbing out the hearth in no time.

The afternoon sun ebbed through the windows, signaling the day would soon be over, and yet, the lord of the manor did not show his face. Surely the man could not be hiding out in his solar all day. He could be in the fields, but she saw no one before she entered the gate. A handful of knights strolled into the hall and carried the trestles to the center of the room. They then moved the benches and paused, their gazes fixed on her.

With a blush in his cheeks, Daniel stepped forward. "My lady, if you would not mind, Sir Rupert and the others would like to move the bench by the tables."

Rose watched as the boy's ears turned red, but she wasn't inclined to move. Her gaze traveled past him to the knights. They were all dirty and caked in mud as if they had been working in muck all day. All had grey hair or had no hair at all. A mass of wrinkles creased their faces, and some had round shoulders and hunched backs. None were of fighting age. Gad. She hoped Agatha was right that no one wanted this keep, for none here could defend it.

Daniel cleared his throat and clasped his hands. His weary eyes shadowed. "Please, my lady."

She sighed heavily and stood. "Oh, all right. When will Sir Theodore return? I wish to speak to him."

The color in the boy's face fled, and he averted his eyes to the floor. "He never comes into the hall at this time."

"Never! Well, when does he return? When does he eat?"

The room became deadly silent, and all stared at her. Why, even the flames on the tallows seemed to stand still. The urge to laugh bubbled in her throat, but she swallowed hard, preventing its escape when no one even wore a glimpse of a smile. The strange seemed to rule here. A pot fell in the kitchen and broke the spell. A few of the knights mumbled to one another before they moved the bench Rose had just vacated. As if on cue, Percival entered with another old man who could be the stable master. Sister Mary Ella hurried to take a seat at the table while Daniel scurried away as his mother approached.

Agatha pointed to the knights who were already sitting on either side of the long trestle table. "'Tis very informal here. We all eat together. Come, so we can begin."

That there wasn't a head table did not give Rose pause, but that they were going to start without Sir Theodore did. "Should we not wait for—"

"Nay, my lady. He never eats with us." Agatha gently put a hand on her shoulder. "After you have eaten, I will take you to him."

Out of the corner of her eye, Rose saw Daniel carrying a trencher of food to the solar. With a swift knock, the boy entered and then exited within moments, empty-handed. He then sat down next to Percival. So the lord of the manor ate alone. Why?

Rose had been told that Sir Theodore had suffered terrible disfiguring wounds while he was in Normandy. Yet those here should be used to them by now. Why then did he hide? Because of her? But Agatha had said Sir Theodore never ate with them. Rose strode to the table and sat down next to Sir Rupert. The quicker she ate, the quicker she would meet the mysterious lord.

A slow smile spread across her face. And the quicker she could make his life more miserable, the quicker she could gain her freedom. After all, had not the nuns cheered when she left? Indeed. Within a fortnight, Sir Theodore would be begging for her to leave.

Three

*But the Lord said unto Samuel, Look not on his countenance,
or on the height of his stature; because I have refused him:
for the Lord seeth not as man seeth; for man looketh on the
outward appearance, but the Lord looketh on the heart.*
1 Samuel 16:7

A MEAL OF FISH STEW, CHEESE, AND HARD BREAD
should not have taken hours, yet it had. Rose had
never eaten with a slower bunch of people. Even Percival
and Sister Mary Ella seemed put out at how long it took for
the knights and others to slurp down the meager meal. Why,
they did not even have wine to soothe one's throat. Instead,
to quench your thirst you were given a cup of goat's milk.
After every few chews and every few gulps, the knights and
servants began rehashing old stories of when the manor had
been a viable keep. Rose suspected their words bestowed
Taine Manor with more praise than it deserved. Certainly,
sheer boredom of lackluster conversation kept Sir Theodore
away at mealtime. Mayhap in the future she too could take
her supper elsewhere.

Finally, Agatha arose signaling the meal was over. A few
knights grabbed stools and made their way to the hearth and
the fire. Sister Mary Ella sighed and began to help clear the
tables. Percival followed suit.

When all seemed to be put in order, Agatha motioned to
Rose. "Come, I will take you to see Sir Theodore now."

Elation jumped in Rose's chest as she hurried to the solar.

26

Finally, she would be able to meet the mysterious lord of Taine Manor.

After a swift knock, Agatha opened the door. "Sir Theodore, Lady Rosemond is here."

The room was dark, the windows shuttered, and a lone lit tallow sat on a table next to an empty trencher. A warm, bright fire blazed in the hearth, yet Rose could not discern the occupant, for he sat away from the light in the dark shadows of the room. With a tight smile, Agatha gestured to a high-back chair near the fire before picking up the trencher. Rose did not move but folded her hands to bolster her courage.

"Is there anything else you will be needing?" Agatha called to the shadowy silhouette.

"Nay, I believe we are fine," a resilient deep voice rang out of the darkness.

Agatha gave Rose a weak smile before she left the room, leaving the door slightly ajar. Even with the warm fire, a chill swept up Rose's spine. She peered into the darkness trying to make out Sir Theodore's features.

"Well, are you going to stand there all evening gawking, or would you like to warm up a bit?"

His heavy pleasant timbre bespoke of a confident man and could be quite soothing to a timid and anxious soul, but Rose was neither timid nor anxious. She jutted out her chin, strode to the chair, and sat. Her back straight. Her shoulders squared. Her will strong.

He laughed.

She bristled.

He laughed all the more.

She rose. "How dare you laugh at me. I have not come here to be insulted. If that is your game, then find someone else to torment. I shall return to Godstow on the morrow." Rose turned and walked to the door, wondering what she had just done. Escaping Taine Manor would be easy, but getting away from Godstow would be next to impossible.

"Sit down, Lady Rosemond. I mean no offense. It is just that I have not seen a woman full of as much spunk as you in a long time."

She had to agree with him. Besides Daniel and perhaps Mistress Agatha, the people at Taine Manor were duller and slower than the sisters at the abbey. Still, he had no right to make sport of her. Keeping her head high, she returned to her seat.

"Would you like something to drink? A glass of wine to take off the night chill?"

Was this hospitality or the beginning of some other vile plan? Lame or not, most men could not be trusted. "Nay. I rarely drink wine." Untrue, but if she needed to flee, she needed her wits.

"Very well. Do you know why you are here?"

"Aye. I am here to aid you in your education of deciphering and understanding the written word." She narrowed her gaze, trying to make out his features.

"And you are agreeable to this?"

"Of course, otherwise I would not be here." She hoped he accepted her lie. She leaned forward. He did seem tall, but she could not be certain.

"I would imagine you are here because it is better than the abbey at Godstow."

"That is debatable," she huffed.

Another low laugh drifted across the room. "Indeed. Plus, Taine Manor is not as grand as Rockbridge Castle."

Rose squeezed the arms of the chair with her hands at the mention of her father's estate. "I would not know, my lord. For I have not seen Rockbridge for almost three years. It could be as broken down as this place."

He laughed again. The fire popped and hissed and danced with merriment. "I hardly doubt it. Your father's circumstances would allow him to keep his holdings in good repair."

She had enough of this idle banter. "I am sure you have not brought me here to talk about Rockbridge."

"You are correct. I was only trying to ease your fears."

"Fear?" She cocked her head to the left, hoping to bring his looks into focus. "Pray tell, what should I be afraid of? I have been schooled on your past. I will not scream and swoon over your disfigurement. Do step into the light."

His chair creaked, and Rose could feel her excitement and apprehension rise within her. He stepped slightly out of the shadows, exposing his left profile. Why, he was not deformed at all. A bright thatch of sandy hair flecked with red hung to his shoulders and caressed a strong jaw. He looked at her from the corner of his eye. In the dim light, she could not discern if his eyes were hazel or green sprinkled with a dusting of gold. He pulled back his shoulder, and the muscles in his thigh grew taut as if he held all his weight on that one leg.

Her eyes narrowed. He did seem to be balancing. "Step further into the light. I wish to see all of you."

He hesitated. His hand curled into a tight fist, then relaxed at his side. He let out a long breath, then slowly turned until he stood fully before her. Rose fought not to gasp or put a hand to her mouth, for never had she seen a more pathetic sight. Where his left shoulder was strong and muscular, his right shoulder drooped forward, weak and feeble. Where his left leg was sturdy and well-defined, his right leg was twisted and bent. His hair hung like a veil over the right side of his face.

"Brush back your hair, for I wish to see more of your face," she demanded.

He hesitated and then complied. Now she understood why he wore his hair so long. The disfigurement of his body could be overlooked, but his face... His right cheek was sunken and withered as if all the bones had been crushed. His right eyelid sagged, and his right brow jutted outward at a peculiar angle. Though he tried to be proud, his whole presence screamed humiliation. Rose thought about reaching out and giving words of condolence and care, but deep down she knew he would scorn them.

Besides, she was not here to offer comfort. Nay, she had to think of her own circumstance. Though Sir Theodore may look wretched, he still had control over her life, and he was the jailer who stood between her and freedom. She tightened her resolve and put a cruel smile on her lips. "I see why you hang in the shadows."

A hurt passed over his eyes, and Rose wished the nuns were about to give her a good thrashing. He managed to move his chair closer to the fire before plunking down. As out of habit, he covered his withered right hand with his left. His left hazel eye studied her with no expression while his right hooded eye clearly held all the secrets. "Perhaps we should discuss your duties."

Duties? A storm rose within her. He deemed to treat her as a servant? Rose tipped her head but held her tongue.

"Each morning, in the hall, we begin with prayers before we break our fast. We will then return here to spend a few hours in study. You will be allowed a stretch of the legs in the courtyard before the noonday meal. Then, as I attend to my holding, your time will be on your own. Unless, of course, I need you to interpret some missives or make accounting of the manor's stock and goods. Even though we did not do them today, usually before we sup we do our evening prayers."

Oh, how typical. Another who wished to exert his control over her. Did he think he could get away with this? She was a lady, the daughter of one of the most powerful barons in England. Her father would skewer him for his lack of respect. She opened her mouth to tell him such when she realized the cold truth. Her father would do naught. He had let her rot for close to three years with the Benedictine nuns at Godstow. He would not lift a finger to help her unless she conformed to his wishes to become a docile maid whom he could marry off to the knight of his choosing. She wanted to make her own choices. Was that too much to ask? In her mind, she could hear her father shout, "Aye, too much."

So be it. She would fight for herself. "My thanks for telling me *my duties*. For I have a few needs of my own which must be fulfilled. First off, I do not arise early, so please do not expect me at morning prayers. I will happily teach you in the morn, but I am not your steward. Please find another to assist you in the afternoon with the keep's accounts. Nor will I be joining you for evening prayers." She gave a quick nod and threw back her shoulders. Discussion over.

A lopsided grin spread on his face as he leaned forward. "Lady, your duties are not open for debate and change. They are as I said. Your father has given you to me in service. You claimed you were in agreement to that service. If you cannot abide, you may return to Godstow." He then had the audacity to cordially bow and lift his head.

Her insides bubbled until a dark mass of anger flowed to every part of her body. Who did this monster think he was to order her about? She shot to her feet. "You know I would rather die than return to Godstow, and you know I am forced to stay here. Fine, then. I shall follow your rules and live within your boundaries. But I promise you will rue the day you set them."

His left brow shot up in surprise. "There are no boundaries here. This is not a prison."

"Really, and if I chose to leave? Would you not give chase?"

He leaned back and smiled. "I wouldn't want you to get lost in the wetlands."

Why, he found this all amusing! Rose thinned her lips and headed for the door. She then turned back, lifting her chin as high as she could. "Fine, then. I will enjoy your limited hospitality and follow your insufferable rules. But there is one request, nay rule, nay boundary, I must insist on. I will only sit on your left side during our lessons, and you will not, under any circumstances, touch me with your vile body. Not your knee, hand, or fingers. Nothing. Do I make myself clear?"

His lips twitched as he stared at her. She feared that at any moment he might laugh. Instead, he graciously nodded again. "Very well, Lady Rosemond. I wish you to be happy here. Is there anything else?"

Her whole body shook. She wanted to slap his ugly face, but she feared that would only give him more pleasure. "Don't not call me Lady Rosemond. I hate that name. I am Rose, and best you remember it." She strode from the room and slammed the door behind her, trying to drown out his loud guffaws.

Four

O praise the Lord, all ye nations: praise him, all ye people.
For His merciful kindness is great toward us:
and the truth of the Lord endureth forever.
Praise ye the Lord.
Psalm 117:1–2

A LONG YAWN ESCAPED DANIEL'S LIPS AS HE HELD up a drab tunic. "I think this one doesn't have any holes, sir."

Theo eyed the coarse garment before glancing at the small pile of weathered tunics spread across his pallet. What his clothing looked like had never bothered him before Lady Rose had joined their company, but now... "Do I not have a more colorful one?"

The bleary-eyed boy yawned again. "There's only the red one, and that has a hole in the sleeve."

Guilt rolled through Theo. The boy should be resting instead of attending his fickle lord in the wee hours of the morning. "That won't do." Theo pushed the old tunics to the side and sat down on his pallet. "Then it will have to be the one you hold in your hands." Theo lifted his arms as high as he could manage while Daniel struggled to drop the brown tunic over Theo's head and stuff his arms through the sleeves.

Usually, Theo dressed himself, grabbing any rumpled tunic and breeches he could find. But today he wanted to look more presentable. Thus, poor Daniel lost his much-

33

needed sleep. Theo rose, and the lad brushed the creases out of the clothing.

"There, sir. 'Tis the best I can do." Daniel's words may have said what Theo wanted to hear, but the boy's voice betrayed him.

"Have no worry. I know I am no prize. Come now. Get my sword." Theo stretched out his arms, but Daniel did not move.

"Sir, you want to wear your sword?" the boy asked incredulously.

Theo tried to tamp down his irritation. True, it had been months since he had belted his sword around his waist in front of others, mayhap a year, but that did not give Daniel the authority to question him. "Did I not say so?" Theo snapped.

Daniel quickly rummaged through the trunk until he found the rough leather belt and worn scabbard. Wisely, the lad did not pull the blade from its sheath. With months of neglect, the sword must look a fright. Carefully he looped the belt around Theo's waist. The weight of the blade caused Theo's right leg to buckle. With haste, Daniel adjusted the belt so the scabbard rested on Theo's stronger left hip. What good would that do him in a real battle since he could not even hold a tallow with his right hand, let alone a sword.

Cautiously, the lad stepped back, but still stood close enough just in case Theo might need some guidance. "There, lord. I think that is better. I am sure Lady Rosemond will be pleased."

Theo wrinkled his brow and feigned indifference. "This has nothing to do with the lady."

"Aye, sir. But she is beautiful." The lad's face beamed with awe, and Theo could not blame him.

Lady Rosemond... Lady Rose was beyond beautiful. She was stunning. Theo's mind skipped back to last night when she had entered his solar. He had been told that Lady Rose was fair, but he had not been prepared for what he saw. Her long black braid fell far past her short sheer veil. The glossy weave of hair was looped over her shoulder like a midnight fur. Her thick, dark lashes protected the most magnificent pair of eyes he had ever seen. Neither grey nor blue, but a fine mixture of both. Eyes of a temptress, sweet and seductive, twisting a man's gut into knots.

If that were not enough, her slender, delicate frame reminded him of a miniature porcelain statue brought from the Far East. Exquisite and delicate beyond measure.

He too had been struck and paralyzed like Daniel by her beauty, until she opened her mouth. Oh, her voice was melodious and could caress a man's ears like a choir of angels, but her words were sharp and cut like a demon's blade. Time and age had taught Theo many things. The first being outward beauty was not the same as being beautiful. Lady Rose's beauty stopped at her flesh. Yet, he could not believe it had always been so.

Theo took a careful step toward the solar door, wincing with pain under the added weight of his sword. He applied more pressure to his left leg and consciously fought to control his limp. He then paused and smiled at Daniel. "A word of caution. Never trust a beautiful woman. It usually does not go well."

"Aye, sir," Daniel mumbled as he opened the door.

The lad's lack of enthusiasm spoke volumes. He would have to learn the hard way like all men. Theo hoped the lesson would be learned years from now and not during Lady Rose's stay. But then youth never seemed to learn…until they were old.

Theo shook off his thought, straightened his shoulders, and carefully stepped into the hall. He was pleased to see the room had been prepared. A rugged wooden cross stood on one of the tables, and all at Taine Manor were assembled for morning prayers.

All, except one.

Lady Rose.

She meant to test his mettle already. So be it. He turned a sharp eye on Sister Mary Ella. "Where is your charge?"

The nun cast her eyes to the door. "Still abed, I suspect. I gave her a nudge this morn, but she would not budge. Mumbled something about being cold and smoky. She said if you wanted her, you would have to fetch her yourself."

By the holy cross, she openly defied him, and all stood with great anticipation to see what he would do. Theo drew in a deep breath and slowly released it. He wanted to storm out of the hall and drag her out of her bed. But the thought of thumping and limping up the tower steps in front of everyone curled his stomach. Yet, he could not ignore her defiance if he wanted to maintain control of the manor.

Theo squeezed his left hand on the hilt of his sword. The grip foreign. In the past, he had always unsheathed his sword with his right hand. But things were different now. "Sir Rupert," Theo bellowed.

The elderly knight lifted his watery eyes and shuffled forward. "My lord?"

"I want you to take a few knights and bring Lady Rosemond de Payne to the hall. If she refuses, drag her."

More than one in the hall gasped, and Sister Mary Ella cackled. Rupert stood still like a stuffed piece of cod.

Daniel jumped forward. "I'll go get the lady." The gleam in his eyes and his over eagerness begged one to wonder if the lad's actions were offered from a pure heart.

"Nay, Daniel. This is not your burden." Theo shot his gaze back to Rupert. "Go now."

The elder knight shook his head and then tipped it sideways to two other knights. The threesome took their good-natured time leaving the hall. The others mumbled, but Theo maintained his stance no matter how the pain in his right leg screamed for respite.

The moments dragged. A small mouse scampered across the floor and stopped briefly, rising on his hind legs. The rodent's nose and whiskers twitched; his dark beady eyes fixed on Theo. The creature probably knew that all this was folly, and he could not wait for Theo to fall flat on his face. Literally.

A loud string of screams and rants filled the air and reverberated through the closed door. Theo puffed out his chest as the door crashed open. The mouse scurried away. One knight hobbled in as the other two held Lady Rose under her armpits. The pair desperately tried to dodge her flailing feet.

"Put me down, you brutes," she roared.

Sir Rupert and the other knights looked to Theo. He nodded, and the knights unceremoniously dumped her onto the floor.

Barefooted and wearing only her shift, Lady Rose stood. Her dark hair a tangled, matted mass. Her eyes a stormy grey. Her slender shoulders quaking with rage. Most would think a wild hoyden stood in their mist. But Theo could only marvel at her magnificence.

She clenched her hand in a fist and shook it in front of his face. "What type of beast are you that you would drag a defenseless woman from her bed? You should be drawn and quartered!"

"Oh my," Agatha said, putting a hand to her mouth.

The air in the hall grew thick and quiet. Every gaze rested on them. Slowly, Theo let out his breath and cast a glance toward Agatha. "Please bring a coverlet for Lady Rose." The woman took off without a word, and Theo turned back to the termagant before him.

"We discussed this last eve. All at Taine Manor partake in morning and evening prayers."

Lady Rose huffed, and she let her gaze travel across the hall and its occupants. "This is not a convent or monastery. We are not nuns or monks. Yet you make us do matins and vespers." She folded her arms over her chest. "I have had enough of this at the abbey. I am finished with prayers."

Her blasphemous words sent tongues wagging. Theo was wholly glad that a priest was not present, for he would have had the lady in chains before they broke their morning fast. Thankfully, Agatha returned at that very moment and draped the coverlet over Lady Rose's shoulders. And praise be to

God, she did not toss the cloth to the ground but wrapped it tightly about her lithe body.

The room fell silent once again. Theo cleared his throat. "Let us begin."

All turned, faced the makeshift altar, and fell to their knees. All, except for Lady Rose. She stood in the rear of the hall, her head held high. *By all that was holy she aimed to kill him.* If he were young and strong he might have forced her to the humble position, but being older and wiser, he knew force did nothing but harden the heart. Instead, he motioned to Rupert and another knight to stand sentinel, lest she think to escape.

Then Theo, with measured steps, made his way to the altar and slowly sank to his left knee, hiding his pain by biting the inside of his lower lip. His scabbard dug into his good thigh, and he thanked God it did not rest on his right side. The muscles in both legs eased. With his composure returned, he began. "Heavenly Father, thank you for sending your son to die for our sins and thank you for protecting us through the night. May we bring glory to your name this day. Amen."

"Amen," the assembly echoed.

Temptation sluiced through Theo. Desperately, he wanted to turn around and see Lady Rose's reaction to his prayer. *This isn't about you, but God.* Guilt washed the temptation away, and Theo leaned over and picked up a parchment which held one of the Psalms he knew. Psalm one hundred and seventeen was the first Psalm Lady Catherine had ever taught him, and it was the shortest, thirty-three words. He read the verses quickly. When he did not stumble over the words, he inwardly gave a sigh of relief. Usually, after reading this Psalm he would pick another, but fearing he would blunder, Theo ended with another short prayer of thanksgiving and carefully rose to his feet.

A shifty knowing smile greeted him when he turned around. Heat rose up the back of his neck, but he refused to let her get the better of him. "Lady Rose, I will meet you in my solar after you have groomed yourself and broken your fast."

He did not wait for her reply but turned and, with restrained steps, walked to his chamber, desperately trying to keep his limp in check. Once behind closed doors, he unfixed the belt around his waist and let the heavy sword drop to the floor. All this had been a mistake. He could not have Lady Rose stay here. But if he did not master the written word, if he could not become a wise and learned man, then he would never be able to pay off his debt to Hugh and Eleanor and he would never be able to make Taine Manor into a worthy keep. Without honor, respect, and worth, he was naught but a rotting worm.

Five

*All scripture is given by inspiration of God,
and is profitable for doctrine, for reproof, for correction,
for instruction in righteousness.*
2 Timothy 3:16

WITH NO ASSISTANCE, ROSE MANAGED TO SHRUG into her bland, brown bliaut and then belt a simple leather girdle about her waist. With a heavy sigh, she fell back on the pallet and closed her eyes. All she wanted was a little rest. In her anger last night, she had forgotten to ask Sir Theodore to change her accommodations and had no choice but to return to the tower chamber. There she found the iron brazier had been moved under one of the arrow slit windows; some of the obtrusive smoke drifted out into the night air, while most still lingered in the room. The fire had indeed warmed the chamber and made it tolerable.

The trouble lay in the bed. Sister Mary Ella had managed to wrap all the coverlets about her like a cocooned moth. Not one sliver of the pallet was free of her bulky form. Rose spent most of the night trying to pull a small bit of the coverlet from the nun's greedy body while struggling for a minute piece of pallet. When sleep seemed close, Sister Mary Ella would leave out loud snorts and gasps. Rose feared each might be the elder nun's last. Yet, she would rally, and Rose would, once again, try to gain some sleep.

This was all that boorish monster's fault. All a show to prove he had authority over her. Being forced to partake in his morning prayers had not been for naught. For she learned some very valuable information. Sir Theodore struggled with his reading, and he meant to hide his lack of skill from those at Taine Manor. He wanted to save face. She laughed. Like any would care if he could read or not. Most lords relied on scribes to take down their words, and they would have their stewards keep track of their coin and goods.

But not Sir Theo. There wasn't a scribe or steward present. He relied on a youthful lad and his mother for help and guidance. Plus, he used a small band of aged knights and a few straggly servants to do his physical work. Rose sat up and brushed her fingers through her hair. What a sham she had walked into.

Or what an opportunity. She stood and swiftly braided her hair. Her hand paused over the sheer veil. Nay, she would leave her head uncovered. The road to freedom would be obtained from here if she didn't do anything rash. Rose smiled inwardly as she opened the chamber door. The cool blast of fresh air flushed her cheeks, and a ray of hope bloomed in her chest. Today she would win her freedom.

With a spring in her step, she descended the tower and entered the hall. She did not mind the warm, watery pottage or the rock-hard bread she was given to break her fast, for her mind focused on her meeting with Sir Theodore. If she was amiable enough, certainly he would give her free rein of the manor. She'd start with the stables...surely there had to be one good horse.

Sister Mary Ella came and sat next to Rose. "I've been thinking. Mayhap I should stay here with you. To protect your virtue."

Rose coughed as a spoonful of pottage bumped down her throat and quickly took a drink of goat's milk. "I was assured by Mother Superior my virtue would be safe here. Are you afraid that Sir Theodore might not be honorable?"

The old nun shook her head. "Nay. I have heard he has not sought out a woman since he returned to England. No doubt, he cannot..."

"Then I do not understand. There is none here that would lay a hand on me."

Sister Mary Ella raised a brow. "There are the knights and that servant boy."

Ah. This had nothing to do with virtue and everything to do with the tower chamber's pallet and warm coverlets. "Not a knight here would touch me for fear of their lord's wrath, nor are they young enough to catch me."

"But as a rowdy band…"

"Nay, not even as a rowdy band, and well you know it. As for Daniel, though he may have the stirrings of manhood, he would not jeopardize his mother's security. Fear not, I will be quite safe here. You can return with Percival to the abbey. When are you leaving?"

The nun frowned. "On the morrow. Mother Superior did not want us to linger." Her spirits rose slightly. "Unless you are uneasy and think we should stay longer?"

Rose stood and shook her head. "Nay. I will be fine. Now, I must go. Sir Theodore will be wanting his lesson."

She headed to the solar and pinched her cheeks one more time for good measure. Thus, from this day forward, she would apply her father's strategy—to win the field you must be a good tactician. With a healthy knock, Rose plastered a sweet smile on her lips.

"Enter," the monster roared.

She brushed her hands over her bliaut. Now the war would begin, and very soon she would have her victory and freedom.

The huge smile on the lady's face put Theo on alert. Gone was this morning's termagant. Her long lashes fluttered in a demure way, and she tilted her head to the left like a shy maid. He wasn't fooled by thinking what happened at morning prayers had softened her defenses. Lady Rosemond de Payne would be a pain in his arse for some time to come.

"Ah, Lady Rose. Please come in and leave the door slightly open."

She nodded her head like a docile doe and quickly complied. "Good morn, my lord. Are you ready for your lesson?"

Her honeyed voice put Theo even more on edge. 'Twas easy to best an opponent when they are openly hostile, but when they slinked about behind cheerful faces with hidden plans…then they are dangerous indeed. He tried to shake off his thoughts. He was not at war with Lady Rose. If he wanted to learn his words, he would have to placate her as much as possible.

Theo sat down at a small table. He motioned to the chair on his left. "Shall we begin?"

Daintily she crossed the room and sat. The sunlight streamed into the window behind her, and colorful sparkles danced off her dark hair, casting an ethereal glow. She modestly fluttered her lashes again. "What have you been studying?"

A great urge to touch her shiny hair and tender cheek tore at Theo's control. But her words of last eve kept him in check. *You will not, under any circumstances, touch me with your vile body.* In her anger, she had shown her true colors; he would not forget it. He pushed one of the scrolls toward her without saying a word.

She unrolled the parchment and shot him a speculative look. "This is the Psalm you read this morn. You know it by heart. We need to work on something you have not memorized."

He feared she would say thus. Yet he had no desire to stumble and bumble over his words in front of her. "Did you sleep well last night?"

She paused, and then a sly smile grew on her face. "Thanks to Sir Rupert and Daniel, they managed to build a small fire in a brazier to keep the chill away, but the room was still very smoky. Even after they moved the brazier near a narrow window." Rose took a deep breath and sighed, letting her gaze travel around the room. "It is not as cozy as this chamber, that's for sure."

Now he knew what she was after. He nodded, thoughtfully. "Perhaps later today I can take a look at your accommodations and see what else can be done."

"Oh, how wonderful. I knew you would want me to have the most comfortable place."

Aye. He did. But he had no intentions of giving up his solar. However, at this time, it didn't seem prudent to give up that piece of information.

"Good. With that settled. Shall we begin?" Not waiting for his answer, she turned her attention back to the parchments on the table.

His throat dried, and his heart began to hammer. Think. How else could he put off the inevitable? A thought flashed in his mind. "My lady, it is unusual, even with a lenient father, for a woman to learn to read. How did you come by such a skill?"

Her brows shot upward, before she settled back in her chair. "First off, whatever you may have heard, my father was not as lenient as you think or I would not be sitting here. To answer your question, I was always the curious sort, and after my mother died, I spent a lot of time with Father Ramsey, Rockbridge's priest."

All knew Rockbridge was a wealthy holding, but it must be more powerful than most to have its own priest. The idea was almost bewildering.

"I pestered the good father until he taught me the language of the Biblical scrolls."

Aye, Theo could see how many would find it hard not to give in to Lady Rose's whims. "You know Latin, then?"

She looked around the room as if she expected the walls to hear her. "Some. And some Greek too. But do not say so loudly, for there are those who would not understand."

True, even with a father like Sir Walter de Payne, some would not approve of her knowledge of the holy language. Some may believe it to be a sin.

"He did some translation, and I helped him. That is how I learned my skills. Though the nuns did try to beat it out of me."

A moment of fury flamed through his body at the thought of Lady Rose being abused. Did her father know of such treatment? Then he saw the twinkle in her eye, and he knew she played him false. He thought to voice his revelation but then changed his mind.

She let out a sigh and turned back to the scrolls. "But I have survived and hopefully have found a safe and secure home here."

Theo remained silent. But he made a mental note to talk to Sir Rupert the moment this lesson was over. The lady would need additional supervision or she would be heading for the wetlands by nightfall.

"Let us see what else you have been reading." Rose unrolled the scroll, and her lips thinned. "Ah, another Psalm."

"That is mostly what I read," Theo said.

Her eyes flared, and her body quaked. She cleared her throat and licked her lips. Obviously, she fought for control. What did she have against scripture and the Psalms? As he thought on it, nor did she bow her head to pray this morn. Apparently, her anger not only rested on her father's shoulders, but on God's as well.

"Is something wrong?" he asked.

With a quick shake of the head, she looked down at the parchment. "Nay. Shall we begin?"

For a moment, Theo wished she would have balked at the Psalm, for lo and behold there in inky scribbles was long and laborious Psalm fifty-eight. "Aye." He sighed and took a deep breath. "Do ye indeed speak right...right..."

Six

Let no man deceive you with vain words:
for because of these things cometh the wrath of God
upon the children of disobedience.
Ephesians 5:6

*J*F SHE HAD TO ENDURE ONE MORE PAINFUL HOUR IN
Sir Theodore's presence as she did this morning, then
insanity would certainly befall her. Rose tore out of the hall
and out into the courtyard, slapping her feet on the hard
ground. Perhaps those long hours of kneeling in the abbey
had been beneficial. For they had taught her patience, which
had been sorely tested by Sir Theodore's bumbling words.

Had you been any different when you learned? The prick
of her conscience gave her pause, but she quickly tucked the
uncomfortable thought away. And Psalms! Why did the
monks and priests always insist on translating the Psalms
before other holy writings? Even Father Ramsey had found
more exciting things for her to read. Oh, the stories he had
obtained when he was in the Outremer. Why, she wagered
that Sir Theodore's skills would improve at a more rapid rate
if he would be reading something more exciting than the
Church's Holy Scripture.

Bah! She sucked in the cool late morn air and pumped
her arms as she walked to relieve her anger. As her calm
returned, her ears pricked at a most liberating sound—the
nicker of horses. She strode into the stable to find Daniel
brushing the coat of a most magnificent animal. Well, not

magnificent, but it was a horse with four sturdy legs.

The lad stopped his chore; his face flushed with color. "Lady Rosemond! Wh-what do you here?"

As she approached the stall, he stepped back and knocked over a bucket of water, giving his foot quite the soak. If possible, his face flamed all the more, and he hopped about like a mad hare. After he settled down a bit, he righted the bucket but receded farther into the stall.

Rose rubbed the neck of the beast and laughed. "I bring you no harm, Daniel. Do come forward. All I wish is to admire this fine animal."

That seemed to have eased his nerves for he stepped closer and touched the horse's back. "He may not be the best destrier in all the kingdom, but he is the best at Taine Manor."

She glanced around the meager stable. The lad had spoken truth. Besides this beast there was two sway back mares, one old workhorse, and a mule. No other creature resided within. "Is this Sir Theodore's mount?"

Daniel made a face. "I suppose so. But he rarely rides him. The horse was a gift from Lady Eleanor given after Sir Theodore returned from Normandy."

Ah, the elusive Lady Eleanor. The woman who had rejected the noble Sir Theodore's love all those years ago. Rose took a handful of grain and gave it to the horse. Mayhap someday she would get to meet this lady. "Does this horse have a name?"

"Aye, my lady. Sir Theodore calls him Triumph."

She frowned. "'Tis an odd name for a horse."

Daniel shrugged and returned to his grooming. "His lordship says if he ever masters riding the beast, it would be a triumph."

Interesting. Sir Theodore did not ride often. A twinge of sadness swept her heart. What was a knight without his mount? Rose gave a mental shake. His infirmities were not her concern nor his troubles hers...to a point. She could not let her defenses down. A soft spirit would serve her no purpose. Sir Theodore was her enemy. She stroked

Triumph's mane. This fine animal could serve her well. "Do you exercise him?"

Daniel shook his head. "I take him out to the larger corral outside the manor and let him run there, but I do not ride him."

Her hand paused on the animal's neck. "Why ever not? Does Sir Theodore forbid you?"

Again, the boy shook his head and this time averted his gaze to his feet. "Nay, my lady. It is a strong-willed beast, and I am not skilled with such fine animals. Only Sir Theodore seems to be able to handle him." Daniel lifted his gaze. "That is, when he does ride him."

If she believed God cared or was even there, then she would say this was divine intervention. Already she could visualize galloping to freedom. She tried to hide her exuberance by picking up another handful of grain and giving it to Triumph. "I used to ride often when I lived at my father's keep. I miss it so." She let out a heavy sigh for good measure and then lowered her lashes.

"I'm so sorry," Daniel squawked, his Adam's apple bobbing up and down.

She trailed a finger along Triumph's back, taking a step closer to Daniel. "Do you think I could ride him? Just once." Again, she dropped her lashes and tried to give him a look of pure innocence.

"Oh that I could allow it, my lady. But I fear Sir Theodore would be furious if I did not get his permission." His voice held a tone of awe and longing.

Rose inwardly huffed. She had not tempted him enough to defy his lord. She stepped out of the stall and turned to leave. So be it. She would just have to slip away some eve and entice Triumph with some tasty oats.

"But I could ask him. I am sure he wouldn't mind if you are as good with horses as you say you are," Daniel said eagerly.

Gads! That was the last thing she wanted, to alert Sir Theodore. "Nay. It is fine. I am sure there are other things I could do to fill up my time."

Daniel dropped the brush in the stall and followed her. "Aye. You can help with the goats."

She paused. Surely he jest.

"Come. I will show you." She followed him not knowing why.

They headed across the courtyard to the neat, tidy little shed with a well-groomed pen around it. The bleating of the creatures would drive most mad, but Daniel's countenance brightened with each painful noise the goats made.

Where Taine Manor may have been lacking good horses, there seemed to be an overabundance of healthy goats. This would explain the goat's milk at every meal. Mayhap the cheese too. "Pray tell, why are there so many goats?" she asked.

"Always has been as long as I can remember. Lord Leonard de Taine had a passion for them. Every day he would come out and spend time with them. He loved to feed them. He'd even take some of the goats to his solar. During the summer, they would be out eating everything around the manor. Many a peasant would become angry when they started eating their fields and homes for that matter." Daniel shook his head. "Lord de Taine would just hand the peasants coin for their lost crops and lodgings. He made sure the goats had soft rushes to ease their bodies when they rested. Of course, they ate those too. When he was alive, this was my primary duty, to help him take care of the goats. Others tended to the horses, and we had more servants to look after other things. But all that changed when he died."

One of the goats came up by the fence and bumped his head against Rose's hand. She gave him a hearty pat. "What happened then?"

"The manor became the property of Sir Hugh de Maury and Lady Eleanor, but they hardly came as they lived at Thornwood Keep. A much finer holding than this." Daniel picked up a pitchfork and entered the pen and began heaving hay into a trough. "But Lord de Taine had a scribe write out the conditions about the goats to the new owner. The animals would be taken care of in the manner they were used to or the keep would have to be given to someone who would."

"But who would want such a place?"

Daniel chuckled and kept shoveling of hay. "I think I have said enough, my lady. It is not my place to say more."

Perhaps, but she needed to know more. This might be the key to her escape or it might mean nothing, but she would not know unless she heard the full tale. She leaned over the fence and flashed a bright smile. "Oh, but I do find it interesting. You have such a fine timbre to your voice, I could listen to you forever. Please continue. I shall not tell a soul. I promise."

Daniel's ears pinked, and he glanced around the courtyard before he cleared his throat. "Well, I think Sir Hugh wanted to get rid of Taine Manor, but Lady Eleanor was fond of the place. She lived here before she married. At one time, she had offered it to Sir Theodore before he went with King Richard to fight the French. I think Sir Theodore wanted more. You can't blame him."

Undeniably. Yet a man like Theodore de Born obviously had few prospects. The goat in front of Rose placed his front hooves on top of the fence. Rose tickled his neck. "Who then helped run Taine Manor in Sir Hugh' and Lady Eleanor's absence?"

"That's when things really fell apart." Daniel wiped his brow. "They appointed a steward, Master Harding. He was a bad man, my lady. He spent most of the keep's funds on wine and merriment, if you get my meaning."

She did, but that a boy would know about such things told much about the environment he was raised in. The goat in front of her scraped his hoof across her arm when she stopped her scratching.

"Get down, Philip." Daniel chased the goat away. "Sorry, my lady. They don't get as much attention as they used to on account I have many chores these days."

"Tell me how did that happen?" Rose tilted her head and gave him an enduring smile, hoping the actions would keep his words flowing.

"Well, when Sir Theodore arrived and saw what was going on, he ran off Master Harding. Most of the knights who were worth their weight in salt left when Sir Theodore cut off their wine and sent all the whores away. There wasn't much left, and Sir Theodore had been honest about it. Those who stayed would have to work harder. That's how I got all these extra chores. But as soon as I am older…"

The longing in his voice she understood well. Mayhap Daniel would be a useful ally in escaping and helping her navigate the wetlands. A plan began to form in her mind, but she had to make sure Daniel spoke the truth and wasn't dreaming of things he would never do. "So, you would leave your mother and seek your own way?"

"Aye, I would. There isn't a future here for anyone." He finished filling the trough and leaned on the hilt of the pitchfork. The goats bumped and jostled against one another to get closer to the hay. "Still, I will miss these fellows."

Rose dropped her gaze to the bleating beasts. "There are definitely enough of them."

"Fourteen to be exact." Daniel placed the pitchfork against the shed and then exited the pen. "One for each apostle."

Rose smiled when Philip came back to the rail looking for more of her attention. "But there were only twelve disciples."

Daniel leaned on the fence next to her. "True, but we have Saint Paul and Matthias too."

"Matthias? I do not remember the priest talking about him."

"He was the disciple that took Judas's place after he hung himself." Daniel puffed out his chest, clearly proud that he knew something she did not.

"Ah, of course. But if there are fourteen, then you must have a Judas too?"

"Aye, my lady. But he is always given to a poor peasant family for Easter. And then we find a young kid to take his place. It is a tradition that Lord de Taine started and the people seem to love and there are always young kids by spring."

She frowned. "For that to be so, then not all these goats are male, even though they carry male names." They both started laughing.

Daniel slapped the rail. "And when one dies or one is given away as a gift, a new kid becomes a disciple. Any extra goats are sold off. Has been that way and will probably continue until Sir Theodore or Master Jude are gone."

Rose cocked her head. "Master Jude? You mean the disciple Jude? Which goat is he?"

"Nay. I do not speak of the goat, I speak of Master Jude. The old man who came from France with Sir Theodore. He is the keeper of the goats." Daniel wrinkled his brow. "When he is here. He comes and goes as he pleases."

That explained why she had not met him nor did she care if she ever did. She turned her full attention on Daniel. "You are a fine young man. You remind me of the lads who came to be pages or squires at Rockbridge."

His eyes lit up at the mention of her home. "Oh, my lady. I have heard it is a grand place."

"Aye, it is," she said, adding a pinch of longing to her voice. "I have not seen my home or my father for almost three years. If only I could see him. I know he would forgive me. But alas, I have no way of getting there." She dropped her gaze and peered at him through her long lashes. She had no intentions of going home. However, those particulars might best be revealed to Daniel later...when they were far from Taine Manor.

"Oh lady—"

"Call me Rose." She placed her hand on his.

He flushed and nodded.

Rose gave him a wide smile. Truly, this was almost too easy. She licked her lips—the taste of freedom was indeed delicious.

Seven

*Iron sharpeneth iron; so a man sharpeneth
the countenance of his friend.*
Proverbs 27:17

HEO EYED THE METAL SHIELD IN SIR RUPERT'S HAND
and then looked at a brazier which was similar to the
one in Lady Rose's room. They had spent the better part of
the afternoon trying to come up with a way to vent the
smoke out of the lady's chamber.

"I am not sure it will fit." Theo leaned against the table in
the blacksmith's hut.

"Nay, sir. We measured that opening three times. It will
fit." Rupert placed the molded shield on the front of the
brazier. "See, it will work."

Before injured, Theo used to be able to draw fairly well.
Often he used his skill of pictures to convey what others
might put into words. Now he could not sketch out anything.
He could not cipher. He could not fight. He couldn't even
carry a bucket of water without falling over. How then could
he survive as lord if he had no skills at all?

Theo looked at his drawing and then eyed the shield with
skepticism. "The peat or wood will have to be loaded from
the back. I'm not sure that is a good idea. I don't want the
lady to get burned if she attempts to stoke the fire in the
middle of the night."

Rupert mumbled something under his breath and then
dropped the shield on the workbench. "I doubt she would do

that. Methinks she would be yelling out the door for one of us to come and do it for her. She's a mite mighty in her ways."

Indeed, it would appear so, but Theo thought her brave bold actions were a front for a very angry and insecure woman. Her father sent her away, and the man she loved had rejected her. No wonder she came across as a tough tart.

The older knight harrumphed. "Why do you care if a little smoke gets into the lady's room? Lady Eleanor never complained about such things."

Obviously, Rupert could not make the distinction that not all women were alike. Theo placed his good hand on the curvature of the shield. "If we form it to angle away from the room, I think it might work. I think we only need to do a little more shaping."

"Aye. I suppose. I'll hammer it some more," Rupert grumbled.

The regular smithy took off when Theo had dismissed Master Harding. From then on anyone who could wield a hammer would take a turn at being the blacksmith. Today, it was Sir Rupert's turn. No matter how hard he tried, Rupert did not have the talent.

"Nay. We will have Sir Gregory help me. I have another job for you." Theo rested his left hip against the bench as he examined the shield. "I want you to keep an eye on Lady Rose."

"Hey? You want me to be a lady's maid now too?" Rupert folded his arms over his sagging chest. "I won't do it. Have Daniel keep a watch on her. He's always ogling the girl anyway."

"That is exactly why he cannot. He would be doing her bidding in less time than it takes you to roll off your pallet in the morning. Nay. You will watch her."

The old knight rubbed a hand on the back of his neck. "I'd rather be working here." He lifted a brow, hoping Theo would honor his plea. "I'm not that young. She could slip right past me."

Theo had to admire Rupert's tenacity. Some other lord

would have dismissed him by now. "Nonetheless, you are my choice. Make sure she knows you are watching her. Then perhaps she may not try to run away."

"You think me watching her will prevent this? She might well slip out at night when the rest of us are dreaming about finer times."

"You might be right, but she is not familiar with the terrain, so I doubt she will slip out alone."

A soft tinkle of laughter floated on the air and into the smithy hut. Theo pivoted and looked out the window. Just as he suspected, Lady Rose was with Daniel. With a dainty finger, she wiped a smudge off the lad's face, and with the bat of her eyelashes, she gave him a coy smile. Daniel was practically drooling.

By the holy cross, she didn't waste time. "Sir Rupert, go out there now and make conversation with the lady and tell Daniel I need his help here."

Rupert frowned and followed Theo's gaze out the window. He started to chuckle. "Well, aren't they a fine pair?"

"Just get out there." A twinge of jealousy sprung in Theo's chest. There used to be a time when he could woo women. Now, they shuddered in his presence.

With slow easy steps, Rupert strolled from the hut and joined the pair. Daniel's face fell as his gaze traveled to the hut. Theo stepped back into the shadows. The last thing he wanted was for Lady Rose to see him. He peeked out again. One could tell from Lady Rose's tight lips that she was ready to explode. Poor Rupert, he would have to take the brunt.

Best he turned his attention back to the task at hand. Theo picked up the shield and struggled to place it above the brazier. He paused when he heard the approach of footsteps. "Daniel, bring over the hammer," Theo said without turning around.

"I'll give you your hammer."

Theo spun about and saw Lady Rose holding the hammer high above her head. Theo held up his left hand. "Now, Rose. We don't want to do anything rash."

"Rash? What do you speak of? My desire to smash the handsome side of your face so it can match the other side? Aye, I think that is an excellent idea."

With one measured step, Theo moved closer to her. "You are angry I am taking Daniel away from you. But you must understand, there are only a few strong enough in the keep who can wield a hammer."

Scowling, she squeezed the hilt of the hammer even more. Her eyes reminded him of two stormy waves hitting a mass of hard rocks. Beautiful. "Don't talk to me like I am a child, *Theo*. You asked that old goat, Sir Rupert, to accompany me around the manor, lest I get into trouble."

He took another slow step forward, she did not back away. "That is not what I said. I asked him to watch you so you wouldn't try to run away."

"Haaa…" She rushed at him with the hammer, and with his good hand, he wrestled the tool from her grip.

She began to rub her hand and wrist. "You hurt me, you brute." Bits of midnight hair escaped her braid; her chest heaved up and down like a wild animal caught in a trap.

Oh, she was a beauty.

To gain control of his own emotions, Theo placed the hammer on the table. "Nay. I did not. I was only trying to protect my…how did you say it? The handsome side of my face." He couldn't help but smile as she gave him a fierce frown.

She folded her hands into fists, and Theo braced himself for another attack. As quickly as it had come, her anger receded when she noticed the molded shield.

"Whatever is that?" She stepped past him and rubbed her fingers along the shiny shield.

"That, my lady, is going to keep the smoke from your room at night."

She flashed him a sidelong glance. "This morning you promised to give me your solar."

Had he heard wrong? "Come again, what did you say?"

Her hands dropped to her hips, and she turned a hard gaze

on him. "You told me I could have your chamber."

Theo allowed his mind to drift back to the conversation they had this morn. He could not remember a single moment where he had said thus. He cleared his throat. "I believe I said I would look into your situation to see what could be done."

"Well, does that not mean I would have your solar?"

He shook his head, cautiously, his gaze never leaving hers. "Nay." He could see a new round of rage brewing in her eyes. "But look here." He lifted the shield and carefully walked over to the brazier. "It will fit on the front, and if I can tip the top toward the window, most of the smoke will go out into the night air."

She bit her lower lip. Any traces of anger fled when she stepped forward. "You would have to tip the top inward just a little more." Her fingers went to the top of the arched shield. "Right here."

"I agree. I think that is the spot."

A thoughtful look crossed her face. "I wonder if it would work."

Good then, her curious nature had saved the day and his nerves from her tirades. "So, do I have your permission to call for Daniel now?"

She shook her head and walked over to the table and picked up the hammer. "Nay, I will help you."

She did indeed help. She was an oddity. Not only did she read and write, she could wield a hammer as good as any blacksmith. It didn't take long for Rupert and Daniel to appear at the smithy door, but Lady Rose shooed them away. "Sir Theodore and I will finish this task. You may go about your other duties."

Her authoritative tone almost made Theo laugh. She sounded like the mistress of the manor. The thought made him somber. For she was young and vibrant and he was old and decrepit. She could not be more than twenty summers old, while he was approaching his thirty-seventh year.

After she had pushed the others out, she could not stop chattering. An endless stream of questions bubbled out of her throat. She helped him check the measurements, and together they figured out how to hammer and shape the top edge of the shield. Once he had heated the upper edge, she would pick up the hammer to pound and shape the metal. So determined in her task, she wouldn't even let Theo help her with the shaping. The work took up the majority of the afternoon. Double-checking measurements, heating the metal again, pounding and shaping, seeing if it would fit.

Finally, it looked as if they had completed their task. They bolted the shield to the front of the brazier, then they stepped back to examine their handiwork. Theo wiped his brow. "I do believe we have done it, my lady."

"Aye." Her face was covered with dark smudges. Matted tendrils of hair were plastered to her sweaty brow. Tiny cinder holes had ruined her gown. To most, she would look a fright. To Theo, she was lovely.

"I do not think anyone here could have formed it any better. Where did you learn such a skill?"

She turned and gave him one of her captivating smiles. "I used to bother the smithy at Rockbridge too."

Theo sat on a tall stool to rest his aching muscles. "Your father should have put you in chains."

At the mention of Sir Walter, the smile dropped from her face. "Well, he finally did, didn't he?"

Cloistering a woman with this much spirit in a nunnery did seem cruel. Yet, Theo understood her father's reasoning. Before her arrival, Theo had received a letter from Sir Walter, explaining the details of her confinement. Had he not done so, who knows how many greedy lords and knights might want to abscond the wealthy heiress. Whoever controlled Rockbridge would gain immense power. No doubt, the man who wanted to run off with Rose did not meet Sir Walter's standards.

"Let us make the best of this. In time, I am sure your father will forgive you."

Her features turned hard and stiff. "He does not need to forgive me. He needs me to forgive him. And that will never happen. But I do not want to speak of this. Let us get this brazier up to my room."

The smile returned and warmed Theo to the pit of his stomach. "We shall need help, go and fetch Daniel and Sir Rupert."

It did not take her long to return with the pair. Rupert's brows shot upward when he took a look at the finished brazier.

Daniel walked over and let his fingers glide over the shield. "Why, I do not think Sir Gregory could have done better. My lady, you are talented indeed." The lad's voice was filled with awe and adoration. Theo would have to watch the two of them even more so.

"My thanks, Daniel. Now let us get this to my chamber." She went to open the door while Rupert and Daniel lifted the brazier.

They crossed the courtyard to the tower. Everyone stopped what they were doing to take a look at the odd contraption. Some offered their approval, while others mumbled its failure. Daniel and Rupert carefully carried the brazier up the stairs. Rose followed, and Theo stopped at the bottom step and leaned against the railing.

When Rose noticed that Theo was not following, she paused. "Are you not coming?"

The last thing Theo wanted was to stumble and clomp up the stairs like a deformed ogre. "Nay, I will wait here. Just let me know if it works."

Rose rolled her eyes and descended the stairs. "That is nonsense. I will help you. Come, lean on me."

Again, Theo shook his head and backed up a hair. "It would take me too long."

Her gazed narrowed. "I do not care if it takes you to Christmas, you are coming." With no further ado, she grabbed his left hand and they began ascending the stairs.

His face flamed with every jerking motion he made. *Thump, clump. Thump, clump.* The sound thundered in his ears, but Rose said nothing and gently encouraged him to take the next step. Each step sent a jolt of pain to his spine and heaps of humiliation to his soul. By the time he had made it to the chamber, his brow and back were drenched in sweat.

"There, you made it. You should practice your steps every day so you can get stronger." She folded her hands and smiled.

"My lady, is that an invitation to come visit you in your chamber?" Though he meant the comment in jest, her face flamed and she turned away from him.

"Oh look," she said finally. "They have put it in place of the other. Now add the peat from the back where there is a small opening. Oh, how I wish we had some coal or oil to burn, but alas, we must make do with what we have."

She ran over and bent down picking up a small bundle of twigs and adding those to the brazier.

Daniel stepped in front of her before she could throw the twigs in. "Here, my lady. Let me help you with those."

At first she held on to the bundle as if it were a precious stone, but then she relented and let Daniel perform his chivalrous act.

Once the brazier was loaded, Sir Rupert used a flint to light the fire. Everyone seemed to be holding their breath in anticipation. Smoke puffed up into the air, some came into the room, but most went out the arrow slit.

Rose clapped her hands and twirled around. "It works. It really works." She hugged Daniel, she hugged Sir Rupert, and then she came at Theo, her arms wide, he flinched, and she stopped. A look of wonderment followed by sympathy filled her eyes. "I would not hurt," she whispered and quickly turned away.

Aye, he knew she wouldn't hurt him. It was just that he hadn't had a hug from anyone in a very long time.

Eight

For if ye forgive men their trespasses,
your heavenly Father will also forgive you:
But if ye forgive not men their trespasses,
neither will your Father forgive your trespasses.
Matthew 6:14–15

HE SNORES OF SISTER MARY ELLA BOUNCED OFF the chamber wall disrupting Rose's sleep. Thankfully, the good sister would be leaving this morn. Rose tossed to her side and stared at the new brazier. The hood had made all the difference. Most of the intrusive smoke went out the arrow slit window, and to her surprise, the room actually felt warmer, as if the hood helped to control the heat within. True, during the night she did have to get up and rekindle the fire, but that was a small price to pay to have a snug, comfortable room.

Another rumble left Sister Mary Ella's throat. There was nothing to do but get up. Mayhap if she dressed quickly she could search the manor without the watchful eye of Sir Rupert. When Conrad and she had fled Rockbridge three years ago, they had done very little planning. She would not make the same mistake twice. This time she would wait and plan until the escape would be flawless. First, she'd find a safe place within the manor to hide enough provisions for her journey. Plus, she had to gain Daniel's trust. If she could get the lad to help her, she knew she could get away…but to where?

Therein lay the problem. She could not go back to Rockbridge. Her father would probably send her right back to the abbey, for she could not conform to his wishes. Never would she marry a man of his choosing.

There was Lady Catherine de Maury; she had been so kind when she came to Godstow. But she was a close friend of Sir Theodore. Her heart tugged as she thought of dear Conrad. She could not go to him, for he had been forced to marry another. Unless he would leave his wife and run away with her? The thought drove a strong longing into her chest. Oh, if only he would be so bold. That would not work anyway, for her father would look at his keep first. There was only one answer. Daniel and she would have to run away as peasants, perhaps to a coastal town. There they could gain passage to Normandy.

Rose winced at the thought. It was wrong to string the lad along, but she didn't have a choice. It wasn't like Sir Theodore was going to let her walk out the gate with a cheery wave of the hand. Again, her gaze shifted back to the brazier. The man was not as thickheaded as she thought. Reading may not be his strength, but he did seem to be good at ciphering numbers and coming up with unique ideas. Too bad about the accident, for his left side of his face and body were quite pleasing. Had he returned from France whole, he probably would have had a line of maids trying to get his attention. Of course, she would not have been one of them.

Nay, she had already decided her future, if she could not have Conrad, she would live her life alone. The French and Italians were much more enlightened. They would find it charming that a woman could read and write. Why, she could teach the wealthy her knowledge for a fair price. She'd belong to no man. She sighed and rose from the bed. What a wonderful dream. If only she could make it come true.

After dressing, Rose slipped down the stairs and into the courtyard. The dim predawn light hid her from scrutiny. Where would be a safe place to hide her provisions? Not the stable or the goat house… Why, of course, with the goats!

Daniel had said he and some old man, who showed up only once in a while, were the only ones who took interest in the goats. With Daniel on her side, they could hide their supplies in the rafters of the small goat shed. An old man would never think to look up, and the others wouldn't even bother to look there. Ever.

With that decided, she only had one other worry. How was she going to get rid of the snooping Sir Rupert? He didn't need to be fast on his feet when one could stand in the middle of the courtyard and see the whole manor. Perhaps she could charm him into helping her too. The absurd thought crashed as fast as it had come. The only thing that would tempt Sir Rupert would be a large bowl of stewed meat. And unfortunately, she had never been the domestic type. She may have searched out the priest and smithy at Rockbridge, but she had always steered clear of the kitchens. Especially after her mother died. Rose pushed the painful thought away.

There was only one thing she could do. She would have to play a sweet and docile creature in front of Sir Theodore. If he believed she was content to stay here, he might be willing to call off Sir Rupert. With that decided, Rose walked to the gate to see how easily it could be opened. However, as she got closer, she heard the groaning of a man. Through a gap in the wooden curtain wall, she saw a man silhouetted in the moonlight. A large broadsword with the blade pointed to the ground was clutched in his left hand. His right hand curled in as did his right bent leg. Only one man fit that description—Sir Theodore.

With a loud groan and all his might, he tried to lift the broadsword up into a striking position, but his left leg could not hold all his weight and the sword's too, so he stumbled to his right and had to use the blade as a crutch to keep himself upright. She watched him try to wield the sword over and over.

Finally, he dropped the blade and rubbed his right thigh. "Mangled flesh! I would be better without this leg."

His cries tore at Rose's heart and brought a set of tears to her eyes. How the poor man must suffer. In many ways he was just like she, a prisoner. She of men who wished to control her and he of his own body. Nay, his was worse. For she could flee her captors where he could not flee his flesh. He took two steps and fell to his knees. Moans of anguish filled the air.

Though it wasn't prudent, Rose squeezed through the large gap in the wall and ran to his side. "Sir Theodore, are you all right? Can I help you?"

His angry eyes flashed in the moonlight. "What are you doing here?" he said through clenched teeth.

"I could not sleep, so I took a walk." She held out her hand. "Here, let me help you."

He growled and turned away from the offered hand. "I don't need your help. Return to the manor."

She squared her shoulders and stepped into his view again. "You claim to be a good Christian. Is that not so?"

"What has that to do with this?" He slammed his hand on his twisted thigh.

"Pride is a sin. And your sin is getting in the way of me helping you." She held out her hand again. "Now then, you can take my hand or you can sit out here all day long."

He laughed and looked up at her. "Lady, I am capable of standing on my own. I don't need your help."

"Maybe not. But I am offering, and it would be very unchivalrous of you not to accept my help."

He shook his head but took her hand. "I am beginning to see why your father locked you up in a nunnery. You must have exhausted the poor fellow."

"I doubt that is the reason," she huffed. She almost lost her own balance as she pulled Sir Theodore to his feet. He quickly circled his left arm about her. He smelled of pine and birchwood. Odd for a man who never seemed to leave the manor. His body warm and inviting, not at all what she expected. She had to look up to make sure this was indeed Sir Theodore.

Once she was right on her feet, he stepped back. "Forgive me, my lady. I did not mean to offend you." He bowed his head, letting his long hair fall over his face.

"Offend me? How so? I would be flat on my backside if you hadn't caught me." She brushed off her bliaut and then leaned over to pick up his sword.

"You asked me not to touch you," he said quietly.

So she had. In an anger meant to hurt. A feeling of loathing cascaded over her shoulders and down to her toes. How could she have been so cruel? "Forgive me. I should not have said that." She held out her arm. "Come, let me help you back to the manor. Put your arm around my shoulder."

He hesitated but then complied. Air hissed from his lips when she wrapped her arm around his waist. And slowly they began to walk over the rough terrain. Rose used the tip of his sword as a counterweight. He winced every so often when he would stumble. She wondered if the face he made was because of leg pain or embarrassment. Nonetheless, he did not pull away from her.

At the partially opened gate, he released her. "You go ahead," he said.

"Why? Whatever for?"

"I am trying to protect your virtue. I'll not have the whole manor gossiping about how I took the fair Lady Rose out into the fields to have my way with her."

Laughter bubbled from her throat and sprang out into the early morning air. "Oh sir, do not worry. There isn't a soul within this keep who thinks you are capable of such harm."

He stopped and stared at her, horror etched on his face. She laughed all the more.

"Lady, I can assure you. Certain parts of my body are functioning just fine."

The laughter expired in her throat, and her heart began to hammer. A strange curl spiraled in her stomach. Shock or desire? She wasn't sure. However, she did not find his revelation all that offensive. In fact, she found it almost pleasing. Perhaps someday he might actually find someone who might overlook all his maladies.

She handed him his sword. "Well, then if that is the case, perhaps you should be looking for a wife instead of a teacher." The shock on his face caused her laughter to return. She sped through the gate, giggling with delight.

The sun shone bright in the high windows of Theo's solar, and still the lady had not arrived. What was taking her so long? It had been hours since she left him standing at the gate like a gaping fool. She was a perplexing woman. Cruel and cunning one moment, kind and considerate the next, and then playful and jovial another. He wasn't fooled; she meant to leave and was indeed cooking up a plot in her beautiful brain, but still, she didn't have to come to his aid this morn.

Rose had a tender side that had been bruised and battered. Whatever the hurt, she kept any of her goodness well hidden. Even now, the waiting was a game to her. She had not been here more than a day and already she was taxing his mental and moral fiber. Baron de Payne had not only raised a beauty, but he had allowed her to gain more knowledge than a woman ought to have. Even with her large fortune, her father would be hard-pressed to find her a husband that would be able to hold her reins.

As if God willed it, the door burst open and the lady rushed inward, a wave of dull, drab grey. Theo frowned. A young lady, such as she, should be wearing bright colors that could accentuate her lovely frame. Mayhap a nice gown would brighten her countenance and decrease her craftiness. Perhaps Agatha could remedy this situation. Surely Lady Eleanor had left something behind. Theo doubted his own thoughts. Nay. Lady Eleanor was shorter and somewhat rounder than Rose. However, he was certain Agatha could find something for the lady.

"I am so sorry I am late, but I had to say farewell to Sister Mary Ella and Percival. I do hope you enjoyed breaking your fast and are ready for another lesson." She flashed him a sunny smile and sat on his left side.

The look so plastered to her face reminded him of a Roman or Greek statue, a liking of a human but fake nonetheless. He wanted to remind her that the pair had left hours ago, but he was certain that was the point of her tarrying, to rile him with half-truths and a false disposition. So the games had begun. Theo bowed slightly and took his seat next to her. "I thought since the Psalms seemed to upset you so perhaps we could try something else."

She leaned forward enthusiastically. "I thought you had nothing else."

He handed her another parchment that she quickly unrolled. The glimmer of hope dimmed in her eyes as she began to read.

"This is naught but more Biblical readings." She sighed.

"Aye, but this is one of the Gospels. Look, the winged angel, the symbol of the Gospel of Matthew." Theo pointed to the picture the Crosswind monk had drawn at the top of the page.

"You mean a winged man," she corrected.

Theo tilted his head to the right. "That is not what Lady Catherine told me. But then I guess that does not matter, only the words are important." He brushed his fingers down on the scroll. "I have been practicing this part. I enjoy it very much."

She scanned the words, and her false sweetness slipped away to reveal her true visage. "Truly these words bring you joy?"

"Aye, and comfort too."

She sat back, and her lips curled. "Read them to me."

Her challenge was given with malice, but Theo was happy to oblige. "For if ye forgive men their trespasses, your heavenly Father will also forgive you: But if ye forgive not men their trespasses, neither will your Father forgive your trespasses." He had read it perfectly. In truth, he had it memorized. It was one of the first passages Lady Catherine had taught him.

Rose pushed the parchment his way. "I see you know these words well. Surely you do not believe this?"

"Of course, I do. They are words from Jesus's lips."

"They are words written by a man and said to belong to Jesus," she said flippantly.

Theo could not believe what he heard; why, her words were heresy. But had he not felt the same when he had left for France? That God's words were for those who did not have faith in themselves. But then he met Lady Eleanor, Lady Faith, and Lady Catherine, they had such a strong faith in God. Even after his accident, when he had returned to England and the devil tempted him with his failures, Lady Catherine had been the rope which held him to God. Theo had come to believe that all women were of a religious nature. Clearly, he had been mistaken.

"You have lost your faith?" he whispered.

A rage so wild filled her eyes with tears. She slammed her hands on the parchment. "You speak as if it is a terrible thing. Does it pay to have faith in a God who wants us to be unhappy? Who lets terrible things happen to his believers? Tell me the truth. Have you forgiven the man that did this to you?" She waved her hand at his marred face and body.

"The man who did this to me is dead," Theo said quietly.

"Then you are fortunate. Your revenge has been satisfied. But tell me, do you not have anger toward God for what has happened to you?"

For a moment he said nothing, for he could not fathom the anger and hate that had twisted her face into a hideous mask.

"Tell me," she snapped. "And do not lie to me. For I saw you beat the ground this morn and cry out in anguish."

Theo took a deep breath and brushed the hair away from his face. His gaze locked firmly on hers. "I do not know why God let the devil destroy my physical body. I do not know why those who love the Lord suffer. But lady, this I do know. Anger, resentment, and revenge twist the soul and bring forth more suffering and pain. God does not make us unhappy; we do that ourselves. I cannot change what happened, but I can change my thoughts and actions. Aye, I have my weak moments. Aye, I wish I were whole so I could be strong. But I never want to be the man I was before. He was bitter and selfish because he did not get what he thought he was owed. A man who hid his resentment through killing, drinking, and whoring. Thank God, I am no longer that man.

"As for the man who pushed me off the battlement, he was a tortured soul, and instead of seeking out love and forgiveness, he searched for revenge. And now, he may be suffering for all eternity because of it."

A wave of emotions flickered across her face—anger, hurt, pain, sadness, suffering, and lastly torment. "Still, could not have God changed your heart another way, without..." She lowered her gaze and then raised it again, this time filled with new defiance. "You may believe God does not seek to harm us. I have seen little where He does good." Her body shook and tears rolled down her face. "I cannot forgive. Not the man who harmed my mother nor a father who destroyed my happiness." She stormed from the room and no doubt was headed for the manor gate.

Theo rose and carefully rolled up the parchment. He still had much to learn, and he did not speak of the reading of words.

Nine

But to do good and to communicate forget not:
for with such sacrifices God is well pleased.
Hebrews 13:16

ROSE PUMPED HER ARMS AND LET THE RAGE SEEP through every pore in her body as she headed straight for the stables. How could Sir Theodore be so complacent with his situation? The anguish she had seen earlier this morn, though heartbreaking, was understandable. A man who desperately wanted to hold a sword, to fight again. All that made sense.

But this God-fearing, all-forgiving man she had just left…why, that was just preposterous. *Seek out love and forgiveness…* Bah. What kind of life did he have cloistered away in a broken-down keep? Why, he was no better off than the sisters at Godstow.

Seek out love and forgiveness… He said those words to make himself feel better for a life he could not change. She wagered that if the Almighty healed him tomorrow, he would leave Taine Manor without a backward glance. He'd return to killing and drinking and…whatever knights of his caliber do.

She heard Sir Rupert wheezing behind her before his figure came into view. "Where are you headed, my lady?"

"Out."

"Out where?"

Rose entered the stable and headed straight for Triumph's

stall. "Out of this manor. Out of the presence of your God-fearing liege lord."

Sir Rupert let out a crusty laugh. "I wouldn't call him that."

The old knight's disrespect infuriated Rose all the more. She snapped about and leveled him with a furious look. "Well, you should. Where would you be if Sir Theodore did not let you live here? He has given you food, shelter, and purpose." Any further words stuck in her throat when she realized she was defending the very man who had drawn up her hackles.

Rose turned back, found a blanket, and threw it on the animal's back.

"My lady, what are you doing?" This time the question came from Daniel, who stood in the stable entry.

"Leaving. Would you like to come? I am sure we can find food and shelter along the way."

Sir Rupert gaped and started coughing while Daniel's face flamed as usual. Rose shook her head and turned her attention back to Triumph.

"Daniel, ready one of the mares for Lady Rose, and Rupert, would you be so kind as to ready my mount? The lady and I would like to take a ride this morn."

Slowly she turned back to the entrance, and there stood Sir Theodore, jamming his curled right hand into a riding glove.

Without a word, both Daniel and Sir Rupert jumped into action, keeping their eyes averted. Sir Theodore held out his left hand. "Shall we wait in the courtyard, my lady?"

She raised her chin and bit her lower lip, but she did not take his offered hand. Lifting her skirt, she whisked past him and stood stiff in the yard. "I wish to leave, not take a ride," she said in a low voice.

"Aye, I know. But methinks it would be wise to plan your escape a little better than to leave without a cape or provisions."

He was trying to hide his insufferable crooked half smile

from her, which he could not. "If you know I am planning to leave, why not just help me along? Then you would not have to put up with my intolerable presence any longer."

He fixed his gaze on hers and tipped his head in a cordial manner. "But I enjoy your intolerable presence, and it would pain me greatly if you would leave."

She rolled her eyes and puffed a wayward curl from her face. "Then you would be the first."

Loud, strong, pleasant laughter escaped his lips and warmed the fall air. "Lady, it is a good thing you speak your mind, for if you wished to cast your woman's web wide with words laced with milk and honey, there would not be a man who could resist you."

Saints alive! She could feel her cheeks heat. Thankfully, Daniel and Sir Rupert appeared with the horses. With little assistance, she quickly mounted the mare. Not so for Sir Theodore. Sir Rupert produced a stool on which he guided his lord. Pain and agony contorted Sir Theodore's face as he tried to mount Triumph. The destrier danced and shook his mane as his master tried to right his seating.

Rose cast her gaze to the ground. Her heart ached. She had caused this scene to happen, such suffering and embarrassment. The poor man.

"Are we ready?" he asked in a strained voice.

Without raising her gaze Rose nodded, turning her mount to the open gate. She trotted next to him across the open countryside even though she could gallop away without him being able to give pursuit. However, it did not take her long to realize that the mare would do whatever the destrier did. If Sir Theodore veered right, so would the mare. If he turned left, so would her animal. Daniel had failed to tell her these horses must have been trained together. This mare would go nowhere without Triumph. No wonder Sir Theodore had no fear of taking her outside of Taine Manor.

Even though he was clearly in pain, he managed to control the beast quite well. With the simple flick of his left wrist, Triumph turned to the edges of the wetlands. The land became mushy, and a thin sheet of moisture rested on her face. Crooked trees loomed before them, and the cackles of crows drifted on the winds.

"Whatever you do, do not venture out into the wetlands. Day or night they will twist you about, and you will not know where you are. It may be the shortest way to the coast, but it is not the safest. There are drop-offs where you think the way is flat and easy. The worst of all is Devil's Cliff. The trees are thick right up to the edge. Many have lost their lives not knowing the cliff was there."

The mare trailed close to Triumph even when she tried to steer it away. "So then you must have ridden out through these lands often to know of such a place."

He shook his head. "Not by horse. But I have come part way by cart with Daniel. It is the best way to survey the land. Though I must admit there were places where the cart could not go. But we do have a rough sketch of it. I always think it is best to have knowledge of what you have been given."

He gritted his teeth. Rose suspected the action was not done in pain but because of his words—*you have been given.* There was his weakness. Sir Theodore may have forgiven the man who maimed him, but he could not let go of his pride. As bad as the land was, it had been given and not earned. He wanted to learn to read, for what? So he could find a way to pay Lady Eleanor and Sir Hugh de Maury for this land? Or did he seek something else? Self-worth?

Neither mattered to her. For she had just discovered that Daniel was truly the key to a successful departure. He helped map out this land. The lad might even know where the map could be found. Perhaps the loss of her temper over the scriptures earlier had not been a foolish act after all, but it could not be repeated if she wished to cleanly escape.

She nudged the horse next to his. "I am sorry for my outburst earlier. As my mother used to say, 'We must do with what we are given.' You only have Biblical writings, so that is what we will use. I think we should return and continue our lesson."

His brows shot northward. He nodded. Nevertheless, his guard was up, and it would take some work to knock it down.

'Twas not admirable, but he could not help it. Theo spent the rest of the morn trying to rekindle her anger. Instead of pulling out a different parchment, he continued with the scroll they had started this morn. Most of the verses he had memorized, but he did not recite it perfectly. He bumbled and fumbled around on even some of the easiest words. Not once did she lose her composure. She sat and instructed like a dutiful teacher so engrossed in her charge's progress.

Her mouth was full of praises for his efforts, and before she left, she patted his left hand. He suspected that right now she was pulling her beautiful tresses from her head.

No matter. The gauntlet had been thrown. She would try to scheme her way out of the keep, and he would disrupt every plan she could possibly conceive. An idea sprung up in his head. He would make her stay here more pleasurable.

He made his way to the hall, and when he was certain Lady Rose was not about, he called for Agatha.

Wiping her hands on her apron, Agatha shuffled from the kitchen. "Aye, my lord?"

"It seems that Lady Rose came with very few provisions, and I am wondering if Lady Eleanor left any clothing that could be made suitable for Lady Rose?"

Agatha took a deep breath. "Lady Eleanor had little herself when she lived here. Lord de Taine did not provide her decent clothing until you arrived to take her to Thornwood all those years ago."

Indeed, he remembered the day. Lady Eleanor had been unbearable with her constant prodding and pushing. He had been given orders to detain and slow her journey as much as possible. Finally, he couldn't take her badgering any longer, and they arrived at Thornwood ahead of schedule, much to

Sir Hugh's chagrin. But then, Lady Eleanor had managed to worm her way into everyone's heart. Theo winced inwardly. His included. But alas, one cannot change the past and one should not dwell on it.

He cleared his throat. "Well, if you do see anything that the lady would like, please let me know and I will compensate you."

Doubt clouded Agatha's eyes. "I shall try, sir. Is there anything else you want of me?"

Theo shook his head. "Nay, that is all."

The woman scurried back to the kitchen as if the fire of hell nipped at her heels. Theo let go of a deep breath. There went another fine woman. Mistress Agatha never complained and went about her exhausted list of duties. If he ever became a rich man, he would set the woman in a fine cottage and give her a few servants of her own. The wishful thought was just that; neither a hope nor a prayer could fulfill that dream, for Taine Manor had barely enough coin to keep going.

Upon leaving the hall, once again a tantalizing laugh drew him to the goat shed. Of course, he should have guessed. Sir Rupert sat propped up against the outside of the shed sleeping like a scruffy old goat. Perhaps he should be dubbed Methuselah. Rose and Daniel sat far away on the fence, their heads together, thick as thieves conspiring their escape. The lad looked at her with eyes full of worship. Did she know what a dangerous game she played?

Theo smiled. Once he, too, was a young lad in love. Even though he had been a squire at a different keep, once in a while Theo would return home on special occasions. One Christmas, he had been love-struck by the miller's daughter; her fair golden hair shimmered like the night stars, and her bright blue eyes captivated his green lad's heart. Nevertheless, his father had told him and his brother that under no circumstances were they to touch one hair of her head or any other maids that resided within their home. Fortunately, or unfortunately, his older brothers had taken him off one night to see a lady of many talents. Though the outing had been successful, it had never changed his desire toward the miller's daughter. A trace of those feelings swept Theo now as he watched Rose flash her sweet, seductive smile toward poor Daniel.

Theo cleared his throat, and Sir Rupert mumbled but did not awake. The pair on the fence flushed with a guilty look. However, Rose managed to school her features quickly. "Daniel, could I have a word with you?"

The lad bobbed his head and jumped from the fence while Rose fluffed her veil and batted her long lashes. The Lord save us. Daniel stood no chance against this siren. Nor did she understand the capabilities of a youthful lad in a fever of lust.

Theo threw his good arm about Daniel's shoulders when he approached. "I want you to deliver a message to Lady Catherine at Crosswind Keep for me."

The lad's face fell, and his gaze drifted back to Rose's. In the past when Theo had wanted Daniel to journey somewhere with a message, he would be filled with excitement, but not today, not since Lady Rose had entered the manor. "Aye, sir," he said despondently.

Ignoring Daniel's temperament seemed best. "I want you to tell the lady we will be attending the festival in two weeks."

The lad perked up. "All of us, sir?"

"Aye, lad. Do I ever go anywhere without you?"

"Nay, sir. But I meant…" Daniel cast his gaze to the ground.

Theo knew what he meant. The lad wanted to know if Lady Rose was coming along. Could the boy be that obtuse? Theo clenched his teeth. What else would tempt him to leave the safety of Taine Manor to be gawked at in such a public place? "I know what you meant," Theo snapped. "Of course, the lady and Sir Rupert and a few of the others will be joining us. Why, I even think your mother would like the jaunt."

The color drained from Daniel's cheeks at the mention of his mother.

"Tell Lady Catherine that Lady Rose will be joining us and will need special accommodations." Theo pulled a bag of coins from his belt, opened it, and took out one coin. "And make sure to give this bag to Lady Catherine to provide the proper clothing for Lady Rose."

Surprise crossed Daniel's face followed by an approving smile. He shook the bag in his hand. "Aye, my lord."

Theo held up the last coin. "And this is for you. Mayhap Lady Catherine can find a fine tunic for you that is not full of dirt and holes. Take one of the mares."

The lad cheeks colored again as he slipped the coins in a pouch. "My thanks," he said before he took off to the stables without giving Rose a second look.

But Theo couldn't resist a look back. She stood near the pen of bleating goats, her arms folded across her chest, and her brow deeply furrowed. Her ire drew him as much as her beauty. "Is there something wrong?" he asked.

"Where is he going?" She tapped her foot on the dusty ground even as a goat, Saint Philip, reared up and placed his front hooves on the fence, bumping his head against her back.

Theo tried not to smile for she did not give the animal any heed. Mimicking her, Theo folded his hands across his chest. "He is going to Crosswind Keep."

Her eyes grew wide, and he could practically see the million questions rattling in her head. However, she did not ask...at least not right away.

With a slight bow, Theo turned and started walking back to the hall.

She followed after him. "Why is he going there? What trade do you have with Lady Catherine? Was the message about me?" She stopped and inhaled deeply. Clearly the rain of questions had left her breathless.

He paused his steps. "Why do you always think everything is about you?"

Her mouth opened and closed, undoubtedly searching for an answer that was probably so foreign to her she couldn't fathom the meaning.

He let out a contrived sigh. "I sent him to accept Lady Catherine's invitation to the fall festival at Crosswind." He continued his walk to the hall.

She raced after him. Her face bright like a sunny day in midsummer. "Am I going too?"

Again, he paused and couldn't help but be pulled in by her infectious enthusiasm. "Aye, I suppose. Though why I would want to take someone who obviously doesn't seem to care about dancing, singing, and making merry is beyond my reasoning."

A squeal of delight left her lips, which drew Sir Rupert from his slumber and warmed Theo's soul. She reached out and hugged him, tight. "Thank you. Thank you. I have not danced since..." Tears hung in the corners of her eyes when she pulled away. She clapped her hands like a child and spun away dancing and singing a delightful tune all the way to the hall.

Theo stood frozen. Fearing if he took one step he would crumple to the ground. The sensation of her warm body and her sweet womanly scent clung to him. His heart pulsed and hammered blood into areas that were better off dead. Even when he had been a green lad pining for the miller's daughter, he had never felt this way. Nor when he fancied himself in love with Lady Eleanor.

"What is she so pleased about?" Sir Rupert asked when he came to Theo's side.

"I told her we were going to the fall fair at Crosswind."

Sir Rupert's head jerked up. "What? You, at the fair?"

A wave of irritation swept through Theo. He headed for the hall. "And you're going too."

"Oh, I'd rather not," Rupert grumbled, following Theo into the hall.

"Like it or not, you are. It is about time you do some hard work here." Theo put his hand on his hips and watched Lady

Rose twirl and swirl around every servant and knight in the hall.

"Hey? What are you talking about? I usually go out in the fields every day with the men." Rupert puffed out his chest and acted like he didn't even see Rose's antics. Perhaps he didn't.

"You go out into the fields, but you sleep while others do the hoeing, planting, and weeding."

Rupert stepped in front of Theo, trying to distract his gaze from Rose's dancing. "I'm giving the orders and guiding their progress and…"

Rose danced. Someone picked up a lute, and before he knew it, others began to sing. Theo caught himself humming.

Sir Rupert scowled. "Aw, the devil have it." With the wave of the hand, he quit the hall.

Agatha came from the kitchen, and she had a blue cloth draped over her arm. She said something to Rose and then handed her the cloth. With the flip of her wrists, Rose shook out the cloth and held up a blue gown with a red ribbon weaved through the neckline. Another shriek of joy left Rose's lips. She hugged Agatha and came over and gave him another hug before dancing away again, holding the garment to her chest.

Her infectious laughter filled the room as she whirled, skipped, and spun about. Agatha came to his side. "Where did you find the gown?" he asked, swaying to the music.

Agatha puckered her lips and paused a long while. "After you left, I went to search the cellar. I remembered some of the…ladies who used to enjoy Master Harding's company had left in a haste after you…came. They left a few of their belongings behind."

Theo's throat went dry. "Are you saying that's a whore's—"

Agatha raised a hand, cutting off his words. "Look how happy she is. Why, we have not had someone that jolly here in a long time."

Rose held the gown with one hand and then grabbed one of the aged knights with the other. They hopped and swayed to the music. She threw back her head; her veil cascaded to the floor exposing her long black braid, which swished to-and-fro across her back. She licked her red lips and began to sing a sweet melody.

A cold sweat trickled down Theo's spine. What had he done? Not only had he made a few simple decisions to maintain peace. He had allowed this young woman to touch his soul. This was more than a dangerous thing... Alas, it was a peril that would need a long recovery. Just like after his fall off the battlement in Normandy. Mayhap it would be better if Lady Rose did escape and soon.

Ten

Behold, I am the Lord, the God of all flesh:
is there anything too hard for me?
Jeremiah 32:27

EADING ACROSS THE COURTYARD TOWARD THE goat house, Rose hummed a merry tune. She clutched a sack full of dried meats close to her chest. Things were turning out better than she had planned. No longer did Sir Rupert follow her about. When Sir Theodore realized how excited she was about the festival, he called the older knight off. It had been years since she had a good time, and she would not leave until she had a little fun. However, that didn't mean she wouldn't leave soon after or during…

If she could figure out a way to hide and take her supplies along to the fair, then she might just slip away one night while everyone else was making merry. There was only one problem with that plan; fairs were never a safe place for a maid to be alone. Who knows what she would encounter on the road without an escort. She needed Daniel. She had to make sure he would not change his mind.

Rose cast her gaze around the courtyard just to be sure she wasn't being followed before she slipped into the shed. Instead of lifting her bag up into the rafters, she found an old man rummaging through the provisions she had smuggled in yesterday.

"Do you have any mead in that sack? This bread is a mite hard." The old man sat on a stool that had not been chewed by the goats. As a matter of fact, two goats sat calmly on either side of him, their noses twitching with their gazes locked on the bread. The old man swatted them away. "Peter and Paul, leave." The goats waddled away through the shed opening to the pen beyond.

With a measured look, Rose shifted her gaze from the goats to the sack at his feet, and then she looked up at the rafters. How did a round-shouldered old man manage to see and extract the sack? Would seem impossible, yet he held her bread.

"'Tis not your bread. Everything belongs to the Lord." He waved the bread before taking another bite.

His words startled her. At first she thought she had said her words out loud, but then noticed his clear, almost colorless eyes fixed on her bag. Rose twisted the sack in her hands and drew it toward her breasts. "It is a sin to steal."

The man wiped his mouth with his fingers and coughed again. "Aye. And that bread and meat you hold is not yours. Is there any drink in there?" He motioned to her bag.

"How did you…" Rose narrowed her gaze. Mayhap Sir Theodore had found a new spy to watch her whereabouts. "If you know I hold meat, then you know I have no drink."

"Ah, you are right, but I have a drink right here." The old man leaned over to his right side and picked up a mug of mead.

Astonishment and fright skittered down her spine, for she was certain that mug had not been there moments before. "Where did—"

"Rose, where are you?" At that very moment, Daniel entered the shed. When he spotted the old man, his cheeks colored and a guttural sound left his throat.

The old man raised the mug in his hand. "Daniel. How nice to see you. The lady was just bringing me some more food."

Daniel continued to stammer without getting a single intelligent word out. How was she ever going to get him to run away with her if he could not muster up one decent lie?

She thrust the bag into Daniel's hands and folded her arms. "The food is not yours. You should not have taken it. I am certain that mead is not yours, either." She looked around the shed. "Though where it came from I do not know," she mumbled.

The old man laughed. "Anything within this shed is mine. If you do not believe me ask the boy."

Finally, Daniel managed to nod his head. "This is Master Jude's home. He is in charge of the goats."

So this was the elusive Master Jude who had arrived with Sir Theodore from France. That this elderly man made it across the channel without expiring was a miracle in itself. Nonetheless, Master Jude must be more agile than he looked in order to sneak around without notice. No doubt, this was the man's true purpose—to spy for Sir Theodore.

Rose raised her chin and looked down her nose at him. "Go back and tell Sir Theodore that even if he foiled this plan there will be others."

"Rose!" Daniel admonished. "He is your elder."

Master Jude laughed again, placing the mug on the ground. "'Tis all right. I take no offense."

He then sharpened his gaze, and Rose could have sworn it sliced right through her.

"I do not need to spy in order to know what I know. Your intentions are plainly written on your face. Now before you say another word that you may regret someday, go and help Daniel fill the hay trough."

Master Jude waved her off and held out his hand to the sack in Daniel's arms. The fool handed it over without a single word. She almost grabbed the bag back, but then decided irritating the man would only make him more tenacious in his spying. Instead, she turned on her heels and marched out of the shed into the pen with Daniel in tow.

"Saints be praised. Who does he think he is?" she ranted.

Daniel picked up the pitchfork and began filling the trough. "Please keep your voice down. He might hear you."

Rose wanted to argue but then thought he could be right. Master Jude may look old, but that didn't mean he was deaf too.

"You shouldn't have talked to him that way. Nobody does."

Rose paced back and forth as Daniel continued to carry out the task. "And why is that? He is just another old man that lives at this keep. Like all the others, except clearly this one is a peasant."

"Nay. That is not true. He knows things others do not. He's a wise man. Often Sir Theodore seeks his counsel." Daniel paused his chore and leaned on the pitchfork. "Some here claim they can't even see him," he whispered.

"What nonsense. You make it sound like he is a ghost. Keep this in mind, ghosts do not eat. While we stand here shoveling hay, he is eating our food."

Daniel opened his mouth. "Pardon, Rose. But I'm the one doing the—"

"'Tis just a use of words. He is naught but a spy for Sir Theodore and full of no more wisdom than you and I. Though I do believe that Sir Theodore and Master Jude do plot their deeds together often. And right now they are plotting against you and me."

Frowning, Daniel shook his head. "I don't think—"

"Never fear. I shall take care of this forthwith." Rose spun about ready to give Master Jude a piece of her mind, but when she entered the shed, he was gone, along with the stool. Two empty sacks lay on the ground. She looked in every corner, but he was nowhere to be found. There was only one entry, and yet he had managed to slip by them.

Daniel poked his head into the shed. "I've fed the goats… Oh, so he has left again."

Rose looked around the shed one more time. "Apparently. Did you see him slip by us?"

"Nay. But that doesn't surprise me. He's always disappearing and reappearing."

She rolled her eyes and then glanced around the shed just once more for good measure. "Like a ghost," she mumbled.

Daniel nodded. "Aye. Like a ghost."

The door to Theo's solar flew open, hitting the wall. Lady Rose stood in the entry with a deep scowl on her face. It had occurred to Theo that he had not seen her wearing that look since she had learned about the festival. But alas, plainly the reprieve from her temper had ended.

Theo dropped the parchment on the table and heaved a heavy sigh. "Is there something I can help you with, my lady?"

"I met Master Jude," she huffed without moving from the doorway.

Theo slowly nodded his head. "And…"

She rushed into the room and pointed a finger at his face, a whiff of straw tickled his nose. "Don't 'and' me. You know full well he is your new spy to replace Sir Rupert."

A laugh stuck in Theo's throat, but he knew better than to send it into the air. "My lady, I can assure you Master Jude is not my spy. He is his own man. I could not tell him what to do more than I could command the wind. The man comes and goes as he pleases."

"Daniel told me you are often in counsel with him." She lifted up her chin and placed her hands on her hips.

Words of defense came first to his mind, but then that would only rile her more. "Perhaps you would like to sit down." He motioned to the chair next to the hearth.

She opened her mouth and then looked down at his right leg. With a snap, she shut her lips and sat. He took a seat in the chair across from her.

"Would you like something to drink?" he asked calmly.

"Nay," she retorted.

"In truth, I know very little about Master Jude. He was the man who drove the cart which took me to the French coast. He decided to join me on my travel back to England. At that time, I thought it was out of pity, but then he was as mysterious on the ship as he is now. There would be days I did not see him at all, and yet, I knew he could not have gotten off the ship."

"Now you sound like Daniel. He said Master Jude was like a ghost." Her bluster dissipated; she leaned back in the chair.

"I would not say that, but he definitely is a mystery. Do you know I do not even know his real name? He told me to call him whatever I wanted. I am the one who christened him Jude."

"If what you say is true, then for sure the man is a villain." She reached her arms out to the fire and closed her eyes.

The firelight danced off her fair face as the afternoon sun faded from the solar windows. Theo's heart squeezed in his chest. He took another cleansing breath to clear his thoughts. "I thought so too in the beginning, but now I do not. He does not lie; his words are plain and straightforward. He does not steal nor does he seem to care if this keep survives or fails. It is as if his thoughts are from another realm."

Rose shrugged. "Shows how much you know him. For he took from me..." Her cheeks and neck turned crimson as she stumbled into her own trap.

"Do continue, my lady."

She dropped her hands and her gaze to her lap. "Nay. 'Tis not important. I just am not sure I believe you."

Theo wanted to reach over and take her delicate hands in his and reassure her, yet her words about touching him still stung sharp in his mind. "I have no reason to lie. He is not following you on my order. If he wishes to converse with you, he has a reason. At times, he appears to give advice when I think I already know the answer, but often I discover I am wrong." Theo shifted in his chair. "This much I do know, his guidance is tried and true."

Her gaze shot up with a twinkle of playfulness in her blue eyes. "Mayhap he is an angel."

"You jest, but I am not sure you are wrong. Sometimes I think he is…" Theo shook his head and looked at the fire. "You would think me crazy if I told you."

"Aye, he is not God."

His gaze flipped to hers. "But the thought came to your mind too."

She rose and smoothed out her lovely blue gown. "I have had enough of this 'God talk.' I will hold you to your word that Master Jude is not your spy." The flames rekindled in her eyes before she narrowed them. "But know this. If I find out you have lied, you will regret it."

With dainty steps, she walked to the door. One would think she was a demure, defenseless maid. But Theo knew better—never cross the lady or there would be hell to pay.

Once again, Rose could not sleep, still fuming over the lost provisions. She would have to collect more, and what better time than now when everyone was asleep. Clearly a new place to hide the food would have to be found, but for the moment she could keep it in her room. In fact, if she did get caught this eve rummaging through the kitchen, she could say she was famished and needed something to curb her hunger.

All the same, she grabbed her slingshot, the only possession she had managed to smuggle out of Godstow. A little added security, just in case she needed it. She scampered down the steps and once again was drawn by the groans and moans she knew to be Sir Theodore's. In the moonlight, she saw the keep gate partially opened. And, like before, beyond the keep was Sir Theodore trying, once again, to raise and wield his sword with his left hand.

Rose bent down and picked up a few rocks before heading through the gate. She placed one stone in her slingshot and flung it at Sir Theodore's feet. Immediately he turned as she continued to walk toward him.

"Lady Rose, you should be in bed," Theo said, huffing and puffing. Even in the dim moonlight she could see sweat dripping down his face

"As should you. But here you stand."

He eyed the slingshot and rocks in her hand. "Do you aim to finish me off?"

She laughed. "Methinks it would take more than these few stones to penetrate your thick hide." Rose regretted her words, for clearly he thought she spoke of his scars. "Nay, I did not mean—"

"It matters not. Where did you get that?" He pointed at her slingshot.

"I made it at Godstow." She shook the slingshot in her hand. "Actually I made two, but the first was taken away from me."

"Why, were you hitting the other nuns with your dangerous stones?" His words were given in jest, but they were not funny to her.

"I began whittling my first slingshot when night visitors started coming to my cell."

The sword went limp in his hand, and a look of horror etched the good side of his face. "Visitors. Pray tell, you were not—"

She held up a hand. "These visitors were hairy with sharp teeth and long tails. Rats. I had learned to make a slingshot from one of the peasant lads when I was around ten summers old. We had much fun killing many a rat and other vermin that entered the keep. So I thought I would do the same at Godstow. We did have our share of rats."

A sympathetic look crossed his face and riled her insides. Like him, she did not want pity, only understanding.

"When I caught my first rat, I marched to the abbess's chamber and proudly held up the dead rat. She was not amused at all. For I had killed a creature that God had placed at Godstow to teach us patience in our earthly suffering. She took away my slingshot and made me do penance."

Theo dug the tip of his sword in the ground and gripped

the hilt for support. "There are some strange beliefs in the Church."

"That is a mild way of putting it." Rose held up her slingshot. "I then made this one and kept it hidden. Many knew I had it, but no one told the abbess. I killed at least ten in our kitchen alone. Sister Mary Jane, our main cook, was very thankful." She wrinkled her nose. "Though even with the rats gone, it was not my favorite place to be."

"You do not like preparing food? I loved the kitchens as a child, for there was always extra bread or potatoes to be had."

A longing crept into his eyes as a sadness crept into her soul. His past gave him comfort, while hers... "Let us think on something else. Why do you keep trying to wield your weapon? When it brings you naught but anguish."

He looked down at his sword and tapped the tip against the ground. "Even though my battle days are over, one never knows when one might have to defend a precious possession—"

"Or a dilapidated keep." They both laughed on this. She thought to give him her slingshot as an easier weapon to use, but his right hand would not be able to hold and aim the sling any better than the sword. "Come, I think you have practiced enough for one night."

He nodded, and once again using his sword as a crutch, they walked back to the keep not knowing that this would soon become a nightly ritual—she and her sling, him and his sword.

Eleven

*Till he fill thy mouth with laughing,
and thy lips with rejoicing.*
Job 8:21

HE SMALL CARAVAN JOSTLED OVER THE BUMPY road as it made its way to Crosswind Keep. Rose nudged one of the mares near the cart where Daniel and Sir Theodore rode on the front bench while Mistress Agatha sat in the rear, fussing over the meat pies, cheese, and other goods they planned to sell at the fair. The closer the festival approached the sourer Sir Theodore had become. He refused to talk about the upcoming affair during their lessons, and he almost shouted the roof off the hall when Agatha approached him about selling a few bushels of grain to help with the manor finances. In the end, he relented and even added two more carts to their party. One hauled wheat and rye to be sold at the fair marketplace and another that carried another brazier and shield and a multitude of drawings that only Sir Theodore and Sir Gregory, who had become the official smithy at Taine Manor, were allowed to see. Whatever the content, all hoped the sale would bring good fortune to the manor.

Even Rose could not tamp down her excitement. Tomorrow she would have a joyous time at the fair, and at week's end, she and Daniel would flee for the coast, even if Daniel truly was a reluctant participant. The task to persuade him had not been easy. When their provisions had been discovered by Master Jude, Daniel wanted to wait until next spring to leave. There was no way she would winter in Taine Manor. The thought of spending the cold season in the drafty tower curled Rose's toes.

With a little more coaxing and a lot of false promises, Daniel finally relented and agreed to stick to the original plan of fleeing before the fair ended. They had found a new hiding place for their food in an abandoned serf's hut not far from the manor. In fact, the spot was better than the goat shed. No one paid Daniel any heed where he went, for he was always scurrying about doing some task. Plus, her talk with Sir Theodore about Master Jude must have served its purpose, for the elderly man had not been seen again.

At the present, most of their goods were hidden in the cart beneath the barrels of wheat while she held a few extras in her own parcel secured to the mare. None were the wiser. Freedom was a few short, fun-filled days away.

Rose held the reins of the mare tight to keep the horse near the cart. "We should be there shortly, should we not?" she called to Daniel.

"Aye, Crosswind Keep is just around the next turn in the road," he said brightly.

Sir Theodore grunted and pulled his cloak tighter about him. "I'll be glad when I am back near the hearth at Taine Manor." The man's bottom lip hung so low that his chin puckered with ugly lines even on the good side of his face.

His grumpy mood could not dampen her spirits. "If you despise this so much, why did you say we could come?"

Sir Theodore tipped his head to the side, glared at her, but did not say a word.

The cross look sent a joyful giggle to her lips. She kicked the sides of the mare, and the horse took off ahead of the party. Sir Rupert's curses followed her as he tried to give pursuit on the other old swayback mare. Around the bend she pulled up on the reins, and Sir Rupert almost crashed his horse into her mare's backside.

Ahead stood Crosswind Keep. Its large, high curtain walls spoke of power and strength. The lush green fields and farms spoke of its wealth. And the banner which flew above spoke of the Templars. Though, a smaller blue and gold banner flew below, no doubt the de Maury colors.

"I did not think it would be so grand," she said.

Sir Rupert leaned forward in his saddle and wiped his brow. "Is not Rockbridge more impressive, my lady?"

"Mayhap, but I have not seen anything as lovely as this in a long time." She pointed to the left of the keep. "See yonder? Are those not archery fields? I did not know there was to be a contest."

"Nor I, my lady." Sir Rupert shifted his weight. "I do know that Sir Hugh is one of the finest archers around. Clearly he learned the skill growing up here." Sir Rupert gave her a thoughtful look. "At one time, Sir Theodore was a fierce competitor too. In a strange way, he lost Lady Eleanor's hand at an archery tourney."

Rose knew of Eleanor's rejection of Sir Theodore, but she did not know all the particulars. Rose's heart constricted. The reasons were no longer important, but the thought of him losing his ability to participate in such a tourney tore at her something fierce. How hard it must be to watch others in their revelry while he stood on the sidelines.

She pushed the uncomfortable thought out of her mind and let her gaze drift to the other side of the keep. Mercers and peasants were setting up tents for the fair. From the looks of things, some were already hawking their wares. She cast a sidelong glance at Sir Rupert. "The last to the yonder tents shall buy the other a tasty treat." Rose did not wait for an answer but took off in a full gallop as her laughter trailed behind her.

At the tents, she pulled up the reins and enjoyed the grumblings of Sir Rupert. "We should have waited for the others. Ye could have been clipped off by one of the Templar archers." He pointed to the guards on top of the battlements.

"Aye, a lady and an old knight are a great danger to the welfare of Crosswind." Rose spotted a tent that was already cooking egg pies. She dismounted and led her horse toward the pavilion. "You lost our wager. You can buy me one of those pies, for I am famished."

"I do not have the coin to fill your belly. I barely have enough to fill my own. Besides, I made no wager." Sir Rupert followed but did not reach for his purse.

Rose's mouth watered at the smell of rosemary, basil, and chives drifting through the air. She had some silver in the bottom of her bag, but that would be needed for her escape. Nor did she wish for Sir Rupert to know about the funds. Best she kept them a secret. She turned away from the golden-crusted pies and walked on as more mercers arrived with bolts of fine linen and silks from the east. Farmers carried bushels of turnips, leeks, and beans. Hunters spread out their fish and fowl. Jesters practiced their juggles and stories to entertain the fairgoers. All hoped to make some profit so they could feed their families this winter.

But the Church and the Templars would gain the most. For without their sanction, this festival could not take place. They would take a measure of every yield and become the strongest overlord throughout the known world. Even King John, who some say robbed many a church coffer to keep his brother Richard in prison years ago, would not overstep the boundaries laid down by the Crosswind Templars.

Nonetheless, Rose could not be angered by the greedy or the thieves who would surely lift a few purses this week. In her opinion, any fair held great enjoyment and she planned to take her fill. By the time Sir Theodore and Daniel rolled up, she was in the midst of singing a merry tune with one of the jesters.

All in the party smiled, except one. Sir Theodore sat with his cloak and hood draped over his body like a shroud. "If you do not mind, my lady. I think it would be best to meet Lady Catherine before we delight in the advantages of the fair."

Rose's spirits dipped a little but could not be hampered by the dreary man. "Of course. By all means, Sir Theodore. Please lead the way. Sir Rupert and I will follow."

If she could have made out his face in the dark hood, she would have expected his scowl had deepened. Without saying another word to her, Sir Theodore ordered Daniel to drive the cart through the open gate. The rest of the party followed in somber silence except for her and Sir Rupert, who still hummed the jester's cheery tune.

Oh, it was going to be a grand fair indeed.

Rose dropped her horse off at the stables and strolled through the bustling bailey. Monks robed with the Templar tunic were everywhere. Not only were they stationed on the ramparts, but they seemed to be in every building within the curtain walls. They were in the stables; they stood in the doorways of the armory and by the smithy. They ran to-and-fro from storage cellars, the buttery, and probably the kitchens as well. She suspected the hall would be likewise—full of them. Like bats in a cave, she mused as she walked up the great hall steps.

Her assumptions were proven true when she entered. Monks raced about preparing for the festival while Sir Theodore stood in the middle, still covered up like the Middle Eastern Bedouins she had read about in one of her father's scrolls. A silly thought skipped into her mind. Mayhap that was the reason Theo kept all those goats at Taine Manor. Secretly, he was not Sir Theodore at all, but a Bedouin who used to herd goats and camels across the great African deserts. A large smile spread across her face, which drew the attention of the man himself and a woman dressed in a fine emerald velvet gown. Her head covered by a wimple of green and gold. The moment she turned recognition flooded Rose's memory. Lady Catherine, still as beautiful as she had been when she came to visit Godstow.

"Rose." Lady Catherine held out her hands, and Rose ran right to them. The older woman gave Rose a hug and then pulled away to have a good look. "How are you?"

"Fine and so excited to be here," Rose exclaimed. Warmth spread up her spine when Lady Catherine's gaze skipped up and down Rose's figure. No doubt assessing her garments.

Sir Theodore greeted Rose with a formal bow, which put Rose on edge. Why all of a sudden did he act the gracious lord?

"You look well fed, but there are other things…" Lady Catherine said, then shifted her gaze to Sir Theodore and gave a conspiratorial nod. "We shall finish our discussion later, Theo. Right now I think it would be wise to take Lady Rose to her chamber."

He bowed slightly to Lady Catherine. "I agree. Every effort must be ensured to make Lady Rose comfortable. If you will excuse me, I have to go and see to the rest of my party."

"Then you do not mind sleeping in a pavilion near the fair? I know it is not as comfortable as your—"

"It will be more than comfortable." He bowed again. "Ladies," he said before he took slow, measured steps toward the hall entry.

Lady Catherine watched him with sad eyes. "I do hope he will be all right. He is such a good, but fragile, man."

Fragile seemed to be a debatable term, but Rose held her tongue. One did not disagree with one's hostess. Gad! She was beginning to sound like Sir Theodore.

"Come." Lady Catherine led Rose up a set of stone stairs. "There are three additional chambers on this level. One will be for my son Hugh and his wife. Mine, which I was going to share with you, but Theo wouldn't have it. He wanted you to have your own chamber." She walked farther down the hall. "So you may use the chamber which used to belong to my son Julian."

Lady Catherine entered the room and pulled back heavy drapes from a few small windows. The room, though modest, was comfortable with a table, a pair of soft cushioned chairs, a large trunk, and a good-size bed in the center, mounded with a heavy coverlet. Above the bed hung a tapestry with a golden-haired boy on his knees; his hands folded in prayer. "Do you know the child, my lady?" Rose asked.

A soft laugh left the delicate woman's lips as she stared at the tapestry. "I should say so. That is my son Julian when he was a young lad." She longingly gazed at the tapestry. "Even then, he was full of the spirit of the Lord."

The religious term made Rose squirm. Just because a man prayed a lot did not make him full of God or bring a person closer to Him. She had prayed often that her father would relent and let her marry Conrad. How hard had she prayed that her mother's life would be spared? In either circumstance, not once did God hear or lift a finger in answer. "Is he not coming to the festival?"

"Nay. His wife, Ariane, is heavy with another child. This will be their fourth. Praise be to God. I do hope this one is a girl. It would even things out. Alas, Julian does not wish to leave his wife." Lady Catherine put her hand on Rose's arm. "Which brings good fortune to you. I usually hold this room for Sir Theo, but he would not take the comfort."

The thanks stuck in Rose's throat as a wave of guilt rolled in her stomach. "With his condition, Sir Theodore should have this room. I have no quarrel with staying with you or even in the women's quarters."

Lady Catherine threw up her hands. "Aye. I tried to tell him you would not mind, but he was adamant. He said you have given up much since coming to Taine Manor, and he wanted you to have a little bit of the comfort you used to have."

Why did he do such a selfless gesture? Surely keeping an eye on her whereabouts would be harder if she resided in the keep while he hunkered down in a tent. Rose strode to the window and looked out into the bright fall day. Though the weather was warm, inviting, and lovely, it could change with a shift of the wind. Plus, the nights were growing chilly and Sir Theodore did not fare well in the cold. "Oh, my lady.

This is not right. I will find him, and I will insist he takes this room. Then, if it is all the same to you, I will happily sleep in your chamber."

"By all means, if you can sway his mind."

"Good. I will go find him now." Rose started for the door.

"Wait," Lady Catherine called after her. "There is one more thing." She walked over to the large trunk at the foot of the bed and flipped it open. "These things are for you."

The trunk was laden with gowns of different colors and materials. Some even had beading, while others were trimmed with gold or silver ribbons. Rose picked up a warm fur-lined cloak only to find a linen chemise lying below. There was also a pair of satin slippers and a pair made of soft leather.

"My lady, your generosity is too great. I cannot accept these gifts." Rose placed the cloak back in the chest.

"The only thing that is from me is the cloak. The rest was purchased by Sir Theo." Lady Catherine held up a sapphire gown trimmed with gold piping. "This one almost matches the color of your eyes."

Rose stared at the dress. Indeed, it was marvelous, even more beautiful than those she had worn when she was young. "I can't. He should not have wasted his precious coin on me. Why did he do such?"

Lady Catherine laid the gown on the bed. "Perhaps he is grateful for what you are doing for him. His desire to read is great. Though his body is beyond repair, his mind is still strong. You give him hope, where before he had none. Graciously accept these gifts. Besides, you know he would never sell them, and I don't think they would fit him."

They both laughed at the silly thought. "You are right, though it may be funny to see. Do you think the color would flatter him?"

"Do stop." Lady Catherine's laughter brought tears to her eyes. "I think he would be appalled if he knew the twist of our conversation. Let me help you change." She motioned to the gown on the bed.

"Nay, I am capable of dressing myself. It is one skill I became proficient at while living at Godstow. However, the nuns would never allow me to wear something so grand."

Again, they shared a laugh. "I would imagine not. All right, I will leave you to it. Later, I will have the trunk moved to my room. I have a feeling you will be able to persuade him." Lady Catherine gave Rose a knowing smile before she left.

When the door shut, Rose turned her attention to the gown on the bed. Lifting the garment, she knew it would fit her perfectly. She went over and pulled out the leather slippers, holding them to her feet. They would fit perfectly too. Sir Theodore had a better eye for measurements than what she would have thought. Her skin heated with pleasure and remorse at the same time. She was flattered that he would take such notice, but sad for she would betray his kindness with deception when she would flee. There was only one thing to do. She would have to leave the gowns behind.

Rose touched the heavy cloak and ran her fingers over the soft thick fur. This she would take, for it would keep her warm on the cold winter days ahead. Furthermore, it was a gift from Lady Catherine and not Sir Theodore. Again, Rose held up the leather shoes. She would take these too, for surely he would not want her feet to freeze either. However, even with the decisions made, Rose could not squelch how her selfishness would inflict pain to those who had only been gentle and gracious.

After she had changed, Rose made her way out of the keep through the bailey to the area where many travelers, merchants, and mercers were raising their pavilions. It did not take her long to spot Sir Rupert and Sir Gregory dragging the brazier, shield, and scrolls into the tent.

"Where is Sir Theodore?" she asked.

The pair shrugged. "He left with Daniel and Sir Hugh a few moments ago. No doubt discussing another extension of payment for Taine Manor," Sir Rupert said. "Seems he had a few unexpected purchases this month which cost him extra coins." His gaze flipped over her clothing, and they both knew where those precious coins had gone.

"I heard them say something about the armory. Mayhap he is finally going to sell his sword. What use is it to him, anyway?" Sir Gregory snickered.

Heat fueled by anger infused her body. "What do you know of his skill? He is a knight just the same as you. How dare you jest about it?" She did not wait to hear Sir Gregory's blubbering. Instead, she turned and walked back to the bailey, skirting around carts filled with rugs and treasures from the east, bleating sheep and nickering horses, squabbling servants and rude knights.

Once inside the gate, she headed straight for the armory, dodging pages and squires going about their lords' businesses. She found the threesome at the entry, Sir Hugh showing a sword to Daniel. The moment she was within earshot the group hushed.

"Lady Rose, what are you doing you?" Sir Theodore's terse statement was followed by a look of contrition. "I am sorry. 'Tis I did not expect—"

The dark-haired man with eyes a striking blue stepped forward and lifted her hand, placing a warm kiss upon it. "I am honored to meet you, Lady Rosemond."

With visible notice, Sir Theodore bristled. "May I present Sir Hugh de Maury?"

Rose pulled her hand away and hid it in her cloak. "You resemble your mother."

"I hope that is a pleasant thing. Many say she is an attractive woman, even at her age."

She could have sworn that Sir Theodore had rolled his eyes at the remark.

"But alas, the true beauty stands before me." Sir Hugh flashed a dashing smile that made her want to laugh but clearly had a different effect on the others. Daniel flamed like a candle, as if that was anything new, and Sir Theodore gave out a sound that was close to a growl.

"I have heard much about you, Sir Hugh. Sir Theodore sings of your praises often."

Sir Hugh lifted his eyebrows at her last comment, and his gaze swiveled to his friend. "Really? He speaks highly of me?"

"Well, not as much as your wife." Rose's last retort soured Sir Hugh's smile and caused Sir Theodore to beam. "I hear she is quite a remarkable woman. I do look forward to meeting her."

"You shall this evening; we shall all sup together, won't we, Theo?"

A darkness fell on Sir Theodore's face. "I have other business to attend to this eve, but I am sure Lady Rose would like the company."

"But surely you must eat?" Rose pleaded.

"Why have you come to the armory?" he asked, avoiding her question.

Indeed, she did come here with purpose. "I wish to speak to you about the sleeping arrangements."

Her comment caused Sir Hugh to cough while Daniel turned purple. With the guide of a hand, Sir Theodore moved her away from the armory to the middle of the bailey. He looked back over his left shoulder to where Sir Hugh stood. "You must choose your words more carefully or you will give others the wrong impression," he said in a low voice.

"I do not care what others think," she said at the top of her lungs.

He tried to shush her, but she would not have it.

"I'll not sleep in a room that was offered to you. I have no issue with sleeping with Lady Catherine."

Sir Theodore scanned the bailey. Besides Sir Hugh and Daniel, a few more stopped to watch them also. "I will be quite comfortable out in the pavilion."

"Are you mad? The cold will do you no good. Plus, with Sir Rupert, Sir Gregory, Daniel, and Mistress Agatha—"

"Mistress Agatha is sleeping in the women's quarters. Do try to keep your voice down."

"Even so, there are other servants from Taine too. All of you sleeping in one tent, you'll be packed in like a barrel of rotting herring. Either you sleep in the chambers offered by Lady Catherine or I'll... I'll give you back all these fine clothes." Rose stripped off the cloak and threw it at his face.

More stopped in their tasks to watch the scene unfold as Sir Theodore caught the cloak with his left hand. "My lady, you must calm down. Look about you."

Without a turn of her head, she knew their audience had grown. She reached for the hem of her gown and began pulling it upward. "Let them watch. If you do not take the chamber, then I will strip off all you have given me."

Daniel and Sir Theodore now both had purple faces. He threw her cloak over his shoulder and then bent down to still her hands at her knees. "My lady, what you do is unseemly."

She glared at him. "Will you take the room?"

"Nay," he said through gritted teeth.

With a yank, she pulled her gown from his hand and started pulling it up her thighs, ignoring the gawking pages and the squires who were licking their lips.

"Cease," Sir Theodore roared.

She froze and so did all in the bailey. "Will you take the chamber?" she whispered. She knew she had him when he gave out a heavy sigh.

"All right," he said.

Rose dropped her gown, and a few onlookers groaned.

Sir Theodore looked about with an evil eye. Immediately all returned to their duties, except for one.

Sir Hugh guffawed and smacked a fist on his chest. "Hail to Lady Rosemond. The victor and fairest maid around."

Twelve

*And as ye would that men should do to you,
do ye also to them likewise.*
Luke 6:31

ONE WOULD THINK THE FESTIVAL HAD BEGUN ALREADY
by the revelry in the great hall. This wasn't the usual
fare of food for Crosswind Keep. Venison and crispy capons,
roasted potatoes and cooked vegetables, all heaped on brown
bread trenchers filled the air with mouthwatering aromas.
The lords and ladies who sat in the hall this eve would not
leave hungry or in some cases sober. Wine, ale, and mead
flowed along with the delicious food. Theo would wager
many would be stumbling into the wrong pavilions when the
feast was over. Yet the monks took it all in stride and so did
Lady Catherine. She sat at the head table with her son Hugh
and his wife, Eleanor. To the hostess's left sat Rose in the
sapphire gown she had earlier tried to shed in the bailey. The
color accented her smoky grey-blue eyes, and her
exquisiteness had caught the attention of many lords and
knights. There was none as beautiful as Rose, but like with
all roses, she did have her thorns.

She sat like a prim, docile innocent who politely
chattered with the hostess. Most would think her so calm, so
delicate, so tender. So perfect. Few could take their eyes off
Lady Rose.

Theo's stomach curled. By contrast, most who gazed
upon him had other thoughts—so frightening, so grotesque,

so callous. So ugly. Once he stepped out of the shadows, the gaiety would be momently paused by gasps and gawks. Few gazed on him more than a second.

Blast! He should have stayed at Taine Manor. But then Rose would not be smiling and his recent invention would be collecting dust. There was nothing for it. If he wanted to earn Taine Manor, he would need to give Lady Eleanor a fair price for it even if she didn't want his coin. He would not stand for charity.

Theo gritted his teeth and stepped into the light. As expected, many stopped their eating, drinking, and carousing to stare at the beast who had entered the room. Nonetheless, he threw back his shoulders and took slow, measured steps toward the head table.

"Theo," cried Lady Eleanor with delight. "It is so good to see you. Come, sit by me!" The knight sitting next to her shifted down, opening a spot. Thankfully, it was a chair and not a bench, for all would enjoy the spectacle of watching the cripple trying to maneuver his bad leg over the plank.

Even so, Theo took the seat with a hard thump. He placed his good arm on the table while the other drooped at his side. A word had not escaped his lips when one of the servants plopped a trencher in front of him and a tankard of ale at his left. Theo pushed the tray away, scanning the tables of merrymakers. His pulse kicked up a notch when he spotted Lord Iron and Lord de Baston. Open-minded and men of novelty pursuits, they could change Theo's fortunes. That they had agreed to meet with him on the morrow was a gift in itself. Though both looked at him with speculative gazes, no doubt wondering if the monster could really produce anything of importance.

Lady Eleanor leaned in. "Theo, where is your mind? You have been sitting here staring at Lady Catherine's guests without touching your food or drink."

"I am not hungry." He shifted his gaze to Eleanor and still marveled at how her lopsided grin could capture every heart in the room.

"Mmm… I wonder at your preoccupation. Is it because this is the first time I have seen you in a room full of people, or is it because you have a most enchanting creature living at Taine?"

Of course, Eleanor would go straight to the heart of the matter. There was no idle talk with her. "I would not be here if I did not have some business to conclude tomorrow."

Eleanor rubbed a finger over her lips. "Really? It is an act of commerce that brings you here? I had heard you usually invite those who have dealings with you to Taine Manor, or if the season was right, you would venture to the lord's keep."

Theo said naught, for Eleanor had a way of burrowing to the truth faster than a tick in one's skin.

"Since you have not attended any festivals since you have returned to England, I would think the lady would be the reason." Eleanor took a drink from her goblet to hide a grin that spread like a wide river across her lips.

"Do not make more of this than what it is. She is educating me to read, that is all."

Eleanor placed the goblet back on the table and still could not wipe the smile from her face. "That is not how Hugh tells it. He said you are besotted."

A puff of air left Theo's mouth. "Clearly your husband's vision has dimmed over the years."

At that moment, a lovely laugh floated on the air and traveled up Theo's spine. Eleanor leaned over to look at the author of its source, then turned back. "Ah. Lady Rosemond has an enduring laugh, does she not?"

Theo turned away from Eleanor's intense gaze. "I would imagine all women sound the same when they are happy."

"Oh, Theo. You know that is not true, but nonetheless, I will not goad you any longer. For I am happy that you have given up your monkish ways. Come, give me a hug." She leaned over and wrapped her arms around him, giving a good squeeze. "Please tell me this means you will come to Thornwood when the winter has ebbed."

"I cannot say what I will do that far in the future." He unwrapped himself from her arms.

She sat back in her chair. "Oh, so true. I could be heavy with child again as I was two springs ago."

Theo scanned the room. "Where is little Henrietta? With that other scamp, Isobel?"

Eleanor chuckled. "In truth, Isobel is mild compared to my daughter and a good influence on her. No doubt, right now Henrietta is probably terrorizing her nurse. I do not know where she gets her energy or her ideas from."

Could she be so obtuse? Henrietta was the epitome of her mother. Incorrigible and completely infectious.

"Thankfully, she takes after her father in looks or she would be in trouble indeed. Truly, who would want her if she was plain like me?" Eleanor asked.

Theo gazed at the woman he once fancied to marry. "If I remember rightly, there were many fighting for your hand."

She reached over and squeezed his left hand. "You and I remember it differently. I think most were after Taine Manor."

The sad state of the manor drifted into his mind. "My lady, that land would never hold more appeal than you."

"You say that to be kind."

"Nay, I say that in truth."

A wash of guilt sluiced over her face, but she did not let go of his hand. "It is my fault. I should have found a better caretaker. I did not know the ill character of Master Harding. It is just that Hugh and I were so busy with rebuilding Thornwood after that terrible fire. Forgive me for not giving you a better home."

The word *giving* grated on Theo's nerves. "Eleanor. Taine Manor is better than I deserve. And I shall pay you for it as soon—"

"Nonsense. Hugh and I were willing to give you the place before you left. You deserve more. I just wish I had more to give." Tears glistened her eyes as she squeezed his hand all the more.

Theo shook his head. "Nay. I am alive because of your charity. If I cannot pay you back within a year, I shall leave."

"Where would you go?" she cried. "Oh Theo, don't be so proud. You are helping Hugh and me. Where could we find a better caretaker other than you?"

Her words were meant to be kind, but they dug deep, like a sword to the gut. "Fear not. I will not leave until I have found the right man to undertake the task."

"Cease this talk. It depresses me. You are going nowhere. I forbid it." She then leaned forward. "Can we not have some music?" she called to Lady Catherine.

"Indeed," Lady Catherine answered back. She rose and lifted her hands. Immediately three monks scurried out of the room and quickly appeared again with a lute, crumhorn, and a frame drum. The small group of monk minstrels struck up a lively tune, and someone called for a carole dance.

Hoots of laughter and voices of glee erupted as lords, knights, and ladies all scrambled to make a circle. Out of the corner of his eye, Theo saw Rose rise and take the hand of the knight sitting next to her. Her laughter and smiles had the knight stumbling around like a green lad with his first love.

Hugh whispered into Eleanor's ear, and soon they rose to join the dancers. Even an elderly knight offered his hand to Lady Catherine, who quickly accepted and stepped to the circle. The music rose in the air, and the dancers started off with their right foot, followed by a rapid strike outward with the left. They moved to the right and then to the left, all the while Rose's laughter floated with the music like an intoxicating melody. The more they danced the more she laughed. Her delicate hips swaying to the gentle rhythm. Her long black braid twisted with a gold ribbon swayed gently in the air. If he were a whole man, he would have grabbed her around the waist and pulled her to the middle of the circle to do a provocative jig.

The thought sobered him like a dunk in a cold river. He truly was an abomination. Even if he were a whole man, he should not be thinking such, for he was at least a good fifteen summers older than her. Yet…he could not stop his lustful longings. Theo closed his eyes to regain his composure. When he opened them, he noticed a boy standing near in a corner clapping his hands to the music.

Theo motioned to the lad, who instantly came to Theo's side. "My lord?"

"Take this trencher and this mug out to my pavilion. I shall meet you there." Theo held up a small silver coin.

Without a word, the boy scooped up the trencher filled with food in one hand and the mug in another.

Rose's laughter drifted toward him again. Theo looked up as the tempo of the dance quickened and she lost her grasp of the knight's hand. Before the man could recover the delicate prize, another knight stepped in to seize her fingers. Another infectious laugh cut the air, and Theo could take no more.

He rose from his chair and lumbered to the entry, gritting his teeth as her playful mirth swirled around him.

Rose saw Sir Theodore leave. His shoulders hunched as he pulled his hood over his face. Though she laughed loudly, inside her heart ached. How painful it must be to watch others dance and make merry. No wonder he preferred the safety of Taine Manor and his solar. There he could forget what it was like to truly be jolly. When the dance ended, she begged off other offers, making her way to her seat. At first she tried to enjoy watching the dancers or making light conversation with Lord de Laund, who had commandeered the seat next to her. Neither offered her any solace. She could not take her mind off Sir Theodore.

Only one thing would give her peace. She reached for a pitcher of ale and grabbed a mug. "Where are you going?" Lord de Laund asked, his lecherous gaze full of hope.

"I promised Sir Theodore that I would bring him some more ale, and I dare not tarry longer."

"Satan's claw. How ghastly it must be for you to live under the same roof with that monster. I am surprised your father allows it." Lord de Laund snorted.

His words stiffened her spine. "I am not there because my father wishes, but because I choose to be." She lifted her chin. "And Sir Theodore is not a monster, but there seems to be quite a few in here."

She smiled all the way to the entry as she heard Lord de Laund stammer and stutter from his chair.

The cool autumn air hit Rose's cheeks as she entered the bailey. Once she passed the keep gate, the music drifted away and was quickly replaced by the chatter of mercers, peasants, and servants preparing for the beginning of the festival. Upon inquiring, one peasant was happy to point out Sir Theodore's pavilion and offered her protection if she should need it.

Rose gave her thanks for the directions but waved off the escort. "I shall be fine," she said. Though the farther she got into the makeshift camp, she wondered if she had made the right decision. Men from all walks of life called to her, making lewd remarks. Obviously, most thought her to be a whore, carrying drink to her protector. Relief flooded her body when she noticed Daniel and Agatha standing next to a fire outside Sir Theodore's tent.

"Good eve to both of you," Rose said. "I did not think to see you here, Mistress Agatha."

The older woman held out her hands to the fire. "When I noticed all of Sir Theodore's knights in the hall, I knew poor Daniel would be out here keeping watch over the pavilion by himself. So I came to give him some company."

"The truth is my mother thinks I might get myself into trouble out here alone." Daniel scowled.

Agatha's cheeks sagged as she looked at her son. "Aye, and you would. You're not used to these thieves and wanton women. You could get yourself in a heap of trouble."

Even in the dark, Rose could see Daniel start to turn pink. Not wanting to get in the middle of the brewing argument, she focused on why she was here in the first place. "Is Sir Theodore about?"

"Aye, he's inside eating his food," Daniel said, still glaring at his mother.

"My thanks," Rose said and turned toward the tent.

"You shouldn't go—" The rest of Daniel's words were lost when she opened the tent flap and stepped inside.

The area was dark except for one lone tallow on a small table. Grunts and gross slurps pricked her ears before her eyes adjusted to the darkness. Standing in the shadows, she observed the sight before her. Sir Theodore picked at a capon and stuffed hunks of it in his mouth. Some of the food dribbled out of the right side of his mouth in a disgusting brown paste. He then tried to wash down what had remained within his mouth with ale. But again, this too came oozing out of the right side of his face.

An ache split the middle of her chest and lodged in her heart. Tears pricked her eyes. This is why he ate alone. The poor man. She turned to leave.

The grotesque chewing stopped. "Hey. Is someone there?" Sir Theodore called.

Rose froze, unsure of what to do. Would he react with anger or embarrassment if he knew she was there? Either way, she did not wish to cause him pain.

"I see you there. Show yourself."

The gruffness of his tone reverberated through her body, and she stepped into the light. The horror on his face almost sent her flying from the tent. He turned his face to the left and wiped his mouth in his sleeve.

"Why are you here?" he growled without turning back toward her.

"I-I have brought you more ale." Rose took a timid step forward and held out the pitcher and the mug.

He glanced over his right shoulder but would not make eye contact with her. "Leave it there. Then go."

The prudent thing would be to do as he ordered, but she could not stop her feet. Slowly she made her way to the small table and placed the pitcher and the mug on top. "I thought we could have a drink together." Her voice sounded like a wounded mouse.

He said not a word, nor would he look at her.

Carefully she poured a few fingers of ale in her cup and added the same to his. All the while he kept his head buried in his sleeve. She raised her mug. "To good company," she said without taking a drink.

When he looked her way, his grizzle glare hit her harder than a dagger to the heart. "Is this why you have come—to mock the monster as he eats? To watch the goo drain from his mouth and sluice down his chin like a rabid dog?" He took his left hand and swept the trencher and his mug to the floor. A fit of coughing took hold of his chest, and a spittle of food oozed from his mouth.

Rose stood and came to his side and placed a gentle hand on his back until the coughing subsided, then with the hem of her gown she wiped his face. His chin began to tremble before he looked away. "Leave," he begged.

"Nay," she said softly. "I wish to have a simple drink with my friend, Sir Theodore de Born. Is that too much to ask?"

He raised his head and pinned her gaze with a sharp glare. "Why? So you can mock me later? So you can tell the world that I eat like a pig at a trough?"

She raised her shoulders and let them drop with a heavy sigh. "You are so dramatic."

That did the trick. His mood lightened as he cocked his left brow. "Here now, the lady who whines about smoke in her chamber and complains about reading scripture is calling me dramatic? Whom do you think has the better case, you or me?"

"Not all scars are physical; some are on the inside and touch our souls..." Rose reached over and picked up the trencher, placing the wayward meats within. She then reached for the mug, which managed to survive the whole ordeal unscathed. After standing, she placed both on the table. "I dare say you cannot finish your meal now. But we can still have that drink." She poured more ale from the pitcher into his mug. Again, she raised her cup, putting her elbow on the table.

"You are a hard woman, Lady Rose."

"As you are, Theo." Her gaze never wavered.

"Bold as the trumpets in heaven too." He glared.

Rose tipped back the mug and took a healthy drink, allowing a healthy amount of ale to roll over her chin. With a thump, she placed the cup on the table and pulled her left hand over her jaw.

A partial smile kicked up his face, and he followed suit, slamming his mug on the table when finished. Both of them started laughing and did not stop until Rose stood again and poured more ale into their mugs.

Again, she put her elbow on the table and held up her mug. "Let's do this together this time, Theo."

He frowned. "Nay. Methinks that is not a good idea. You are not used to the drink, and with the familiarity of my name on your lips, some might think ill of what is happening here."

The moment the words left his lips, they both started laughing. For no one would think such a thing. She downed the drink the same way she did before and so did he. They repeated the process one more time. Both Rose's front gown and his tunic were soaked with ale. None of that seemed to matter, for she could not remember having such fun.

When the ale was gone, she rose from the table. "Come. I will walk with you back to the keep."

"I still am thinking of staying here," he said, refusing to budge from his seat.

She plunked down in her chair. "Then I shall stay too."

They both glared at one another and then busted out laughing. "You are the devil, my lady."

"Rose," she corrected. "Nay. I am your friend."

Thirteen

He that hath a bountiful eye shall be blessed;
for he giveth of his bread to the poor.
Proverbs 22:9

THE NEXT MORN, THEO AROSE AND CALLED FOR
Daniel. He looked at the burgundy doublet and dark
breeches he had picked out for his important meeting this
day. If Lord Iron and Lord de Baston did not find his
invention worthy to finance, then his days at Taine would be
few. Again, he went over his opening speech. "My good sirs,
often we have battled with smoky rooms where hearths
cannot be present."

A knock on his door stilled his words. "Enter, Daniel,"
Theo called as he pulled down his long shirt, reaching for the
black breeches. "We must make certain that I look…" The
garment felt like a stone in his hand when he turned to see
Rose standing in the doorway, wearing a plum-colored gown
with a trencher of food in her hands. The heat of hades flew
up his face. "Lady—"

"Rose. Just Rose. Remember, we are friends now."

He hid his bare legs behind his breeches. "Either way,
you should not be here, it is unseemly. Where is Daniel?"

"Here, my lord." The lad poked his head into the door.
"Lady Rose grabbed the tray from me and—"

"You must eat before you dress." She brushed right past
Theo and placed the tray on the table.

Theo shifted the breeches left and then right trying to hide his appendages. "My lady…" She lifted a mean brow at him. "Rose. I do not have my breeches on," he shouted, waving the material before her.

She smiled and blushed just a bit. "I see. Well, I shall leave while Daniel assists you with those." Immediately she turned to Daniel. "Do not put his doublet on as we must eat first."

We. What did she mean by that? Theo could not digest his thoughts further as she left the room, quietly closing the door behind her.

"Come then, my lord. Best do as the lady says. Neither of us will find peace unless we follow her orders." Daniel took the breeches from Theo's hand and held them out, offering a shoulder for support.

Dumbfounded, Theo did not move. Somewhere between last night and this morn he had lost all control. She spoke to him as if she were his wife. At first the thought shocked him, but then sluiced through his body like a warm wine. *Preposterous!*

Theo put his hand on Daniel's back and then painfully shrugged into the breeches. The lad immediately went to the door. "Where are you going? We must finish dressing."

Daniel shook his head and opened the door. "My lady, he is ready."

She marched into the room and sat down on the opposite side of the table. "Thank you, Daniel. I shall call when we have finished breaking our fast."

What the devil was this? There was no breaking one's fast before morning prayers. She knew that. "We must all attend this morn's mass."

Rose waved a hand in the air. "It is a festival ritual. We will not be missed. I have already told Lady Catherine that you were not feeling well last night and will not make the opening ceremonies this morn."

"Opening ceremonies. You speak as if spending time with the Lord were as important as going to a—"

"Fair? Aye, it is. Come now. Sit down and have a bit of cheese and bread. It will be a full day." Rose broke the cheese apart and placed half on his side of the trencher while she placed the other half in front of her.

By the cross, she planned to eat with him. "This is ridiculous. Listen carefully, I will not eat with you and I will not miss the mass. Lord Iron and Lord de Baston will be attending. I have important business with them later, and if I appear ill or incapable in any respect other than the obvious, they will not fund my venture, and without their help..." He pulled a hand through his long hair. He was giving her more information than he wanted her to know.

She bit her lower lip and then stood. "You are right. Forgive me." She strode to the door and called for Daniel before turning back to him. "However, afterward we will break our fast together." With that, she raised her chin and marched out of the room like a queen.

Spending a great deal of time gawking after Rose, Daniel then stood stump still.

"What are you waiting for? We have a mass to attend," Theo roared.

The lad snapped to attention and picked up the doublet, shoving it over Theo's head. After helping Theo jam on his boots, Daniel stepped back to the table. "Do you want me to remove the food?"

Theo straightened his shoulders as best he could and thumped to the door. "Nay. Leave it." For he did not want Rose to make a scene later, which might make the angels in heaven cringe.

A little over an hour later, Theo found himself back in his chamber with the termagant sitting on one of the chairs rubbing her knees. "I thought the prayers would never end. My knees ache something fierce from kneeling on those hard stones."

"I would think you had good practice at Godstow." Theo leaned against the doorframe, trying to hide his own aches. His left leg throbbed as much as his right.

"Aye, but that doesn't mean it gets easier. Sometimes I don't know what is worse, standing for hours or kneeling."

"Sir Hugh's sister, Lady Breanna, put benches in her chapel."

Rose stopped kneading her knees. "What a brilliant idea."

Theo shrugged. "Maybe so, but I doubt you will ever see such a thing come to pass in any other chapel or church in the country."

"Aye, but we can still hope." Rose narrowed her eyes. "You must take off that doublet before you eat. Come, let me help you."

Theo held up his hands and backed away. "What? Nay? I shall call for Daniel, and then you must leave."

She rolled her eyes and stood. "Don't be foolish. Daniel is in the hall breaking his fast. I will help you, and none will be the wiser. It is not like you are stripping naked. You will still have your shirt on. I shall not leave, and I am certain you do not want me to make a fuss."

Indeed, he did not. There was naught to do but her bidding. He sat down on the chair and let her help peel the garment from his body. His skin blazed like a pyre. He kept his eyes averted to the table.

When finished, she sat down across from him with a delicate sigh. "Please do not tell me you are praying some more."

Nay, he was not, but now that she mentioned the subject, he thought it was sound. *Dear Lord, let me get through this meal without making a fool of myself or breaking her neck.*

"Come now. It should not take that long. Just say thank you for the food."

Those words had never crossed his mind. He looked up at her.

She examined the food before them, then lifted a piece of cheese in her hand. "Now then, I have been thinking. If you take small bits of cheese, you will be able to eat without difficulty. Watch me." Rose took the cheese to the left side of her mouth and chewed slowly, trying not to use her right side. After some time, she swallowed. "There. Now you try."

"It will not have the same effect. Besides you still were able to use your whole jaw to chew."

Rose slapped her palms on the table. "Please do try."

Taking a deep breath, Theo picked up a small piece of cheese and popped it into his mouth.

"Use your left side," she instructed.

With his tongue, Theo rolled the cheese to the left. By now, the bit had crumbled to nothing and was easy to swallow.

Her face lit up, and she clapped her hands. "You did it! Not a morsel fell from your mouth. Now try the bread." She held up a small hunk.

This would not go down as easy as the soft cheese. Yet, he could not deny her. Theo broke off a small chunk and again rolled it to the left side of his mouth. He chewed once and then tried to gulp down the bread. The chunk lodged in his throat, sending him into a fit of coughing.

Rose cried out, sprang from her seat, and came around to hit him between the shoulder blades. The soft taps did naught. Finally, he leaned forward and massaged his neck, which always seemed to help when he bit off a large portion of food. The bread bumped down his throat.

"There. It helped," she cried with glee.

He did not correct her false assumption.

"Do remember the food must be small." She demonstrated by breaking the bread into small pieces and chewing on the left side of her mouth. When done, she smiled a smile that would make the saints sigh. "See? 'Tis easy. Now, try again."

And he did over and over. When the food got stuck, she would daintily tap his back and not once did he stop the futile action but relished in her tender touch.

Fourteen

For we walk by faith, not by sight.
2 Corinthians 5:7

THE BRIGHT BLUE SKY HELD NOT A SINGLE CLOUD. The fall winds had turned warm, lifting the spirits of all fairgoers. Rose meandered through the crowd as mercers and peasants alike hawked their wares and goods. Minstrels sang lively tunes while jokers juggled apples, daggers, and small loaves of bread. Maids giggled and fluttered their eyelashes to nobles and knights. Nothing could possibly ruin this day.

Even eating with Theo had been a pleasure. He did try so hard to apply his learned skills, and she knew in time he would be able to eat with others without fear of reprisal. It was the least she could do before she left. A small twinge twisted in her heart—she would not be here to see his progress. Would he continue without her, or would he return to his barbarous ways once she had left? Oh, she hoped he would not.

Nonetheless, she and Daniel had a plan. They would slip away during the archery tourney. Rose looked about. In fact, she would wager they could slip away anytime and not be caught. For she did not spot Sir Rupert or Sir Gregory. Even so, they would stick to their plan, ensuring an easy escape.

A brilliant yellow ribbon at a mercer's cart caught her eye. Rose weaved through the crowd and stopped in front of a cart laden with fabric and rugs of materials she had never seen before. She lightly touched the ribbon—soft and silky, yet shiny and bright.

"Ye won't find a better strip anywhere, my lady," the mercer offered.

"What is it?" she asked

"Comes from eastern Asia, a place called Zayton. Made from silk. I hear King John favors the material."

"Indeed, who wouldn't?"

The mercer licked his lips. "Would you like to try it on, my lady?"

With a heavy sigh, Rose let the ribbon slide through her fingers. She would love to, but she did not have the coin to purchase it, and she feared if Theo came by he would insist she have it. "Nay, not now. Perhaps later."

The glee in the mercer's eyes faded, but he would not be deterred. "'Twould look lovely against your dark hair."

"Aye, Rose. I think you should give it a try."

The familiar mellow voice sent her heart fluttering, and a prick of sweat developed at the nape of her neck. She turned. "Conrad," she cried, the fabric forgotten.

He laughed and immediately enveloped her in a huge hug before stepping back. "You are as beautiful as ever. Magnificent, if I must say. The color of that gown against your pearly skin makes me deliciously hunger."

His lewd words made the mercer gape, and Rose felt her skin turning as purple as her bliaut. She pulled him away from the cart. "What are you doing here?"

He gave another casual laugh and put her arm through his. The sparkle of his golden eyes and his sunny hair made her chest ache. Oh, how good it was to see him. They had always been good friends when they were younger. His father had been a good friend of the family, and often Conrad and his brother would come to Rockbridge for a visit. Not until she was about fifteen summers did his interest seem to grow in a different way. Conrad would always defend her, where his older brother would tease her. Rose nestled close to his side as they strolled down the makeshift street.

"So I hear you are still a prisoner, but this time of that retched monster, Sir Theodore de Born." His body shivered. "How awful for you."

The words spoken in sympathy did not soothe. Quite the contrary. Her ire rose at his callous statement, and she was sorely tempted to wash the smile from his face. "It is not all that bad. He is very kind when he wishes to be."

"Then for your sake I hope he wishes often. For I fear I would vomit every time I had to look at him."

A chill swept through her at his cruel words. 'Twas comments like these that kept Theo hidden from the world. She opened her mouth to give defense when Conrad pointed to a bushel of apples.

"I'm famished." In no time, the bartering was done and he held up two ripe apples. He bit into one, sending a trail of juice down his handsome cleft chin.

When juices oozed down Theo's chin, she had nothing but pity. Yet when they sluiced over Conrad's strong jaw, her heart filled with admiration. With a quick wipe of the back of his sleeve, the liquid was gone.

"They are quite tasty." He handed the apple to her. "Try it."

His sultry voice sent a quiver down her spine. Her hands shook as his fingers touched hers. His eyes begged, and his lips became full in a deliberate pout.

"For me," he whispered.

How could she not? Juice streamed from her mouth. Conrad gently took two fingers and wiped the trickle away. Her lips throbbed at his touch; she closed her eyes.

"Hmm… Conrad, what is this?" a strange nasally feminine voice asked.

Rose opened her eyes as Conrad took two very healthy steps away from her.

"My dear, where have you been? I have been looking high and low for you," Conrad simpered.

The young woman narrowed her eyes and then turned her glare on Rose. "Who is this?"

Conrad's apple fell to the ground before he wiped his hands on his breeches. "Lady Rosemond de Payne, allow me to introduce my wife, Lady Jocelyn."

Conrad's wife's head was covered with a heavy brown muslin veil; her body heavily cloaked. Deep dark circles hung beneath her eyes, and thin frown lines were forming around her mouth. Tiny and fragile to the point she might break in half like a clay pot. "What a pleasure to finally meet you. I have heard much about you from Conrad and others."

Rose lowered her chin. "All pleasant words, I hope."

"Oh aye. Many say you are quite spirited and give in to your whims most often." Lady Jocelyn smirked.

Why, she had never. Rose threw back her shoulders. The woman had almost called her wanton.

"It is quite cold out here." Jocelyn pulled her cloak tight around her and let her hand drop to a large round belly, heavy with child.

Rose's heart gave a sickening lurch. She could not unfasten her gaze from the round woolen bump in the middle of Jocelyn's body. Through the wall of noise swirling around them, Conrad said something about hoping to have an heir soon. Rose finally managed to look away, but not before she saw Jocelyn's lips curl into a nasty smile.

Mumbling words of congratulations, Rose turned and raced away from the pair. The merry calls of the mercers and peasants that held delight moments ago seemed foreign and bizarre. Her head ached, and her vision blurred as tears rushed over her cheeks. What was the matter with her? She knew Conrad had married. She knew sooner or later he would have a family. Rose sniffed back her tears. He had moved on with his life, while she sat in limbo. Truly if she did not get away now, she would wind up in a convent for the rest of her natural days.

Brushing the tears from her eyes, Rose ran to Theo's pavilion. Surely Daniel would be there. However, she stopped behind another tent when she noticed Theo standing at the entry with Lord Iron and Lord de Baston. She had forgotten about the meeting. Stretching her neck, she looked past the men to see if Daniel was about. Her eyes did not find him, but she did spot Agatha making a pottage over an open fire.

When the party of men went into the tent, Rose ran to Agatha. "Is Daniel about?"

The older woman blinked several times. "What is the matter?"

"Nothing," cried Rose. "I just need to speak with Daniel."

Again, Agatha stood still, holding a ladle in her hand.

"Please," Rose begged. "I must speak to him now."

"Child, if you have a problem, surely I can help or Sir Theodore?" Agatha motioned to the tent. "Would you like me to get him?"

Rose shook her head and tried to compose herself. The last thing she wanted to do was alert Theo. She bit her lip. "I just want Daniel's opinion on a ribbon I am thinking of purchasing."

A wave of relief fluttered over Agatha's face. "Oh, well, you should have said so straight off." She motioned with the ladle again. "He is with Sir Hugh over by the armory."

Rose did not wait to hear more but took off like a hare being chased by a hound. Racing through the gate, she weaved between servants hustling with baskets heaped with carrots, cabbages, and onions. Likewise, squires sprinted with shields, crossbows, and maces. Through the chaos she managed to locate Daniel talking with Sir Hugh and another squire.

"Daniel," she called. "My pardon. A word please."

The lad had the audacity to glare at her like she was a wintering loon.

"My lady." Sir Hugh nodded. "Is there a problem?"

"Nay. I mean, aye." Rose laced her hands in front of her, continually rolling her thumbs. "Sir Theodore wishes to see Master Daniel immediately."

Sir Hugh gave another nod, though this time more slowly. "Then by all means." He turned his attention to Daniel. "We shall continue later."

Daniel dropped his chin to his chest and shuffled his feet as he followed Rose away from the armory and prying eyes. She pulled him toward the side of the stable. "We must leave immediately."

The lad's eyes grew wide, and he opened and closed his mouth like a fish stuck in the muck. "What? Ah. I thought you wanted to leave during the tourney?"

"I have changed my mind. We must leave now. While I change my clothing, you go get our provisions. I wish to be gone within the hour."

Daniel pulled a hand through his hair. "Rose, I-I can't."

"What do you mean you can't?" Rose placed her hands on her hips. "What matters if we leave now or if we leave in two days? No one is watching us. None will be the wiser until later this eve. By then we will be halfway to the coast."

His cheeks began to splotch with color. "You don't understand. I am not going at all."

Either her mind was beginning to unhinge or her hearing was faulty. "What do you mean you are not going?" She waved a finger in front of his face. "For heaven's sake, start acting like a man and not a foolish lad."

His spine snapped straight. "I am, Rose. Sir Theodore has arranged for me to become a squire to Sir Hugh." A huge smile splashed on his face. "I am going to become a knight someday."

It took a moment for Rose to shuffle all the pieces into place, but then understanding shone bright before her. This explained why no one followed her about at the fair. Theo had planned to woo Daniel into staying by offering him what every peasant boy dreamed of—a chance to change the course of his life.

She reached for his hand and fluttered her eyelids. "Do you not wish to be with me?"

"I-I…" He pulled his hand away. "I think you are a lovely lady, but Sir Hugh thinks I would be a fine knight."

Awk. There was no use for it. His head had been turned, and his mind was lost in the glory of being a great knight riding a mighty destrier like Triumph. Her eyes shifted left, then right. She reached out and grabbed Daniel by the front of his tunic. "Very well. You stay here if you wish, but you owe me something."

The lad's eyes almost popped out of his head. "Rose, I think—"

"You will go and get our provisions while I change my garments." She poked him hard in the chest, tears beginning to run down her cheeks. "Then you ready Triumph for me. Do you understand?"

She turned away without waiting for his answer and fled to her chamber. Once within, she stripped out of the plum gown Theo had given her. With care, she spread the garment on the bed and brushed her hand over the silver piping. He had been kind, and now she would repay that kindness with cruelty. But she could not stay.

Jagged cries escaped her throat as a waterfall of tears refused to stop. With haste, she put on her old worn brown bliaut. She let her hand drop to the plum gown once more, her fingers gliding over the soft muslin fabric. "I'm sorry," she whispered. "I'm sorry I could not stay and teach you. I'm sorry for being so mean."

At the door, she took a deep breath. Once more she brushed the tears from her eyes. Perhaps this time if she ran fast enough she might truly escape her past.

With his presentation completed, Theo held his breath as Lord Iron and Lord de Baston examined the crude drawings of his new brazier design. Lord Iron grunted once, but they gave no other indication if they thought the design held merit or not.

"You say this will clear any room of smoke and make the room warmer?" Lord de Baston asked without looking up from the parchments.

"Aye. And if you look at this drawing, I believe we could

build larger iron braziers that could heat to any room." Theo pointed to one of the sketches.

Lord Iron stroked his goatee. "Seems almost impossible."

"Like this simple brazier, only larger with piping." Theo pointed to another drawing.

He then sent up a small prayer of praise and hope while Lord Iron and de Baston began discussing the dimensions of the piping. If they could only see the possibilities. This could make all the difference, not only to Taine Manor but also for every lord and peasant who shivered in the winter months.

Lord de Baston held up the rough sketch of the contraption that would send heat to every room in a keep. "How will this work?"

Theo pointed to the drawing. "If you look—"

"Sir Theodore." Daniel stormed into the tent. "You must come. Lady Rose is leaving on Triumph!"

All thoughts of the meeting fled his mind. *Fleeing on Triumph. The girl could get killed!* Theo turned back to the table where the men still held the parchments. "Excuse me, my lords. I have something that needs attention immediately." Without waiting for an answer, Theo thumped from the tent with Daniel at his side. "What happened?"

"I'm not sure. She…just decided to leave."

Theo shot Daniel a speculative glance as they entered the bailey. "And you had no knowledge she would do such a thing?"

Daniel's Adam's apple began to bob up and down. "Forgive me, sir. We were going to flee at the end of the fair, but I changed my mind and—"

"She decided to leave now." With as much speed as Theo could muster, he headed to the stables.

"Nay, sir. I hadn't even told her, right off. She was all out of sorts when she came to find me. Something at the fair must have upset her."

Indeed, and Theo already knew what that something could be. Right before his meeting, he had met Lady Jocelyn de Laval, Conrad de Laval's wife. Theo planned to gently tell Rose this eve of the woman's condition, but apparently the knowledge came forthwith before he could explain.

Theo paused and turned to Daniel. "Go find Sir Hugh. I may need his assistance." With a nod, the lad took off toward the armory.

"Get that horse ready now." Rose's voice could be heard even before Theo entered the stable. "I need to leave immediately."

Theo stepped into the stable. "Rose," he said softly to her back. "What are you doing?"

A stable boy shirked away. Rose's shoulder snapped back, but she did not turn. "I am leaving, and you can't stop me."

The crack in her voice tore at Theo's heart. A fair young maid should not suffer so much agony. He inched closer and closer. "Where will you go?"

She shrugged, and then her shoulders shook. A heavy gasp escaped her throat. Her knees began to buckle. With his strong left arm, Theo pulled her into an embrace and let her tears soak his doublet.

"I cannot stay here," she cried.

Theo patted her back. "Aye, I know. Shh, please don't cry." He could not resist it, he kissed the top of her head. The simple act seemed to have soothed her, for her wails became soft sniffs.

"Em. I was told my help was needed here."

Heat flushed Theo's skin, but he did not release Rose. Hugh stood in the entry. For once there was no smug smile on his face, only concern.

"Aye. I must leave immediately, and Lady Rose wishes to accompany me. Would you please inform my knights and servants? And please give my apologies to Lady Catherine."

Hugh nodded. "Indeed. I shall have Lady Eleanor help with Lady Rose's things."

Within the hour, Theo, Rose, and Agatha rumbled out of Crosswind Keep. Sir Rupert, Sir Gregory, and the others would follow later after breaking down the pavilion and gathering up their unsold goods. Not a word was said through the long journey home, nor did they offer up answers to those surprised at the early return.

Theo led Rose to his solar and then called for food and drink. "You will sleep here tonight."

Rose lifted her ghostly gaze to him. "Where will you sleep?"

"It doesn't matter. Perhaps in the stables or with the goats."

A tiny smile drifted on her face. "You jest," she said weakly.

"Aye. Not with the goats. But do not worry. I shall be fine." A servant arrived with a warm bowl of pottage and some hard bread. He placed it on the table next to her before leaving. "You should eat a little. It will make you feel better."

Rose stared at the pottage; a lone tear trickled down her cheek. "You should have let me leave. Everything is ruined because of me. Hardly any of the goods were sold, and you did not get to complete your business with Lord Iron and Lord de Baston."

Theo sat in the seat across from her. "Rose. None of this is your fault. Why do you wish to put guilt on your shoulders? All is God's will."

A storm started to brew in her eyes, and Theo took that as a good sign. "God's will. What type of God would strip a good man like you of his livelihood and his dignity? Why do you blindly follow Him? Today, you have been robbed of your success."

Theo dropped his hands to his lap. "God doesn't call us to be successful, Rose. Just faithful."

Fifteen

And he said unto them, Why are ye troubled?
and why do thoughts arise in your hearts?
Luke 24:38

HE NEXT FEW DAYS WERE BUT A BLUR TO ROSE. Though Theo insisted she stay in his solar while he slept in the stable, Rose returned to the chamber in the tower the next day. The tiny sanctuary gave her solace, for she could not look upon the people of Taine without guilt and grief. The money they would have made from the sale of grain, cheese, and other goods would have helped them through the winter to buy more and better supplies and food. Now, they would have to rely on their own goods and hope it would be enough.

On top of all this, she had heard from Agatha that Lord Iron and Lord de Baston had passed on offering coin for Theo's invention. With no new offers, the project seemed to be doomed. Already, peasants claimed that Theo was preparing to leave in the spring and had already informed Sir Hugh and Lady Eleanor. Nonetheless, whatever the outcome of Taine Manor, she would be stuck here until spring too.

With a heavy sigh, she rose from her pallet where she lay almost every afternoon after her morning lessons with Theo. No rest would come, so she headed toward the goat pen. She wondered who was taking care of the animals since Daniel now lived at Sir Hugh's keep. Saint Philip started bleating the moment she entered the pen. He kept nudging her hand, looking for a treat.

"I have nothing for you," she said, scratching his neck. With a quick look around, she noticed the trough was empty and Saint Paul was gnawing on one of the fence posts. The water trough was almost bone dry. "This will not do," she said to Saint Philip. "We cannot have the disciples eating their home and dying of thirst."

Rose picked up a bucket and made her way over to the courtyard well; after she returned, she poured the water into the trough. Then she headed to the stables and picked up a bale of hay and used the pitchfork to fill the trough. The goats took to the water and hay like a pack of demons, heads bumping and pushing against their fellow goat brothers.

"What is this? Have you not heard to do unto others as you would have them do to you?" The goats continued to ignore her and shoved their way closer to the trough. Rose shook her head and laughed before walking into the shed.

There she found Jude, the old man, sitting on his stool with a staff in his lap. "Good afternoon, Lady Rose."

She folded her arms across her chest. "I would say the same to you, but I do not offer a greeting to a man who would let his charges starve."

The skin around his fathomless eyes crinkled when he lifted his lips. "But they are not starving. You have fed them."

"Aye, but it is not my task but yours."

"Ah, but we are all supposed to bear each other's burdens."

The man was impossible to reason with. She placed her hands on her hips. "You do know that Daniel is gone."

"Indeed. He will be sorely missed, but his prayers have been answered." Jude raised the deep hood over his head and dug his staff in the ground. His legs wobbled when he tried to stand.

Rose quickly rushed to his side to offer support. "Perhaps Sir Theo should find another to help you with the duties."

Jude made his way to the entry, and immediately the goats calmed down and, almost like perfect gentlemen, began taking their turn at the water and feed troughs. "I am thinking you could help."

Of course, his comment was absurd. A lady did not labor with goats. She opened her mouth to say so but then realized things were truly different at Taine Manor. Knights worked shoulder to shoulder with peasants in the fields. They cleaned the stables and worked as servants. Agatha managed the household like a steward. Why then should she not help with the goats?

"All right, Master Jude, I will assist you, but I shall not replace you."

He nodded, but he did not seem surprised at her answer. "Let us take them out into the pasture."

She had never herded goats, and she wasn't sure that Master Jude at his age could do so either. "Do you think that is wise?"

Master Jude looked at her and cocked an eyebrow. "But of course it is." He opened the gate, and the goats filed out in an orderly manner—no butting heads, shoving, or running away. They stayed close to Master Jude and switched directions when he did. Once through the gate, they made their way to the top of a small hill that overlooked the wetlands. "We will rest here." Jude sat on a protruding rock as the goats began to pull on the grass around them.

Rose chose to sit in the grass in front of him and lifted her face to the warm fall sun. "You should put your hood down and take in the glorious sunshine. I fear we will not have many more days like this."

"We shall have a few more, but then it will be a harsh winter."

The words unsettled her. A harsh winter would not be good for the people at Taine Manor. "Perhaps you will be wrong."

Master Jude shook his head in the dark hood. "Nay. It will be harsh, but fear not, all will be well."

If what he said was true, it would not be well. Rose scanned the goats munching away. They might be slaughtering all of them to stave off the hunger of a long rough winter.

"Not one hair of their heads will be lost before their time," Master Jude said as if reading her mind.

"How can you be so sure of things? I fear the whole manor will be lost if the weather is bad. But then, it may be lost anyway once Sir Theo leaves."

Master Jude placed the staff next to him on the rock. "Mayhap it will be better."

She opened her mouth, ready to contradict him, but then stopped short. "I do not understand him. He let Daniel go when he is desperately needed here. Sir Theo sacrificed the well-being of the manor for me by leaving the fair early."

"Sir Theo puts others before his own needs. The manor, nor its people, will not be destroyed."

How could he be so sure? Unless he knew something she did not. "You speak as if something or someone will appear to change all this. Even if Taine finds a savior, who will help Sir Theo? He plans to leave in the spring."

"Aye, I know. And he will."

Master Jude's nonchalant words made Rose want to throttle him. It was by Theo's good graces that Jude had a home at all. And here he sat, speaking as if Theo's future wasn't important at all. "Stop. 'Tis not true. You know as well as I a poor deformed knight has no future. He will starve."

"He has friends that would take him in. He could also become a monk."

Rose blanched. She knew well the cold and meager conditions of being cloistered away in a convent. The condition would be the same, if not worse, in a monastery. The monks would not bother to teach Theo to read, and he could not write well with his left hand. He would not be able to translate scripture into the written word. Rose started ticking off the months until spring. If she could get him to hold a quill properly in his left hand... Oh, there would not be enough time to train him to write well enough to be a valuable member in the monastery. The cold would cripple him with pain, and he would be naught but a liability.

"Do not say such. He will die if that is his fate," she cried. "He does not deserve to die alone in some damp and dismal cell in some drab monastery."

"I am sure it will all work out. His faith is strong."

Rose sprung to her feet. How could he just dismiss Theo's future? "Faith and God have nothing to do with this. I have seen firsthand that God does not answer prayers, and He lets the innocent suffer."

"God knows what has happened in your past. Everything that has happened and will happen has to do with God and you. Open your eyes and see. If you do not, you may not see the cliff before you." Jude picked up his staff and dug it into the ground. "Come, we must go. For we will be having company soon."

No one would be coming to Taine Manor this late in the season. Rose helped Master Jude to his feet. 'Twas pointless arguing with an old man who clearly was losing his wits. He did not know his future was just as precarious as Theo's. Rose and Master Jude walked in silence back to the manor with the goats following just as orderly as when they had left.

At the gate, a loud rumble from the west drew her attention. A party of knights with familiar colors were galloping toward them. She narrowed her eyes. It could not be, but it was. By all that was unholy, at the front of the column rode the devil himself. Her father.

The rumble of horses' hooves drew everyone's attention. As quickly as he could, Theo made his way to the middle of the courtyard. Rose stood like a pillar of salt staring at the lead knight draped in a black tunic embossed with a red wolf.

The man removed his helm and glared at Rose. "Hello, Daughter."

But she did not reply. Instead, Rose stiffened her back and curled her hands into fists.

Believing an ugly scene would soon follow, Theo stepped forward. "Baron de Payne. What a pleasure."

Sir Walter de Payne dismounted and passed his mount off to his squire. "Aye. I thought to see you at Crosswind, but when I arrived, they said you had left." Even though he spoke to Theo, his gaze remained firm on Rose.

A gust of wind whipped through the courtyard and matched the chilly expression on her face. She shuddered.

Theo wanted to put his arm around Rose, but instead he directed his attention to her father. "I had a pressing matter to attend to here."

Sir Walter's brows shot northward, and for the first time, he took a good look at Theo. To the man's credit, he did not wince, gasp, or step back. All he did was grunt. "That is not how I heard it." His gaze traveled back to Rose.

Before Theo could offer a defense, she bolted toward the tower and raced up the steps, slamming the door behind her.

"I see my daughter still has much to learn," Sir Walter said dryly.

"You must forgive her. I am sure she will come around. Just give her a little time. She will greet you properly this eve." Theo pointed to the hall. "You must be weary from your travel. Come."

Sir Walter followed Theo into the hall. "I have the parchments you asked for. They are a few of Rose's favorite stories about the exotic east. Some are so worn thin it is hard to read the lettering. I also have this for her."

The older man pulled a bundle of cloth and handed it to Theo. On closer examination, Theo noticed the cloth had been formed into a rabbit. A child's toy?

"It always gave her comfort when she was a young girl. Perhaps it might still have the same effect on her. I have another possession that the nuns at Godstow gave to me." He held out a tiny silver cross. "This belonged to Rose's mother. The nuns thought it held too many memories to allow her to keep it. Give these to Rose when I am gone." Sir Walter eyes turned glassy, and he stared off into the distance.

Theo hesitated. What a strange request. He took the toy and stuffed it in his tunic, while carefully holding the necklace in his left hand. The bag of parchments sat on the floor next to him. "Many thanks. I am hoping all will make Lady Rose a more amiable teacher. Though I must say, lately she has been quite patient during our instruction." Theo motioned to Agatha to bring some ale and food. Sir Walter plunked down near the hearth, and Theo took a chair across from him.

"I see little changed." The older man took the ale from Agatha and waved off the food before giving her a grateful nod. "No matter. There is another matter I wish to discuss with you." A series of heavy coughs and gags pulsed through his body and produced a small spittle of blood on his lip. With a healthy drink and the wipe of his hand, the red mucus disappeared. He let his head fall back against the chair.

In this brief moment, Theo took a closer look at the man. At one point in his life Sir Walter de Payne had been a fierce warrior. Tall and of strong build, a chest as wide as barrel of ale, his hands large and meaty. The minstrels sang of a time when Sir Walter could crush a man's head between his palms. Truth or not, Sir Walter was a force to be reckoned with, a wild temper that made him infamous. But now, his skin hung on his large frame. His cheeks drooped. Dark circles beneath his eyes matched the grey color within. Trails of fine veins crisscrossed his once-noble hawk-like nose. His grey-black hair lay matted against his sweaty forehead.

None of this surprised or shocked Theo, except for one feature that made Sir Walter a kindred spirit—a long jagged scar curved up the left side of his face. For a moment, Theo wondered if Rose only sat on her father's right side.

When Sir Walter's strength seemed to have returned, he leaned forward and glanced around the hall. "I remember this place used to be a thriving manor. Close to the channel, but difficult to breach. King Richard saw worth here where others did not. Do you know why?"

"Indeed, I do. He feared his brother John and the French king would try to slip through the wetlands and invade England from this point."

"Ah, you are a smart one. No wonder King Richard took you with him into battle. But then he had to get himself killed, the vain puff. Prancing around like he was invincible. He should have been working on producing a legitimate heir. Now we are left with that mongrel John."

Theo wondered what Sir Walter would do if he knew there really was one living in Normandy and married to Sir Darrin de Longue. But the lady did not want the crown, and Theo had been sworn to secrecy once told. A secret that would go to the grave with him.

"Methinks if my daughter is to stay here, we need to spruce up this place a bit," Sir Walter said before another fit of coughing overtook him. More blood rested on his lip, which again he washed away with another drink.

Theo sat back. "I shall not take more charity. I already owe much to Lady Eleanor and Sir Hugh."

"And yet you plan to leave come spring to save a pride that is as broken as your body."

A pressure bubbled within Theo, which in the past would already have this man on the floor with a sword at his throat. "So Lady Eleanor and Sir Hugh have told you."

Sir Walter waved off. "Aye, but I mean no offense. The truth is not always taken easily. I am here to make an offer for your service. Trust me. You will earn every scrap of timber and every pile of iron to make this keep worthy again."

The anger in Theo's gut subsided as trepidation rolled in. "What do you speak of?"

Sir Walter leaned forward all the more. "Do you have a place where we can speak privately?"

Sixteen

*And they said, There is no hope: but we will walk
after our own devices, and we will every one
do the imagination of his evil heart.*
Jeremiah 18:12

OSE PACED HER ROOM BEFORE SHE REALIZED IT would be better to face the beast head-on. Why after almost three years would her father wish to see her? No doubt he was pulling Theo into his evil plan. Had not the poor man suffered enough?

When she entered the hall, she found her father sitting by the fire whispering something to Theo. Already her father was fast to snare his prey. How he had changed. When she was young, he would chase her around the keep and grab her like a wild bear whose form of torture would be to tickle her. Whenever he went off fighting for The Crown, he would always return with some bright bobble or a pretty gown. Once he even brought her a fat goose, whom she promptly named Gertrude. Though in truth, the goose should have gone to the cooks, but when she desired it, her father could not refuse.

Oh, they would dance and sing and play games. Life was one long merry adventure at Rockbridge Castle. But all that changed one sunny day when her father was gone on a campaign and, like always, he left his steward, Master Bruce Dunken, in charge. With a lean body and dark unholy eyes, he always seemed to be slithering about. At age eight, Rose thought he was really a snake and not a man at all. When no one was watching, he would glide his hands over her shoulders, down her chest, and in other places too. It was one of the reasons she would seek out Father Ramsey. Master Dunken would never come near the priest.

However, one day she had skipped into the storage room near the kitchens where they kept the grain and other fodder. She hoped to sneak out a few extra oats for Gertrude when Master Dunken entered. The look in his eyes said this time he would want more than just a few strokes of her chest.

When she tried to run, he grabbed her around the waist. She screamed and kicked as he lifted her skirt. That's when her mother had entered…

Rose squeezed her eyes shut, trying to block out the awful memory. Her mother's cries for help were heard too late. Beaten, bloody, and torn apart, she died before Rose's eyes. Master Dunken was immediately caught and thrown into Rockbridge's dungeon and just as swiftly executed when her father returned.

Things were never the same after that. Oh, her father still bought her bobbles and pretty gowns. But his hugs were now those of anguish, and his leniency was born from guilt. And as she grew older, he pulled away from her as if knowing where the true guilt lay.

Then he sealed her away for good. First in her room, away from Conrad. Later in a convent, away from the world. Now at Taine Manor, away from hope. Slowly he was killing her, and he did not care.

The bridge between them was harsh and wide. Today she would cross over and meet her father head-on. No more secrets. She would know his purpose here. With her head held high, she strode to the hearth. "Father, why are you here?"

As if startled by her sudden presence, he sat back in his chair and let his steel gaze travel over her form. "Such a greeting, Daughter. Did you not learn anything with those nuns?"

Rose clasped her hands, digging her fingernails into her palms. This time he would not fluster her or gain the upper hand. "Aye, they taught me much. Just not how to greet a father who never cared to visit."

He grunted and turned his attention back to Theo. "I see her tongue is still sharp. I thought by now you would have beaten that from her."

Theo shifted in his seat. His brows furrowed. "I am not in the habit of beating anyone, my lord. If that had been your desire, then you should have found a different home for Lady Rose."

"I am standing right here, Father. Speak to me of what you want, not of what you think others should do to change me."

Once more, her father's gaze rolled back to her. He rubbed his chin before a fit of coughing rattled through his body. An odd feeling tugged at her stomach. When he curled forward, she raised a hand to place it on his shoulders but caught the action in midair, returning her hand to her side.

When the coughing subsided, he reached for his mug and gulped heartily. "This travel when the winds come from the north is more than my body can take. I'll be glad when I have returned home."

Rose thought to point out that the weather lately had been relatively mild for this season, but what would be the point. Her father would just create some other reason to explain the fit. No matter, the color had returned to his cheeks. However, she did note the deep circles under his eyes. "Then perhaps you should state your business quickly so you can leave."

This time he roared with laughter. "So fast are you to see me leave? Fear not, I will not tarry long. I will leave you in peace very shortly."

Her heart plummeted to her toes, and a deep sadness filled the empty space. Without knowing, he had crushed a hope she didn't even realize she held—she wanted to go home too. But clearly that was not his purpose. "Which brings us back to my original question. Why are you here?"

He stared at her a few moments as if committing her face to memory. He then pointed to a bag of scrolls next to Theo's chair. "Sir Theodore sent word that you wished to have something else to read than the word of our Lord. So I have brought them to you."

Before he spoke, she knew immediately they were her beloved stories that she had read over and over when she was young. But she hid her glee, feigning indifference.

"If you do not want them, I can take them back," her father barked.

"Oh, nay." Her fast eager words produced a wide smile on his face. She bit her lip, taking several measured breaths to regain her calm.

A series of guffaws led to another fit of coughing. He turned away. Mayhap there was more to this coughing than the autumn winds. Her father slid a finger over his lips before he turned back. Another odd twinge crept into her chest.

Theo rose from his seat, his eyes filled with unease. "Perhaps you would like to rest a little from your long journey. I shall show you to my quarters."

Her father nodded, before glancing her way. "We shall talk later. I am a mite weary." He stood and followed Theo to the solar.

Rose tipped her head to the side. Round-shouldered and worn, her father had aged much over the past three years. However, her concern was not for him but for Theo. As long as her father was here, poor Theo would be spending his nights in the cold stable or this drafty hall.

That eve all worry of her father's health fled. He entered the hall with a spring in his step, wearing a velvet doublet of dark green. A heavy gold chain hung about his neck and made him look more like a royal than a baron.

Rose narrowed her eyes. Her father, the great Sir Walter de Payne, had always been King Richard's man. All knew he cared nothing for King John. Many of the other barons in England felt the same way. Was that why he was here? Looking for alliances to overthrow the king? She dismissed that thought. What could her father gain from a broken-down keep like Taine Manor?

Yet the thought niggled her mind. Even though the wetlands were hard to navigate, Taine Manor was close to the coast. Could her father be aligning himself with the French in hopes to strip the crown from John? Nay. Her father hated the French more than King John.

Her father made straight for her and planted a light kiss on her hand. "You look lovely this eve. Did you purchase that gown at the fair?"

Rose glanced at her plum bliaut and almost told him the truth, but then thought better of it. He might send her back to Godstow if he thought she and Theo were becoming too close. "The dress came from Lady Catherine. She thought I should have a few gowns to wear at the festival other than my drab brown one."

Her father frowned. "What happened to the others you had? Did you outgrow them?" Again, he appraised her appearance. "Though I don't know how that can be. I think you are thinner than I remember, and I don't think you have become taller. You could have had them taken in instead of throwing them away. If you needed new clothing, why did you not send word?"

A light laugh left her lips. "The nuns did not think my garments were appropriate for the abbey. So they took them. What they did with them I do not know, and they would not permit me to contact you even if I had the desire to do so."

Her father mumbled something under his breath before directing her to the table where the usual participants were waiting. "Come, let us sit and sup together."

Rose looked to the doorway. "I usually eat with Sir Theodore."

"Aye, I know. But tonight he has begged off and wishes to eat with his goat keeper." Her father shook his head. "I have to say, Sir Theodore is an odd man. Whoever heard about eating with a peasant when it wasn't a holiday or special occasion? But the man has been through a lot and can eat with whomever he chooses." Her father's nostrils flared. "After all, who am I but a baron who could change his circumstances?"

She reached out and placed her hand on top of his. "Nay, Father. You have it wrong. He never eats with anyone."

"Except you and the goat keeper," he said dryly.

"But there is a reason…"

Her father raised a hand, signaling this conversation held no importance anymore. A new dilemma had overtaken his thoughts. The hall was brimming with knights. Most of which were young and bawdy. An uneasy thought twisted a knot in her stomach. Unless her father was going into battle, he never traveled with so many knights. Surely he would not attempt to challenge the king before winter set in? Another thought sent another roll within her middle. Did he plan to winter here? Nay. He could not. Poor Theo would not be able to stand the cold sleeping out in the stable.

Her father gazed around the room and at the three trestle tables full of knights and a few peasants. "Where the blazes is the head table?"

"There is none," she said, raising her voice to be heard above the racket.

"There is none? I have never heard of such a thing. What a sorry state this place is." At the end of one table, he grabbed a knight by his tunic and pulled him off the bench. "Eat by the hearth where you belong." A hard steel look sent another to the hearth as well. Her father motioned to the two empty seats. "No wonder Sir Theodore eats with the goats. Better than eating with these buffoons."

Rose almost pointed out that most of the buffoons were his men, but then why gain more of his ire when she needed some answers.

While the knights made merry, there was a group that ate in silence. Sir Rupert and the rest of the older knights ate in a corner far from the tables. Their usual lively banter and silly songs were not heard. After eating, they left the hall. Poor Agatha and the few other servants ran to-and-fro trying to please the remaining guests by filling their mugs and trenchers.

Her father called for food, but none came. "This keep needs better servants."

Rose slammed her hands on the table. "Or perhaps it needs better guests." Ignoring his protest, she stood and went to the kitchen, returning with two trenchers of food and plopped one in front of her father. Again, he opened his mouth to say something, but she had already left and returned with two mugs filled with frothy ale.

"No one acts the high and mighty here. We all do our part at Taine." She sat down across from him and picked up a chicken leg, waving it in his face. "So do your part or leave."

For a few moments he just watched her eat, then he threw back his head and let out a belly laugh. "Oh Daughter, you have changed indeed."

If he had been drinking, she would have said his words were those created by the ale. But he had yet to take a sip. "I know not of what you mean."

He rubbed his chin but still did not attack his food. Most unusual.

She dropped the chicken leg to the trencher. "Why are you really here? You could have sent those stories with a messenger."

"I was concerned about your welfare. I wanted to see what type of place you were living in." His eyes became hooded, and his gaze swept the hall from rafters to floor. "This place is a falling down mess. But that will change." He leveled his gaze on her.

Rose swallowed hard.

He licked his lips and wiped his mouth absentmindedly.

141

His eyes took on a distant stare, but just as quickly, they returned to her. "I was going to give you the stories at the fair, but you are right, I always planned to stop here. I wanted to see...if you were safe. I am thinking you are not."

Nay. Her safety wasn't in danger. He wanted to make sure she could not leave. "As you can see, the wetlands are impossible to navigate unless you know them. The only ones capable of doing so are Sir Theo and..."

"And whom?"

She clenched her teeth. "It does not matter, the lad is gone. I won't be able to leave, at least not until spring."

Sir Walter lowered his chin and narrowed his gaze. "You would do best to stay close to Sir Theodore. There will be changes in the future that will affect all of England."

Truly, he was thinking of dethroning King John. If her father could do so, then he would be the most powerful man in England. For certain, she would be a pawn in a dangerous game.

The wind rattled through the hall. Soon winter would be upon them. Surely, he would not attempt a fight before then. But when spring came... Oh, she had to find that map of the wetlands so she could make it to the coast as soon as the early spring boats would attempt the waves of the channel. If she did not, she would never get away from her father's evil grasp.

"Excuse me." Rose stood, her appetite gone.

Her father circled her wrist with his hand. "Where are you going?"

Before she could answer, Theo walked into the hall. "What goes on here?" he roared.

The hall grew silent, except for Agatha who gave a heavy thankful sigh.

"This home is not a place for whoremongers." Theo kicked a few chicken bones across the floor. "All who live here respect this place and one another. Do not throw your leavings about unless you plan to pick them up. If you wish to eat and drink yourselves into oblivion, then be prepared to plant the fields and harvest the crops to make them. No one is idle at Taine Manor."

Her father let out a quiet calculated laugh. "Spoken like a true commander."

Seventeen

Thou hast neither part nor lot in the matter:
for thy heart is not right in the sight of God.
Acts 8:21

THE COLD BLAST OF NIGHT AIR THAT HIT THEO square in the face and filled his lungs suited him just fine. Perhaps it would clear his mind, which was filled with terrifying knowledge and too much drink. He stumbled down the steps and cursed his own foolishness. Once he had left France, he swore never to overindulge again. In his opinion, there was nothing more repulsive than a drunk cripple. But he could not banish Sir Walter's request.

After Theo reprimanded all within the hall on their rowdy behavior, Sir Walter quickly called for a pitcher of ale and two mugs. Theo didn't plan to take a drink until he saw Rose sitting next to her father with a deep scowl on her face. If father and daughter were not separated soon, there would be more trouble. But as if Sir Walter had read his thoughts, he asked Theo to join him in the solar. An excellent idea at the time, but...he should have stayed in the hall.

What Theo learned and what he agreed to had him tipping the mug more than he ought. In the beginning, most of the ale stayed in his mouth by taking careful, slow sips, but as Sir Walter revealed his desires, all thought of decorum fled and a great deal of the ale wound up on his tunic. He scrubbed a hand over his face as he swayed toward the goat pen. For once he truly deserved to sleep with these animals.

He paused at the fence. The pen was deserted. Who ushered the goats into the shed? In truth, it didn't matter. The goats were the least of his concerns.

Theo tripped over the entry and into a glowing warmth. There, seated around the sleeping goats, sat Master Jude, eating a hearty stew.

"I have been waiting for you. I thought you might need something else besides drink to fill your belly." Jude pointed to a small bowl next to his feet.

"I wondered when you would show up. You have been gone for quite some time." Theo sat down and picked up the bowl to find hot stew within, although there was no fire about. Over the years he had learned all things seemed to be possible with Jude around. Theo raised the bowl. "My thanks."

"You are more than welcome. So how is Lady Rosemond and her father getting along?"

Theo wiped his mouth and set the bowl down. "Not as well as they should be, given the circumstance. Her father is not well, and I fear if they do not make amends…"

Saint Peter gave a dreamy bleat, his legs pumping at the air. Jude placed a gentle hand on the goat's head and instantly Saint Peter settled down. "A rift in any family is always troublesome and could lead to more hurt and pain later if it is not resolved. Mayhap you should have a word with the girl."

"I cannot without breaking a confidence." Theo paused, wondering if he should tell Jude what Sir Walter wanted. A spasm shot through Theo's right leg, which he quickly tried to ease with a few rough massages.

"Then speak without breaking your vow." Jude reached over and lightly tapped Theo's thigh; instantly, the pain left.

Theo let loose a heavy sigh. Indeed, Master Jude could do almost anything. Often Theo wondered what other healing arts the man possessed. "My thanks, again."

Jude nodded. "We were speaking of the vow and the lady."

"Aye." Theo leaned forward, placing his hands on both thighs. "What if the vow was made in haste without much thought? Would it not be wise to tell her the truth?"

"The secret is not yours to tell."

Theo sat back. He had not said a word about what Sir Walter had told him, and yet, Jude seemed to know all the facts. The man must be a sorcerer from the devil or an angel from God. Theo lowered his head and dismissed the foolish thoughts. No angel would live at this forsaken place.

"Don't be too sure."

The muscles in Theo's neck snapped upward. "What?"

Jude waved off. "We were discussing your problem."

Theo shook his head. The grogginess of the drink must be playing with his mind. "If you knew what Sir Walter expects of me, you would not be asking me to hold back the truth from Lady Rosemond."

"What I know or don't know is not the problem here. Sir Walter asked you to do something in confidence, and you accepted. You had a choice, and you made it."

As if the heaviness in his heart was too great to bear, Theo's shoulders slumped forward. "Aye, but in truth, he offered me something I could not reject." Sir Walter had knowledge of the brazier project and offered to fund it. With the venture financed, all of Theo's problems would be solved. Not only did Sir Walter offer coin for the project, but also for fixing up Taine Manor—for Rose's comfort, Sir Walter said, but Theo suspected it was for her security as well. "What if I made the wrong choice?"

"Search your heart. Was there another choice that would protect the lady?"

Nay, there was none. In his heart he knew all others would exploit her and do her harm. Yet, had he not done the same by accepting Sir Walter's assistance? "When she learns what her father has asked of me, she will hate me."

"Ah, there is that pride again. Is this about you or her? Only time will tell what will happen. But you must make one more plea to heal the bond between her and her father because you know it is the right thing to do. Whatever the outcome of that plea is out of your hands. Remember, Lady Rosemond has a will of her own too. Let her exert her own desires and beliefs, only then will she see and learn the truth."

Of course, Jude was right. He always was right. Theo rubbed his eyes. "I will speak to her on the morrow." His eyes grew heavy, and he closed them for a moment. When he opened them, Theo was alone. Again, this did not surprise him, for it was Jude's way. Theo stretched his back and lay down. *Oh Lord, give me the right words to bring peace where there hasn't been any for many a year.*

After morning prayers, Theo did not have to find Rose, for she found him. Actually, she cornered him near the stables.

"I must speak to you alone," she whispered, keeping an eye on a few of Sir Walter's knights leaning against the stable wall. "The day is somewhat mild. Perhaps we can take a ride."

Theo lifted his gaze to the sky. Heavy clouds rolled over the sun, and a stiff wind blew from the north. The day wasn't good for anything but hunkering down by a warm hearth. Besides, the thought of mounting Triumph in front of these men did not appeal to Theo at all. Yet, he did not want to disappoint Rose, and there were few private spots left in the manor since Sir Walter and his men arrived. "If you are not opposed, I am thinking it would be nice to take one of the carts."

Her face fell; his heart sank. A free spirit like her should not be kept under lock and key or riding like an old woman in a cart next to a heap of a man. He could full well understand her desire to gallop away. Often he wished he could run away from his own circumstance, but he could not. Nor was it in his power to set her free…not yet.

"All right. A cart ride is better than staying here." She

pulled her cloak tight around her body as one of Sir Walter's knights had the audacity to stare at her boldly.

Theo clenched his left hand into a fist. "Get a cart and horse ready. The lady and I wish to take a ride," he barked at the cheeky knight. At first the knight did nothing, but then Theo bared his teeth and gave out a low growl. The knight's eyes widened, and he scrambled into the stable followed by the others.

A soft laugh sailed on the air, and Rose lightly touched his left arm. "My word. Must you always be so terrifying? These men will be gone soon enough."

That was not the case. These men would be here for quite a while, but he did want to bring up that subject in the middle of the courtyard. Right now, her protection and security were his utmost importance, and one wrong word or action could cause her to run. "Always stay close to those you know. Some men, when their passions are up, will stop at nothing to have what they want, no matter if their decisions are foolish."

Fear swept over her face, and Theo wished he would have chosen different words. However, the point had been well taken, for she stepped closer to him.

Within a few minutes, the knight had returned with the cart and horse. He offered to help Rose to the seat, but she refused. Instead, she grabbed a stool and helped Theo take his place. Afterward, he leaned over and offered his left hand, which she happily accepted.

She wiggled her hips on the seat, bumping against his left hip. "Move over. I have but a little room."

A warm glow flooded through him as they moved forward. At that very moment, every eye that turned their way held admiration, wishing they were Sir Theodore de Born.

⚜

Theo had not planned to go out this far, but she insisted. The closer they got to the wetlands, the worse the weather got.

The air grew heavy as light fog seeped about them. "I do not think we should go farther. This place has a way of turning a man on his head."

Rose strained her neck, peering into the misty land. "I guess you are right. I had hoped to see…"

"See what? Nay, Rose. This is no place for you to run to. I have told you that before, and I did not say so in jest. The ground swoops low and is covered by a large bog. If you are successful in navigating through, the land rises quickly, but on a day like this, the clouds will linger low and you will not see the danger before it is too late. Never run to the wetlands, Rose. Never."

"You lecture me of their dangers yet you plan to use them to assist my father in his foolhardy plan to take over control of England." A tingle shot up his arms when she leaned over and grabbed both of his hands. "I'm sorry you lost Lord Iron's and Lord de Baston's interest in your brazier invention. But helping my father is foolhardy. It will get you killed."

Theo sat dumbfounded. This is what she believed? Why, it was almost just as preposterous as the truth. "Your father is not trying to take control of England."

"No? Then why all the secrecy? Why does he come here with a group of over twenty knights?"

"There may be more coming, with carpenters as well," Theo mumbled.

"What? Do not tell me my father plans to stay the winter," she shrieked.

"Well, nay, though I did offer." She pulled her hands from his, and instantly Theo felt the chilly wind kick up the hairs on the backs of his hands.

"Are you mad? You cannot sleep with the goats all winter. It would kill you. Tell me now and tell me plainly, what is going on between you and my father?"

Theo could not, nor could he even think it as the plan terrified him as well. He lowered his chin to his chest. "I cannot speak of it. I swore an oath."

A shiver swept through him as her eyes became like two chips of grey-blue ice, her body a rigid frozen sculpture. Whatever rapport they had built since her arrival was smashed and destroyed like a ship hitting an iceberg. He wanted to reach for her to stop the sinking, but he could not stop her from being washed away in the waves.

"Rose, please. Talk to your father. He can explain all."

The thaw came with a crack of thunder. "I do not wish to speak to him. I asked you. Since when have you become a man of riddles? A man who hated charity now laps it up like a dog. Why would you give him your allegiance? Has he offered to fund your heating device?"

"He has, but that is not the reason. He thinks the project has merit." He reached for her, but she leaned back.

A crack of lightning lit the sky. "Do not touch me, you bag of broken bones." She scrambled from the cart. Tears ran down her face as the sky burst open, shedding its own sorrow. "I was beginning to trust you. But you are no different than the rest. All men say they care, but their actions speak differently. You have sold my friendship. Be careful, for my father will sell yours to the devil."

Theo's shoulders slumped. How could he make her understand without betraying his confidences?

She turned toward the wetlands, and Theo thought she would bolt. But she did not. She just stood as the chilly rains filled the bog.

"Come, Rose. Staying here will only make you ill." He held out his hand, but she did not look his way. Instead, she headed for the manor on foot while he dutifully followed by cart.

Eighteen

Be not overcome of evil, but overcome evil with good.
Romans 12:21

THE RAINS DID NOT STOP FOR THREE DAYS, AND when they did, a winter wind took hold with a vengeance—frosting the fields and stiffing the mud. Rose had spent most of her time in her tower chamber, avoiding her father and Theo. However, her curiosity got the better of her, and she could not resist peeking out of the narrow window at the bustling courtyard.

Theo had not lied. Tradesmen filtered into Taine like ants burrowing into a piece of soft wood. Through the cold and the rain they sawed and hammered logs into all the holes in the curtain wall. More knights stood guard. More squires and servants appeared to do their bidding. All because her father, the great Sir Walter de Payne, had deemed this place important.

If not to prepare for battle, then why? Why did her father care about the condition of this manor? More than likely he had started this scheme long before she set foot within Taine's walls. He could say it was for her comfort, but there had to be more. If Theo would not give up his secrets, then she would have to get them from her father. She took a long shuddering breath and left her chamber, walking straight to the hall. With a brief pause and a quick question, she discovered that her father was in Theo's solar.

Without a knock, she stepped inside to find her father and a few other knights poring over some maps. *No thought of war, indeed.* Ah! Here was the proof. Why else would he be surveying maps?

Rose folded her hands in a tight grip. "A word with you, Father."

All stopped and stared, but no one moved a muscle. Least of all her father.

She swallowed hard to ease the growing lump in her throat. "Please."

Her father mumbled something to his men, and they left. He then motioned to a chair next to the hearth. "Please sit. I was beginning to think we would never talk again."

"Are you leaving?" she asked as she quickly took the chair.

A low chuckle left his lips. "Do not sound so eager." He leaned against the table. "But, aye. I leave on the morrow and hope to make Rockbridge before the weather sours more."

In her opinion, the weather was as awful as it could get, but experience had taught her to keep her opinions to herself in the presence of her father. She stared at him, not certain how to begin. "Then Sir Theodore can have his solar back." A stupid way to start, but alas her lips had finally broken their fearful seal.

He placed his hands next to him on the table. "You care for him a great deal, don't you?"

An odd curl gripped her chest and set her heart in a rapid gallop. She let out a small hoot to ease the sensation. "I care nothing for him. He is but my jailer."

A thin lean smile settled on her father's pale lips. "He speaks highly of you. Tells me you are an excellent teacher."

The beat of her heart kicked up again and this time sent a warmth down to her toes. *Must be the hot fire.* "I am surprised he said thus. We have not had any lessons since you have arrived and few before then to make any real progress."

"Perhaps that will change now that you have your favorite stories to teach him."

She opened her mouth to say she would rather be drawn and quartered than to read with the insufferable traitor, but she held on to those words when her gaze caught a small gap in the wall where a piece of soiled parchment stuck within. Could this be the map of the wetlands and bog Daniel had spoken of? Did Theo hide the map, knowing she was searching for it? If so, then...

She turned her attention back to her father. "Aye, I think Theo... I mean, Sir Theodore will make grand progress when he is entertained instead of reciting dull scripture."

"Hmm, we shall see if *Theo* does appreciate your stories as much as God's word. Sir Theodore is a marvel. Despite all he has been through, he still is a strong man of faith." Her father let out a heavy sigh and made his way over to the chair across from her. "Something I should have nurtured when I was younger and feel feeble to do so now."

"Then perhaps in spring you should return and spend time with Sir Theodore. He loves to speak and analyze God's words." She paused a moment, then wrinkled her brow. "And give lectures too."

Her father's stomach shook with silent laughter and then gave way to a string of coughs. Quickly he covered his mouth. Rose squeezed the material of her gown between her fingers, taking shallow breaths. When his fit stopped, he turned away and wiped his lips. When he swiveled back, his eyes held a hollow stare. His cheeks fell in as he gasped for air.

"Mayhap Sir Theodore is right; you should stay for the winter."

"What and let your pupil freeze with the goats?" Her father shook his head. "Nay, Daughter. I have much to set right before... You look healthy, Rose. Being here seems to agree with you."

She narrowed her eyes. He changed his words on purpose. She would have to change them back. "Your eyesight is failing you. You can fix this place up as much as you like, but Taine Manor is just another prison like Godstow." She twisted the folds of her blue gown between her fingers until the material was a tangled mess in her lap. "Except I dress better here."

He grunted. "Aye. You are indeed lovely, like a perfect jewel that many a man would want in his hand. That is why you shall stay here. Safe until... Well, until everything is set and done."

Her stomach began to roll as his words took on a whole new meaning. The building, the protection, the desire to help Theo... He did not wish to conquer England by the sword. Nay, he planned to gain control through power. Through her.

Rose stood and brushed a hand over her wrinkled gown. "Until what, Father?"

He looked away without an answer.

"You plan to marry me off, don't you?"

"No, child, that is not it." His words came out in a feeble whisper; his eyes fixed on the flames in the hearth.

"Who, Father? Who is the man you have sold me to?"

On shaky legs, he made it to his feet. "You speak foolish. I have no husband planned for you. Though your sharp tongue has me thinking that is just what I should do. Find you a husband that will teach you some control and respect for your father!"

Rose began to back away. "All I did was ask for the truth. If I am not betrothed to a powerful lord, then why are you here? Why all of a sudden are you interested in me when for three years you cared naught? Tell me, Father. Tell me."

A swift knock on the door interrupted his words. "My lord, come quick. There has been a terrible accident."

Rose and her father rushed to the courtyard to see Theo lying beneath a large log. A soft cry left her lips as she raced to his side, falling to her knees. Blood oozed from his forehead, and his skin held a pale sheen. "Theo, Theo, can you hear me?" she cried.

"What happened here?" Sir Walter asked a tradesman.

"We were trying to raise the log to the top of wall, for extra support, when one of the ropes slipped." The tradesman pointed to a young knight standing off to the side. "It would have hit Sir Stephen, but Sir Theodore knocked him out of the way."

With gentle fingers, Rose brushed Theo's long hair away from the wound. "Please, Theo. Say something."

A low moan escaped his lips, and his eyes fluttered open. He blinked before shutting them again.

"Theo!" Rose cried, grabbing his left hand. "Please, try to stay with us." She looked to her father. "We need to clean this wound and see what else might be wrong."

"Get the man inside," Sir Walter roared. Immediately a handful of men rushed forward and carried Theo back into the great hall. "Take him to his solar."

Rose called to Agatha who brought forth a bowl of water and a cloth. "I'll get my apothecary jars," Agatha said, handing the bowl and cloth to Rose before scurrying away.

The men laid Theo on his pallet, and Rose daintily began to clean the gash on his forehead. She gave a sigh of relief when she realized the wound was not that serious, but that did not mean he would be fine.

"What do you think?" her father asked.

"I'm not sure." Rose looked at Theo's entire body. "The gash is not deep, but that does not mean there isn't deeper trouble. His body should be examined."

Theo moaned and mumbled but did not open his eyes.

Just then Agatha came into the room with her jars. "How is he?"

Sir Walter shrugged. "My daughter says we need to strip him. What say you?"

Agatha placed her jars on a small table and took a close look at Theo's head before nodding her agreement. With care, she removed Theo's tunic and then his shirt.

A cry stuck in Rose's throat as she gazed upon his chest. His left side looked strong and hard with well-defined muscular lines while the right was a mass of peaks and valleys where the ribs at one time had been broken or crushed. Red and brown scars laced his chest, some from battle and others from his accident.

As if knowing what was happening, Theo opened his eyes and cried out. "Leave off," he shouted. "I am fine."

Directly his gaze found Rose's. He quickly looked away, but not before she saw the humiliation in his eyes. She wanted to reach out to him and tell him he had nothing to be ashamed of, but her father pulled her away from the bedside.

"You should not be here. Let Mistress Agatha tend to him," her father said.

"Nay, I wish to stay," Rose protested. But her father would not be gainsaid. He nodded to a few of his knights who quickly pulled Rose away to the entry. "Please, Father. I wish to stay." But he did not relent.

While others went back to their tasks or took seats near the hearth, Rose stood for the next hour staring at the solar door, waiting for word on Theo's condition. Her last words to him came back to her in a haunting echo. *Do not touch me, you bag of broken bones.* Tears stung the corners of her eyes. How could she have been so cruel? Perhaps if she offered up a prayer... Her spirits fell. God never listened to her. Why did He always persecute the good while letting the evil thrive?

Still, through it all Theo remained faithful to his God, and if he survived this, he would continue to be steadfast. Why he did, she could not understand.

The door finally opened, and Agatha and her father came forth. "He'll be fine. Just a good knock on his head. He's a little groggy, but in a few days I am sure he will be his old self again." Agatha beamed.

"Aye. He's strong and thanking God that it was not worse," her father added.

Of course, he was. "I wish to see him." Rose stepped toward the door.

"No, Rose." Her father blocked her entry. "He does not want to see anyone, especially not you. Let the man rest."

An ache spread through her. *He hates me.* And she could not blame him. She added more to his torture than she did to ease it. She was the monster, not him. She turned to leave as a damning heat pricked her soul.

"I guess it will be I who will be sleeping with the goats this eve," her father said as another fit of coughs racked his body.

She stopped at the hall entry. "Nay, Father. You will stay in the tower chamber. I shall sleep in Mistress Agatha's hut."

"I am not sure that is a good idea. Perhaps you can sleep in the tower with me. We can have another pallet brought up."

She shook her head. Monsters, like she, did not deserve comfort.

Nineteen

I said in mine heart concerning the estate of the sons of men,
that God might manifest them, and that they might see
that they themselves are beasts.
Ecclesiastes 3:18

*S*IR WALTER STAYED ON ANOTHER FIVE DAYS MAKING
sure that Theo was fine. But alas, soon the day arrived
for Rose's father's departure. Not surprisingly, Rose was
nowhere to be found. Theo had been told that every night
father and daughter ate together, but the moment the meals
were done, Rose left the hall. When they were together, their
conversation was formal or nonexistent. No matter how
Theo urged Sir Walter to talk to Rose, neither seemed to put
forth the effort. Not only did Rose avoid her father, but she
avoided Theo as well. In fact, she stayed away from
everyone. At first, Theo thought she might be worried about
him, but the prideful thought quickly was dashed to the rocks
when she calmly said, with a bland face, that she was happy
he'd recovered, before she drifted away like an apparition.
Perhaps her father's departure caused the melancholy, but
once again she gave no sign of joy or sorrow when asked
about it. Nay, something else ate at her, but what remained a
mystery.

"Well, I am off," Sir Walter said as he took to his mount.
His gaze surveyed the courtyard as it had done all morning.

"I am sure the thought of you leaving is too painful for
her," Theo said.

Sir Walter chuckled. "'Tis a shame your circumstance keeps you here. You should be at court. Always trying to smooth things over. A true man of diplomacy."

"You would not have said that had you known me in Normandy. My words were quite brash and my behavior extremely crude."

A sadness entered Sir Walter's eyes; his jaw slacked. "Life changes us all."

"For the better, I think." A frosty wind whipped around the courtyard and howled out the front gate. Tiny flakes of snow glistened in the air. Theo pulled his cloak tight around him. "If the road becomes too rough, please return."

Sir Walter leaned over and held out his hand. "What is the worse that could happen? Freezing to death?" He looked to the handful of knights that would ride with him. "We shall make it. These men are hardy." He then cast his gaze up to the tower one more time. "I know you will protect her. She will need your support when this is all over."

Theo grasped the man's hand. "I will do my best. I pray the winter will be kind to you."

The old man nodded as he turned his mount to the gate and wintry landscape. He would leave without the goodbye and forgiveness he sought.

When the gate closed behind Sir Walter, Theo gave up a simple prayer. *Lord, give your servant safe passage and keep him strong.* He then turned his gaze upward to the window where Rose certainly stood, peering past the gate. *And give me wisdom to fulfill the duties her father has bestowed on me.*

It was not more than three months later when winter had a firm grip on the land that word came. Sir Walter was dead. The time had come for Theo to fulfill his obligation.

For the past three months, a quiet understanding passed between Rose and Theo. Every morning after prayers they would have a reading lesson. Oddly enough, Rose refused to read any of the stories her father had brought but chose to read scripture. Even when Theo said he would like to read the other stories, Rose's jaw would clench and she offered one word only, "Nay." And that was that. In the afternoons, she would either spend time with the goats or up in her chamber. Once he caught her in his solar riffling through his things. When he asked her why, she just shrugged her shoulders and marched away like a queen.

Not once did she venture into his new workshop where he would tinker on his inventions. When he would offer an invitation, she would flatly say, "Nay, I have no wish to be in any structure built and paid for by my father."

Ah, it had been a cold three months indeed. And now it was about to become frigid. Theo folded the message bearing the sad news and placed it on the table in his solar. Earlier, he had expected her to come running to his workshop to see what the message held, but she did not. She had to have known the messenger came from Rockbridge, for he bared its colors. Yet, she stayed away. Why? Because she did not care or she already knew what bad news the message held?

In either case, Theo ordered Agatha to slaughter a fine goose and prepare the fixings as if having a feast. He called for wine to be served and a formal verbal dinner invitation to be sent to Rose. One of the young squires helped Theo to dress in a fine doublet of deep blue and tan breeches. His boots were shined, and his hair combed. A hearty fire was placed in the solar hearth, and tallows were lit to give the room a bright inviting glow. In hindsight, he had done everything wrong, but at the time, he thought she would take the news better if her surroundings were comfortable. He placed the cloth toy rabbit and the tiny silver cross on the table near her seat.

Her eyes were hooded, and her manner guarded as she stood in the doorway, refusing to enter. Tonight she wore no veil but had simply plaited her deep ebony hair. A gold circlet graced her head. Artless. Elegant. Dressed in an earthy green gown, Theo thought she was a nymph from the forest. Willowy, but not overly such. Curved, but not plump. In other words, she was flawless.

His lips grew thick. He motioned to a chair near the small table. "Come, Rose. Let us dine together this eve. Cook has prepared a fine meal to chase away the winter doldrums." Shaking, he poured wine into a silver goblet and held it out to her.

She took a tentative step forward, crossing the entry, turning to make sure the door was left open as always. "It has been months since we have eaten together. Why now?"

Again, Theo motioned to the chair with his head and held out a chalice with his left hand. "Please. Take a drink and then sit."

Rose took the cup but did not sip or sit, her gaze hard on him. In an old wooden cup, he poured some more wine and took a long drink without spilling a drop.

A tiny smile creased her lips. "You have been practicing."

"Aye." Theo placed the cup on the table and sat. "Please, Lady Rose. Join me for a splendid meal."

'Twas then she spotted the rabbit. "Bit!" All manner of hesitancy gone, she placed the goblet on the table and picked up the rabbit and clutched it to her chest. Then she spotted the tiny silver cross necklace. "How did you…this was my mother's. I thought the nuns had given it away. They must have given it to my father. So the messenger brought these. I thought…" She hugged the cloth animal again and whirled around, laughter escaping her throat. "You do not know how happy this makes me!"

Theo did not join in her merriment. His chest ached at what the sad news would do to her. She sat and placed the rabbit next to her plate and quickly fastened the cross around her neck. "Oh, this will be a grand meal indeed."

Theo motioned to the servants to bring forth the succulent goose and a sweet honey sauce. There was soft wheat bread and pickled herring. She raised an eyebrow. "I know the fare has changed somewhat since my father's visit, but I did not think we would have such a festive meal until the winter ebbed. What other news have you from my father? For it must be impressive indeed for him to go through all this trouble."

"Aye, this may be a little extravagant, but sometimes a good meal soothes our troubled souls." Theo picked up a piece of goose and took a bite without a hint of juice or food oozing from his mouth.

"Ah, another improvement. Soon you will be eating with the nobles."

Her words were said in jest, but a sharp jab seized his throat, and he began to cough. Quickly she shot from her chair and slammed him hard on his back like she had done the first time they ate together.

"There, there," Rose said. "Do remember the pieces must be small." She returned to her seat and took a small piece of fowl and placed it in her mouth, chewing slowly, rhythmically. Her lips glistened, and the knot in Theo's throat grew.

He grabbed for his wine, taking a healthy swig. The liquid sluiced down his chin and dribbled onto his tunic.

"Well, perhaps, not yet with the nobles." She laughed, giving him a rare smile. But as quickly as her merriment came, it disappeared; her mood turned serious. "Do not tell me this means my father will be coming for another visit this spring? Please say the fine meal is just to chase away the melancholy of the weather. Or maybe it is because I have been reunited with my precious Bit and my mother's beautiful cross." Rose touched the cloth rabbit's ears, then fiddled with the small silver necklace.

'Twas at that very moment Theo realized he had made a grave mistake. He should have met her in his usual dress and ordered a more simple fare. But he thought if she was comfortable, the news would be easier to accept. He picked up his cup and took another, more modest, sip of wine. She did not follow suit.

He placed his hand on the message. "Rose, about the message from Rockbridge—"

"Aye?" She gazed around the room, and she became cool. "It must be bad news or you would not have gone through all this trouble. Out with it. What awful lord has my father betrothed me to?"

Theo let his fingers glide over the missive. "None," he said quietly.

Her skin paled, and her eyes grew wide. "Well then, what is this all about?" she asked barely above a whisper.

"Your father…"

She closed her eyes and wrapped a tight hand around the rabbit.

Theo swallowed several times and tapped the message. "Your father is dead."

For a moment, he thought she had not heard, for she sat with her gaze transfixed on her animal. Then just as suddenly, she gave a brief nod. A jagged breath left her throat, her shoulders slumped, and she wrapped the toy in both her arms. In the candlelight, he could see her eyes glisten; her lips quivered. Theo wanted to take her in his arms and hold her until the pain was gone.

"Well then. I guess it is over. Excuse me." She started to stand, keeping the animal close to her chest.

Theo reached out, then swiftly withdrew his hand. "There is more."

Rose plunked back down and let out a heavy sigh. "I suspected such. If nothing else, my father was a thorough man. What were his last wishes?" She brushed the rabbit against her cheek.

Oh, how Theo wished that Sir Walter had only left wishes and not detailed instructions. "Your father…has made you a ward. He did so with the approval of King John."

The tears that had filled her eyes moments ago dried. Color crept up her neck and flooded her cheeks. The rabbit fell in her lap. "Who? Who will be my new jailer?"

Theo rubbed his right leg with his sweaty hands, his heart hammering to the point where he thought it might leap from his chest. "It's me," he said hoarsely.

Again, she sat like a marble pillar.

Theo took a deep breath. Waiting.

In a flash, she rose and threw the rabbit at him, then turned the table on its side. "You snake. You viper. This had always been your plan. Why settle for a broken-down keep when you can gain control of Rockbridge. No doubt you plan to make yourself my bridegroom. I would rather marry all the demons in hell than be yoked to a beast like you."

Theo gripped the arms of his chair and rose to his feet. His whole body shook as he tried to gain his control. Then deep within something snapped; a bright red hue cloaked his sight and raged through his body. "I'm the beast? Madam, let me tell you what I have seen these past months. I have seen a young woman shout, wail, and scheme. A woman who would tease and ply her womanly charms to turn the head of a green lad. A woman who showed no respect to her dying father whose only concern was to take care of his daughter. A woman who has rejected God because He deemed her actions and ideas harmful. Nay, lady. I am not the beast. You are!"

She picked up her silver goblet from the floor and threw it at him. She sputtered. Her eyes bulged with tears. A sharp, jagged shriek escaped her lips before she turned and fled the room.

Theo fell back into his chair and moaned. He rubbed his aching forehead. What had he done? He had sworn to God that he would never lose his temper again. An oath broken by a beauty with a beastly temper.

But how could she be otherwise? She did not know her father loved her above all things. She did not know her father was only trying to protect her from the day she tried to flee Rockbridge with Conrad de Laval. She did not know the handsome knight was a greedy, self-serving slime.

The truth broke through Theo's own walls. He was no different. Had he not brought Rose here for his own gain?

First to learn and then…as a means to gain his own security. Was that not part of the agreement with her father? He offered to rebuild Taine and finance his brazier project as payment for agreeing to take Rose on as a ward. He could have refused, but he didn't. Instead, in her time of grief, he yelled and roared, called her the vilest things. He was worse than Conrad de Laval.

Theo pushed his hands against his forehead. He could have said no to Sir Walter's request. He could have done the honorable thing and let her go. He could have told her the truth.

But he didn't.

Because he loved her, and he didn't want her to leave.

Theo dropped his chin and wept. Aye, he was a beast inside and out.

Twenty

The Lord is nigh unto them that are of a broken heart;
and saveth such as be of a contrite spirit.
Psalm 34:18

$\mathscr{I}$F THE DEVIL WALKED THE EARTH THIS EVE, HE FOUND his resting place in Taine Manor. Theo thumped up the tower stairs and begged Rose to let him in. She refused after calling him a number of beastly names. All of which he was sure were true. Finally, as the wind grew frigid and his bones turned brittle, he gave up and returned to his solar.

The place had been set to right, and all traces of their argument erased. Theo grimaced. This meant only one thing; the whole manor had heard their fight. He went over to the table and tipped the flagon. Not a drop came out. He slammed the pitcher on the table and sat down in his chair. A weariness settled over him, and he thought to take to his pallet. Mayhap in the morning light all this could be set straight.

He had slept a few hours when a swift knock rattled the door. "My lord, my lord. Lady Rosemond has left the manor."

Theo bolted from his bed and quickly donned his clothing. At the door stood Sir Rupert and Agatha, their faces pale and full of concern. "She's gone and left us," Agatha cried.

"Snuck into the stable and took the brown mare. She sweet-talked the guard at the gate to help search for her cloak. When he wasn't looking, she smashed him over the head and took off." Rupert dropped his chin. "These young knights will fall for a pretty face every time. And in this weather!"

Theo turned his face up to the winter sky. Aye, the night had turned foul indeed. Sleet splattered the rooftops, and the wind howled like a woman giving birth. What the devil was she thinking? He grimaced. She wasn't. Blast her emotions, and blast his miserable hide for not being forthright with her right away.

"Get Triumph ready and rouse every able man. Have them search the forests and farmlands. You and I shall search the wetlands. We're the only ones who can navigate them safely," Theo said grimly.

"Aye, in good weather, but not at night and not in a mess like this where everything is a blur. Wait until morning to check the wetlands. This isn't the type of weather you should be traipsing about in. She probably didn't even go that way."

In his gut, Theo knew that was exactly the way she went. She had a fascination with the wetlands and the bog beyond. It was the fastest way to the coast. He had not been fooled a while back when he caught her sneaking about in his solar. Daniel must have told her about the map. From then on Theo kept it on his person.

He gritted his teeth. "Get the mounts ready. I'll not leave her out there to die." Then he returned to his solar, dropped to his knees, and folded his hands. *Dear Lord, let me find her. Let me find her safe. I promise I will never hold her against her will again. I'll set her free.*

The stinging sleet pounded Theo's face, and his wet cloak felt like a yoke on his shoulders. The endless time spent on horseback and the cold had every muscle—good and bad—screaming in his body. They had ridden as far as they could into the bog before the marsh turned to a slick paste that threatened to break the horses' legs.

"We dare not go farther," Sir Rupert shouted through the pitting sleet. "The animals cannot take more. Besides, we have lost her tracks."

Theo scanned the muck before him and on either side. If they could not make it through, neither would have Rose's mare. Carefully he slid from Triumph's back and began to walk the edge of the heavy mud. He had not gone more than fifty paces when he found the sign he had been searching for. "Look here, this large splat. She dismounted the horse and continued on foot." He gave Triumph's reins to Sir Rupert. "Take my horse and look for the mare. I shall go on a little farther by foot."

Rupert grabbed Triumph's reins. "Are you mad? You have a hard enough time walking on dry land, let alone trudging through this muck. You'll die out there."

"Maybe so, but I must try. Search for the mare. If you do not find it within an hour, return to the manor and do not come back until the morn. I shall meet you at the manor."

"And if you don't?"

"Then search for us when it is light. Hopefully, the weather will be better then." Theo took one step in the mud and almost fell, but he would not stop.

Sir Rupert shook his head. "Mule-headed fool," he muttered. "May God protect you."

Theo took another step, praying Sir Rupert's words would be answered.

An eternal amount of time passed. The sleet had turned to a heavy rain and then finally stopped. Theo was ankle deep in mud, yet he slugged on, calling out Rose's name. No answer came. She could be anywhere. His bearings were lost as a fog rose from the bog, clouding his sight. Finally, his feet hit dry land, and he began a steady climb, the foliage becoming dense. His heart kicked up a rapid beat; his mind began to register his location. He must be near Devil's Cliff. If Rose came this way...

Ahead of him he thought he heard a cry. He slowed his step. Nothing. Only the wind howling over the brush. Nonetheless, Theo thumped on, trying to pick up his pace even as his right leg dragged and burned with pain. "Rose," he cried out. He perked his ears, yet no sound came. Through the thick misty fog, Theo managed to spot a cloak caught on a low branch. Even caked with mud, there was no denying this was Rose's. A chill swept through his innards. If she did not die at the cliff's edge, she would freeze to death. He pulled until the garment broke free from the tree limb.

He dared not tarry. His gut curled and rolled when he realized she indeed was headed for Devil's Cliff. "Rose," he yelled to the wind. "Where are you?" He struggled on, desperately trying to increase his pace. *Merciful God, please let her see the drop before it is too late.*

The fog parted like the Red Sea, and there she lay at the cliff's edge, weeping. A shout of joy shot from his soul and leaped out of his throat. "Rose!" As fast as he could manage, he made it to her side, falling next to her.

"I can't get down. I can't get away. I can't do anything right." Her cheeks were smeared with tears and mud. Her hair matted and filthy. Her eyes held a wild, eerie gaze. Yet she seemed whole. *Praise God.*

Theo threw the cloak about her shoulders and then took her into his arms. "It's all right, Rose. It's all right. I promise everything will be different."

She shook her head. "Nay, I am hurtful and evil." She waved her hand frantically in the air. "I lost the mare. She could be dead. I destroy everything. I'm a beast."

Theo winced at her words. His words that he flung at her so carelessly. *You're a beast.*

Even as his right arm screamed in agony, he tightened his hold about her. "Shh, Rose. That's not true. You did not destroy the mare, and you certainly are not a beast."

"My father…" she wailed. "I-I-should have—"

"Stop, Rose." Theo placed a gentle kiss on top of her head.

And then a torrent of tears rolled down her cheeks, and heavy sobs racked her body. Every muscle in his body begged for release, yet Theo held her. Until she could cry no more.

Twenty-one

The Lord will strengthen him upon the bed of languishing:
thou wilt make all his bed in his sickness.
Psalm 41:3

HE CUP OF WARM BROTH SLID DOWN ROSE'S THROAT
and heated her stomach. They had managed to make
it back to Taine Manor just as the sun began to pink the
skies. At times, she was certain he carried her, and then
again, she swore she held him up. But they were back, and
Theo had insisted that she stay in his solar while he guarded
the door and only allowed Agatha entry.

"There, child. You've had a terrible fright, finding out
your father has passed. No wonder you took off. But there
now, all will be better. You'll see." Agatha held out a bowl
of pottage. "Drink this. It should fix you right up. In time,
you will be your usual self." Agatha stood and watched Rose
drain the contents of the bowl.

Usual self. That was the last thing Rose wanted to be. She
looked forlornly at the doorway where Theo was sleeping.
Sitting on a chair, both good and bad leg strewn out in front
of him, his head hanging in a precarious way, sure to give
him a neck ache when he awoke.

Rose handed the empty bowl to Agatha. "I think I should
return to the tower so Sir Theo could get some proper rest."

"Aye, he needs it, but that is not going to happen until he
thinks you are well." Agatha let her gaze slide toward the
door. "It's his way—not putting his own needs above others.

171

Had he done that in France, he wouldn't be in the shape he is today." Agatha shook her head and wiped her hands on her skirt. "Only God knows why certain things happen."

Indeed. All the more reason why she rejected her faith. Her past confinements were nothing compared to what Theo suffered. Well, he would suffer no longer on account of her. "Bring me something to wear but do so quietly. I do not want to disturb Sir Theodore."

"If you think you are going to sneak out of here without him hearing you, you have another thing coming." Agatha tapped her right ear. "He has the ears of a warrior. You'll not sneak out of here without him knowing."

"Nonetheless, I will try." Wearing only a clean shift, Rose threw back the coverlet. "Even if he does awake, he'll not catch me."

"Aye, but he will be as mad as a bull. Don't you think the two of you have fought enough? Your constitution is strong, but his..." Agatha turned away. "I'll get you some fresh clothing." She slipped past Theo, and his left eye popped open briefly registering who left the room. Satisfied, his eye closed.

Rose let her feet dangle on the side of the bed while she watched Theo's chest rise and fall at a steady rate. Dark circles hung like shrouds below both his eyes. The handsome side of his face seemed etched with almost as many lines as the right side of his face. A smell of mildew drifted off his dank and dirty clothes. *Foolish man. He should worry about himself, not me.* But alas, it mattered not what she thought. From now on their lives were tangled together until she married...if she would marry.

Agatha returned with the clothing, and this time Theo did stir from his rest. "What are you doing?" he asked.

"Lady Rosemond has asked for some fresh clothing." Agatha wrinkled her nose. "Something I think you would benefit from too."

He pulled a face and stretched, coming to his feet. "I do not think Lady Rose is well enough. She needs her rest. Take those away."

Without moving, Agatha turned to Rose and lifted a brow. "What did I tell you?"

Rose grabbed the coverlet from the bed and wrapped it around her. "My thanks, Agatha. Please leave the garments on the pallet."

"Nay. You need rest," Theo countered.

With a heavy sigh, Rose walked to stand in front of him. "I am leaving this room. Clothed or not. Now, you can order one of your newly acquired younger knights to manhandle me and force me to stay, but I don't think that would be a wise thing to do, do you?"

A muscle in his left cheek twitched as he gritted his teeth. "It is good to see you are well again, my lady."

She nodded. "Agatha, after assisting me with dressing, please draw a tub of hot water and bring it here. Sir Theodore will require a bath and some clean garments."

He clenched and unclenched his hands, but he did not offer up another word. Instead, he left the room and closed the door behind him.

"That went a lot better than I expected." Agatha walked over and picked up a blue bliaut. "Let's get you dressed before he catches his death wearing those wet clothes."

Rose lifted her arms and thought about the shadows under Theo's eyes. 'Twould not be the wet clothes that would strip his health, but the lack of rest. If Theo did not get sleep, he could become as ill as her father. The foreboding thought skittered up her shoulders and crept into her heart. Nay. Never. Not as long as she drew breath.

Nonetheless, that very eve, Theo began to run a fever.

"My lady, my lady. You must come. Sir Theo has fallen ill." Sir Rupert rapped on the tower chamber door. "Mistress Agatha needs your help."

Rose threw off the coverlet she had wrapped around her body to ward off the winter chill and flew to the door. The concern on Sir Rupert's face sent her feet swiftly down the stairs. Moments later, she entered the hall and rushed to Theo's solar.

There she found Agatha standing over the bed. "I came to bring him his dinner, and there he was lying on the pallet, flushed and clammy. All that time chasing…"

"Go ahead and finish it, chasing after me," Rose said, placing her palm on his hot forehead. "You do not have to tell me whose fault this is, I already know it is mine."

"Child." Agatha reached out, but Rose brushed her hand away.

"Do not try to make me feel better." Rose turned her attention back to Theo. Often while she was at Godstow peasants would bring their ill to the abbey. There she learned much about remedies that could cure many illnesses. "Besides the fever, what else have you noticed? Any rashes, boils, or greening of the skin?"

Agatha shook her head. "Nay, and I took a good look before you came. Besides his deformity, there is naught but the fever."

All good signs, but it may still be too earlier to tell. "If none of these things appear, then I think he will recover within a few days, but if some do appear…"

"May God have mercy," Agatha said, making the sign of the cross over her chest.

This time, Rose hoped the woman's actions would indeed bring God's mercy, for if Theo's condition worsened, then all in the keep could be in danger. For boils would mean the Black Death, greening of the skin could be Saint Anthony's Fire, and a rash could mean Small Pox. But a fever alone, as long as it did not affect the mind, could be a mild malady.

"Go fetch some cool water and rags. Bring both a cup and a bowl. After doing so, check to see if there is chamomile or coriander seeds about." Rose's words were given with such authority Agatha did not argue. The older woman could be heard barking out commands to all in the hall.

In no time, Agatha returned with the water, bowl, and cup. "I think I have some chamomile. Would you like me to heat some up? For the other spice, Sir Rupert is checking with the knights who have been to the Holy Land."

Rose dipped a rag into the cool water. "Aye, do that."

Agatha scurried to the door.

"My thanks," Rose called.

The older woman turned back with a smile. "Don't worry. He'll pull through. He's a lot tougher than he looks." With that, she left, and Rose hoped her words were true.

With no time to waste, Rose wiped the wet rag over his skin and then placed another on his forehead. One of the sisters at Godstow believed if you placed a cool rag on the back of the neck as well, you could pull the evil away from the brain. Not knowing if it was true or not, Rose applied another wet rag to the neck area. She then dipped the cup in the water and tried to make him drink to keep the fires of hell from his throat. Mayhap none of this worked. Mayhap all of this helped. Either way, she did not plan to leave Theo's side until he was well or dead.

"Do not die on me," she whispered in his ear. "For I would miss my jailer dearly."

Twenty-two

To the Lord our God belong mercies and forgiveness,
though we have rebelled against him.
Daniel 9:9

AYS HAD PASSED BEFORE THEO FINALLY OPEN HIS eyes. A weakness flooded his body. He wasn't even sure if he could raise his head. Nonetheless, he managed to turn onto his left side when he heard a soft humming on the other side of the room. There, in one of the straight-back chairs, sat Rose, reading a parchment. Long tendrils escaped her braid, her gown rumpled, and dark circles hung beneath her eyes. Surely she did not spend her days and nights watching over him?

"Is that one of the stories your father brought?" Theo asked, trying to clear his dry throat.

She dropped the parchment on the table and sprung to her feet. "You're awake!"

"Aye, it would seem so, though it does feel as if the whole French army has marched over my body." With effort, he hoisted himself up on his left elbow.

"Do not exert yourself." She rushed over to the bed and placed a gentle hand on his chest, pushing him flat on his back. "You still need to rest. We don't want you falling ill again."

"How long…" Theo cleared his arid throat. "How long have I been ill?"

Realizing his struggle, Rose stepped back to the table and poured him a cup of water. "Here, drink this," she said, returning to sit on the edge of his pallet, lifting him up behind the shoulders so he could take a cool drink. When finished, he lay back down. "You started running a fever three days ago, but it finally broke last eve. We are all grateful it wasn't more serious. I do believe you are on the mend. Though you must stay in bed for a few more days."

Theo struggled to sit up again. "Three days! I cannot lie here any longer. I have a manor to run."

Again, she raised her hand to stay him. "Fear not. All is well. Sir Rupert has taken to managing the carpenters and knights, though I must say they have slowed their pace since white patches of snow have appeared in the courtyard. Winter is definitely here." She gave out a heavy sigh. "As far as the other parts of the manor, Agatha has never needed your help with the servants. Sir Gregory and I have commandeered a few men to continue to work on your heating contraption. So you see, all is running smoothly while Sir Theodore de Born, Lord of Taine Manor and the warden of Rockbridge Keep, is recovering."

A grimace settled on his face at her last words. "Rose, about Rockbridge."

She held up a hand. "Nay, we will have plenty of time to discuss the future of Rockbridge later. Now, you need rest. Worry not, I shall watch over you." With a nod of the head she rose. "Now sleep and regain your strength."

Though he was tired, Theo truly wanted to keep his eyes open so he could feast on Rose. For even in her rumpled state she was a beauty. He wished he could touch her soft shiny braid, enjoying its silky feel against his fingers. What a fine thing it would be to wake up each morn, gazing at this lovely lady.

A heaviness settled in his chest. For shame to think such. For even though he controlled her lands, she would never be his. The time would come to set her free and let her find her heart's desire. He fought to keep his eyes fixed on her as she read, but soon sleep did overcome him and he dreamed of being whole with Rose in his arms.

The next time his eyes opened, Agatha was sitting in the chair darning a tunic and humming a dreadful tune. He coughed and waved a hand, Agatha lifted a brow. "Fine time you awake. I never took you to be a slugabed."

Besides the fire in the hearth, a few candles flickered in the room as the wind shook the dark pane in the window. "Is it night? How long have I been asleep?"

Agatha dropped her mending on the table and came over to the pallet, placing a cool hand on his forehead. "Most of the day. I had a hard time getting Lady Rosemond to leave and get some rest, even though you slept peacefully with a foolish grin on your face. I'd give up a few precious coins to know what was on your mind. It is beyond me why the lady wishes to stay with you. Mayhap she hopes you will give her more leeway than her father did if she is nice to you."

"Then you know she is my ward too," Theo said, staring past her as the firelight danced off the ceiling.

"Have you forgotten your argument with the lady a few days ago? The whole manor heard. None are surprised. Why else would Sir Walter offer to fix up Taine Manor? What will be your plans for the keep once you have gone to Rockbridge?"

Not once had Theo thought about leaving Taine, though he knew sooner or later he would have to go to Rockbridge to inspect the holding. Of course, all would think the finer keep would become his permanent home. Most would think he would force Rose to marry him so he could become one of the most powerful lords in England. Why, he even had King John's seal of approval.

"No one is going to Rockbridge until spring," Theo growled.

Agatha stepped back. "A little testy, are we? Nobody is judging you. Even a full-bodied man would jump at the chance. Just remember, you will have challengers."

"Enough. I do not wish to discuss this," he roared.

A laugh left Agatha's lips. "Ah, good. Your lungs seem to be nice and clear. Are you hungry?"

He wasn't, but anything would be better than listening to this woman's mumblings. "Aye. I am."

With a curt nod Agatha left, humming like a badly strung harp.

Theo swore it had been seconds before the door popped open again. "I've changed my mind. I do not want the food," he grumbled.

"I have no food for you, but I am so glad you are awake again." Rose stood in the doorway, wearing a fresh green gown that reminded Theo of spring grass. The circles underneath her eyes had faded, and a bright smile lit up her face and seemed to illuminate the room as well. Her hair had been neatly plaited, and a short sheer green veil covered her head.

He was sorely tempted to tell her to remove the veil, but he could not be so bold. "How are you this eve, my lady?"

"La, do not stand on ceremony just because our stations have changed. Please continue to call me Rose."

For a moment, his countenance soured. She spoke of his newly acquired power as well. "Rose, we must talk about…"

Agatha stormed into the room with a bowl of pottage and some dry bread. "Here, this should help you regain some of your strength."

"Put it on the table. My thanks," Theo said.

She stalled in the middle of the room, bowl still in hand. "What is this? You're all sweet like honey now?" Agatha cast an eye at Rose. "I see the rabbit has tamed the bear."

His ire rose as heat flushed Rose's skin. Blast Agatha for making light of a serious situation. "You may leave," he said more gruffly.

Agatha dropped the bowl on the table, amusement glittering in her eyes, tilting her head toward Rose. "Good fortune with this one. He is in a mood this eve." With that, the older woman quit the room, laughter trailing behind her.

"Sometimes that woman vexes me." Theo kept his gaze fixed on the door, trying to develop a blank mask that one sight of Rose would shatter.

179

"She means well." Rose picked up the pottage and came to his side. "Are you able to feed yourself, or do you need help?"

Theo slowly sat up and shook his head. "I am not hungry. I just said thus to get rid of Agatha."

The sides of Rose's lips curled upward. "She cares for you deeply and was very worried about you."

Theo turned his gaze to the wall behind Rose's head. "She cares for her place at Taine. Her place is secure as long as I am lord of the manor."

"Perhaps she worries what will happen once you leave for Rockbridge." Rose placed the bowl back on the table. "I see you are not ready to eat."

"I do not wish to speak of Rockbridge. That is all."

Slowly Rose returned to his side on the pallet. "We need to speak of it sometime. Avoiding it will not change the situation."

"Aye." Theo's closed his eyes briefly, trying to gain some control. Best just to tell her so she would stop pretending to care about him. "Rose, I will not—"

"I think you are right. Let us not speak of this now. I should let you rest some more." Without warning, she stood.

Quickly Theo reached out but paused just before their hands touched. He dropped his arm to his side. "I have slept enough." His chin dropped to his chest. "Please don't go."

Rose looked around the room like a confused lost lamb. "Then how about I read a story to you." On the other side of the table lay the parchments she had been reading earlier. Picking one up, she returned to the bed, sitting next to him once again. Her shoulder warm against his. "This one...used to be a favorite. I have not read it for some time. It is about a maid who is forced to live alone on an island because she is said to be very wicked." Her words were weak and hesitant as if a sad shroud had been placed on her shoulders.

"Is she truly wicked?" he asks, trying to lift her spirits and still take in the sweet scent of lilies wafting from her hair.

"Do not ask me. All will be revealed." Her eyes began to glow. "Once there lived a maid called, Namha. She was said to be very beautiful, but very evil. Every morn she would sing a beautiful tune that would woo all the young men to her doorstep. With the curl of her finger, they would cross the threshold of her cottage. There, she would cut their throats and drink their blood."

"By the cross, your father would let you read such? This is not a story for a young girl. It is barbaric."

Rose put a finger to his lips. "Shh, you are ruining the tale." She turned back to the story. "Their blood would make her the loveliest maid in all the land. But then a true tragedy struck."

"What could be more tragic than a woman killing young men?"

"There are no young men left in her village."

Theo slaps the bed with his left hand. "But of course. Now what will the wicked wench do?"

Rose turned back to the parchment and pointed to the words. "Namha was quite cunning, and she did not want to starve or lose her beauty."

"Could she not just slaughter a calf and use some eastern berries to brighten her lips?"

An exasperated huff left Rose's lips. "Let me finish." With Theo properly disciplined, she continued. "So Namha began to charm the children to enter her home. There, she would cut their throats and drink their blood."

"God's teeth, how can you say this used to be one of your favorites? What a gruesome tale only a…" A deep sadness transfigured Rose's face, and Theo choked down the word that had caused the transformation.

"It is fine to say. Namha was a monster. A terrible wicked monster." Tears flowed down Rose's cheeks and hung on her lips. "I am as wicked as she. No wonder I used to love this story when I was young. Only a monster could enjoy such a tale." A painful wail sprung from Rose, and she covered her face with her hands.

The racking in her shoulders tore at Theo's soul; he pulled her into his arms and patted her back. "Hush now. It is only a foolish story that a lady of your sensitivity should not have been reading. Your father should have forbidden it."

More tears rushed from her eyes and wetted her cheeks. "Do you not see? I pestered him and nagged him until he gave in to me. He could not deny me anything. And how did I repay him? I ran away. I screamed at him. I dishonored him. I refused to talk or listen to him." She sat up on the edge of the pallet; her eyes red-rimmed and wild. "He was trying to tell me...but I would not listen." Her sobs became chokes and gasps. "I would not listen."

Deep within, Theo's heart cracked. His sorrow rushed outward and mixed with her grief. He gave her a tight squeeze and placed his left cheek against hers. "Rose," he whispered softly in her ear. "None of this is your fault. You are not a monster. We all make mistakes."

She pulled back, placing her hands on his chest. "I hurt my father, and now he is lost to me forever. I am exactly like Namha. My father sent me away because he knew I was wicked and I would drain the heart and soul of all who lived at Rockbridge. Why could I not see it? I hurt him so, and he died...alone."

Quickly, Theo pulled her back to his chest and let the puddle of tears soak his shirt. "Rose, listen. For I have a story to tell you too. Long ago, there lived an evil tax collector. He cheated the people in the land. If they owed ten pieces of silver, he would charge them twenty. He would suck the life out of the people until all about him were poor and he was the richest in the land. He was a monster because people treated him as a monster. Then one day a man came to town, and all the people praised this man because he was wise, honest, and good. But instead of eating and sleeping with the respectable people of the town, he went to the tax collector's house and ate and slept there. The man accepted the tax collector for who he was and helped him to change his ways. The tax collector returned all the money to the village people. He then went and followed the man. Forgiven and loved."

Rose wiped her eyes and hiccupped. "Only you would recite scripture at such a time. You speak of Jesus and Matthew."

"I speak of all of us. Not a man breathing is without sin. We all do things we wish we did not. Not one of us is better than another. In God's eyes, you are perfect because of the blood of his son, Jesus. Rest easy, Rose. Your father loved you and forgave you long before you thought to ask. And our Lord has forgiven you too. He is waiting for you to come back to him."

She nestled closer to Theo, easing him back down on the bed. "It was easier to blame God than to blame myself. Truly, do you believe he will forgive me?"

"If He forgave the likes of me. He has already forgiven your small infractions."

"Small infractions," she whispered, snug against his chest. "Only you would say that. You are a kind, kind man, Theo de Born." She closed her eyes, and in moments, her breathing became easy.

She slept, and Theo tried not to move a muscle to disturb her rest.

Time passed, and finally Agatha entered the room and stared at the bed. "Well, if this isn't a pretty scene. If she does not leave now, her reputation will be lost."

"Then take a seat in yonder chair to quell the gossips. For I will not wake her from this much-needed rest." Theo gently rubbed Rose's shoulder.

"You're going to be stiff as a bench in the hall come morning." Agatha harrumphed and then took the chair next to the hearth, folding her arms over her chest. "Methinks you should be quick in marrying the girl. For my backside does not take a shine to sitting in this hard chair."

Twenty-three

*And he that searcheth the hearts knoweth what is the
mind of the Spirit, because he maketh intercession
for the saints according to the will of God.*
Romans 8:27

ROM THAT DAY FORTH, THEO AND ROSE HAD A
great understanding. Every morn, Rose would show
up and by all appearances had given her soul back to God.
Their lessons were lively with readings and discussions
about scripture, Crown affairs, and other important matters
of the day. Sometimes they were in total agreement, and in
other things they were like wolves at each other's throats.
But through it all, their admiration grew and all thought it
would be just a matter of time before their bands would be
announced.

And most confounding was that Rose insisted on sitting
on his right side instead of his left, squeezing his curled
useless hand often.

At times, Theo ate in the hall with ease, not a drop of
food or drink dribbling down his chin. Still, often Rose and
he would eat in his solar enjoying each other's company. By
winter's end, his reading had improved and he could manage
to scribble out a few sentences with his left hand. Her smiles
his great reward. Theo wanted this simple life to go on
forever.

But as the winter winds became mellow and the earth
became supple from the spring rains, mud always had a way

of seeping into the most pleasant places. The riders showed up one sunny day while the birds made their nests and sung a cheery tune.

Theo made his way to the top of the battlements as the alarm was given. There, coming from the trees, rode a good twenty men, and Theo suspected another hundred remained hidden. "Who are they?" he asked Sir Rupert.

The yellow banner with a red serpent pressed in the middle fluttered in the spring wind. Rupert rubbed his jaw. "I have seen these colors before. I just can't place them."

"It's Conrad!"

Theo and Rupert turned to their left to see Rose flying up the battlement stairs, a wide grin on her face.

Dressed in a light blue gown, clapping her hands like an enthusiastic child, she exclaimed again, "'Tis Sir Conrad de Laval."

Rupert leaned toward Theo. "The cod who caused all the ruckus at the fair. What's he doing here?"

"Why do you think he has come?" Rose asked, her eyes aglow of pleasure and excitement, but a slight wariness as well.

Why indeed. Every cautious bone in Theo's body stood at attention. He wanted to order the guards to start boiling tar, but these men did not approach the gate as if ready for battle.

In two long rows, they trotted forward. One rider broke from the middle and galloped to the gate. He removed his helm, and a shock of blond curls fell about his handsome face. "Hail to Lord Theodore de Born and all within. I am Sir Conrad de Laval and have come to seek your good company."

Rupert turned his back to the wall and pointed to a line of weapons in a corner. "I can take that yonder spear and end his prattle. You know he is up to no good," he muttered in Theo's ear.

Theo placed his left hand over his crocked lip. "Do you wish to incur the wrath of Lady Rose? Look at how she beams as she gazes down upon him."

"Ah, you are as soft as a pile of goose feathers when it comes to her. The lady doesn't even know what's good for her."

"Maybe not, but I will not dash her hopes," Theo said under his breath. "Open the gate," Theo roared, and immediately the guards complied.

Rose squealed with delight as she headed to the courtyard.

"I hope you know what you are doing? I can smell their foul odor from here." Rupert walked slowly and patiently next to Theo.

"That's your own stinking arse that whiffs in your nose." Though as they thumped down the battlement steps, Theo wasn't so sure that Rupert had spoken false. The men wore chain mail, and each had a sword ready to draw at their hip. Sir Conrad sat tall and straight on a spotted-grey destrier. He flashed Rose a charming smile, and she all but melted at his feet.

Theo wanted to smash the pup into pulp.

Instead, he ordered a stable boy to take hold of Sir Conrad's horse. Once the knight had dismounted, he rushed to Rose's side and grabbed her hand, placing a long and languid kiss into her palm.

Rupert rolled his eyes. "What a peacock," he mumbled.

Theo touched Rupert's shoulder. "He is our guest. Behave yourself."

What followed even surprised Theo. Rose threw her arms around Conrad and boldly kissed his cheek. A collective gasp rose out of all who were present in the courtyard. Theo clenched and unclenched his left hand. Did she not know such an open act of affection would send the tongues wagging all the way to London?

Pulling back his shoulders and taking even, measured steps, Theo made his way to the couple. "Sir Conrad, welcome to Taine Manor."

The younger knight blanched at the sight of Theo but quickly recovered. He untangled his arms from Rose's and shook Theo's left hand. "I have heard much about this place, but I am pleasantly surprised the rumors have been false."

"What have you heard?" Theo asked.

A slight pink tinge crept into Sir Conrad's cheeks. "I, ah, heard that this manor was falling apart like…"

It did not take a scholar to figure out the rest of the sentence—*like its owner.* Theo frowned when Rose again slipped her arm through Conrad's.

"Sir Theodore has been slowly repairing the manor. Is it not a grand little place?" She smiled at the blond knight like he was an angel who had just stepped from the heavens. Could she not see this lad was nothing but a vain puff?

Conrad patted her hand and looked about. "It is a fine, modest place." His golden gaze came to rest on hers. "But a woman of your caliber should be in the most glorious of keeps. Like your home, Rockbridge."

The words were so melodiously delivered Theo knew no good could come from this visit. "Sir Conrad, how is your lovely wife?"

A cold spring rain could not have sobered the mood better. Rose glared at Theo as if he had just told her she would have to spend the day sweeping out the goat shed.

Conrad dropped his chin to his chest. "Alas, my wife sadly died in childbirth a few months past, but at least God mercifully saved my son. Perhaps it was God's will. Though it seems wrong to leave a child without a mother."

A horse's behind could not have asked a dumber question. At least Conrad had the decency to show a little contrition, but Rose beamed like the sun. Did no one feel the sting of the poor woman's death?

Rose squeezed Conrad's arm. "How terribly awful. You must be grieving so."

Conrad nodded and peered at her through his lashes like a lost pup. Rose lapped it up.

Horse manure to be sure.

"Come. You must be tired from your journey. We have plenty of food and drink for you and your men," Rose said, leading the handsome knight toward the hall.

"This is all folly," Rupert whispered as they followed the pair. "Let me stab him now. It will save us the trouble later."

"Nay. He is our guest," Theo repeated. "Rose seems quite fond of him."

"Aye. All the more reason to get rid of him. Mark my words. No good will come from this visit."

Theo said naught but knew Rupert had spoken the truth.

A dream could not have been better. Rose sat and watched Conrad stuff his mouth with rabbit, while the greasy drippings slipped down his chin. Oh, he was still the most beautiful man she had ever known, and he still sent her heart into a panic. She may still burn in hell's fire to be filled with joy at learning that his wife had died, but she could not help it. Conrad was free once again.

Over the months she had thought about praying, asking God to open her heart to His truth. Verily, she didn't expect answers, so she did not pray. Nonetheless, here sat Conrad. An answer to a prayer she should have given? Rose could not be certain. For she had not thought about Conrad since her father had died. 'Twas all foolishness. Yet again, perhaps three years ago she was not mature to become anyone's wife, but now...

Her gaze slid to Theo, who sat silently, almost brooding, taking small sips of mead and glaring at his guest. What was wrong with him? Usually Theo greeted all with graciousness, but today he looked like he was ready to tear Conrad apart. Truly Theo could not be jealous. Not once had he expressed more than a mild admiration toward her. What did he fear? Her leaving him? A strange warmth spread through her, and then the truth hit her square in the gut and an ache spread up to her heart.

Conrad was a threat to Theo's control over Rockbridge. Being his ward had given Theo great power. If she became Conrad's wife, that power would shift and Theo would once again be regarded as a lowly, broken-down knight with a modest holding. Surely she meant more to him than a mighty castle, wealth, and the power that came with it? Had every act of kindness been a lie to keep her compliant and cooperative?

She gave a mental shake. Nay, Theo was not that way. If she wanted to marry Conrad, Theo would not stop her, would he?

Conrad leaned toward her, his cheek close to hers. "What are you thinking about, my love? Pray tell, is it about us? For I have never stopped dreaming about you. Though I was married to another, I have always loved you. Certainly, Sir Theodore is a decent man and will see what all within this hall can see."

Rose turned until her face was less than a butterfly's wings from his. "What do they all see, Conrad?"

A breathtaking smile slid across his glorious face. "Why, that we love one another, of course."

Did they? Did she? Had she not always loved Conrad since she was young? Her gaze slid to the brooding Theo, wondering what his thoughts were on the matter.

Later that night in her chamber while staring at the smoke slipping out the window from the brazier, Rose made a decision. In the morn, she would talk to Theo and tell him just how she felt about Conrad. And for the first time in years, Rose prayed, for her decision did not settle well within her heart.

When the morn did come, Theo was nowhere about nor was Conrad. No one was assembled for morning prayers. However, the hall was so quiet one would think mass was being said. "Where is Sir Theodore and Sir Conrad?" Rose asked Agatha.

The query was met with a slight shrug before Agatha returned to her work. In the courtyard, Rose found Conrad's men in swordplay while Theo's knights and those from Rockbridge carried out their regular duties. Her inquiries fell on deaf ears or vaguely answered. No one seemed to know where the pair had gone. She searched Theo's workshop, but they were not there either. They weren't in the stables or the smithy. She even checked the goat shed, but that was empty as well. In fact, Theo and Conrad were missing from the manor altogether. She made her way to the gate where she spotted Jude whittling.

"I am certain you know where they are?" she asked, shielding her eyes from the rising eastern sun.

"Aye," he said nonchalantly, not taking his eyes off his work. "They left early before daybreak. On foot."

"On foot? Why, that is absurd. Sir Theo will not last long on the rocky ground."

Jude paused in his whittling. "And yet, they have been gone a long while."

A wintry chill skipped down her spine. Theo could be hurt. Fallen. If so, would not Conrad help him? "Which direction did they go?"

"Toward the marsh," Jude said, returning to his task.

"Why would they go there? It is the worst in the spring, for one never knows when a fog might roll in."

"Theo knows his way. He will be careful."

"In a cart, aye. But on foot, 'tis foolish." Rose squinted her eyes as if that would bring Theo into view.

"You worry much about Theo but have not said a word about the other."

Rose shrugged. "Conrad is a strong man. He can take care of himself."

Jude blew the wood shavings off his creation. "Are you sure about that? He does not know the wetlands, and they can turn a man around. Even the strongest can become lost within, and yet, you do not seem to worry over him."

Aye, he spoke the truth, but she had no answer, so she

changed the subject. "Where are the goats? They were not in the pen this morn. Nor do I see them in yonder field."

"They were in the field, but when Theo and Sir Conrad came out, the beasts followed them."

"What?" New fear bubbled from her soul; not only was Theo out on the rough terrain, but he had taken a whole herd of goats with him. "That is lunacy. Why didn't you stop them? Those goats can become quite feisty. Some could run off into the marsh, and you know Sir Theo would pursue them. Such foolishness."

"Indeed. Running forward without thought usually causes much folly."

Rose wasn't sure if Jude was talking about the goats anymore or what happened last winter. "A human will learn quickly from their mistakes; an animal is not as swift."

Again, Jude paused in his task and lifted a grey eyebrow. "In my experience, I have found it to be the other way around. Man has a habit of making the same mistakes over and over. It would be better if he were silent and opened his heart. The truth is always before him, but his own thoughts and mouth usually get in the way."

What did an old man know anyway? Where would a person be without his thoughts and his speech?

Jude chuckled. "A lot better off than he is today."

Though she did not voice her question, she was certain he answered it. "Are you speaking to me?"

"Do you see anyone else about?"

Sometimes Jude could be so impertinent. "Do you not think we should look for them? I can call Sir Rupert and get a few other men to search—"

"They will return safely. Worry not. Go about your daily tasks."

Rose fixed her gaze toward the wetlands. "That will be impossible since I start my day instructing Sir Theo." She then turned her gaze to Jude. "Then I feed the goats because their keeper is usually not around."

"That is not true. I always have an eye on them." Jude then held up a small wooden bird. "Here, I made this for you."

Rose took the perfectly sculpted creature in her hand. Etched on the bird's side were fine lines that looked like feathers. They were evenly placed on both sides and perfectly sculpted. The beak smooth and impeccably manicured. The eyes looked as if they could spot a worm wiggling in the soil. "I did not know you had such talent. Why, this bird looks almost real."

"Of course. How do you think I made them?"

She smiled, used to his silly quips as if he had made every bird in this world. "I thank you. I shall treasure him always."

"Let him be a reminder to always think before you give flight. For the direction you take may not be the one your heart wishes to follow. Now go and continue what you were doing last night."

Rose cupped the bird gently without taking her gaze from it. "Last night I ate and drank in the hall and then went to my chamber to sleep. I am not hungry or tired."

"Nay, after that. You prayed. It has been a long time since you have done so."

Her hands fell to her sides as the chill returned to her spine. "How did you know—"

"Do not be afraid. Praying is always a good thing and something all should do more often. Now go. Both Sir Theo and Sir Conrad will be back within the hour, unharmed."

An argument settled on her lips but died before she could produce the words. She gazed at the bird in her hand, and a great peace settled over her. "Very well, I shall pray for their safe return."

"Do not forget to pray for your heart," Jude said, placing the whittling knife in the folds of his tattered cloak.

"My heart?"

"Aye. For it to see what your thoughts and tongue have clouded."

Twenty-four

Let all your things be done with love.
1 Corinthians 16:14

IT WAS AN UNCHARITABLE THOUGHT, BUT THEO could not help it, he did not like Conrad de Laval. In the few hours they had spent walking along the edge of the wetlands, Theo had learned much. Rose's father had been right. Sir Conrad only measured a man's worth by material possessions and power. Not once had the young knight talked about Rose's attributes without attaching her fortune to it. The closest compliment the lad could muster was, "It is a bonus that Lady Rose is so beautiful along with having a great fortune."

Theo wanted to sock the greedy goat in the mouth, but instead, he held his patience. Was he any better? Having Rose as his ward gave him much. Once again, Taine Manor thrived. The debt to Lady Catherine was almost fully paid, even though she didn't want the coin. Before his death, Sir Walter had funded Theo's invention, allowing the work to continue. Aye, there was profit in having control over Rose. No wonder she fought so hard to be free.

But Theo did not want control over her. He wanted her to be happy. To follow her dreams and to love whomever she chose. Sir Walter believed Theo to be wise and that he would protect Rose from evil. Eventually selecting the right man for her when he came along. As sound as those words were, wisdom never understood the affairs of the heart. Rose

193

loved Sir Conrad. And even though he was a covetous cow, he did not seem to have a mean bent. Conrad would not hurt her, but neither would he love Rose completely as she deserved. Would that be enough to have a sound marriage?

Theo pulled his left hand through his hair. 'Twas a dilemma. But he had vowed that day searching the wetlands for her that he would let Rose have her freedom. If her choice was to be yoked to Sir Conrad, then so be it.

He had not entered his solar and placed his right leg on a stool when the door swung on its hinges and Rose entered. "A word with you, my lord." She folded her hands in supplication, but they shook with anger all the same.

"What is it, Rose?" he asked wearily, rubbing his right thigh.

A wrinkle creased her lovely brow. "You should not have walked so far. What were you thinking?"

"Of your future. I was thinking of your future. Sir Conrad wishes to wed you."

Not a stitch of emotion crossed her face. No happiness or gaiety. No sadness or anger. Nothing. She did not nod or shake her head. Nay, she stood like Lot's wife, a pillar made of flesh and blood instead of salt.

"Your thoughts would help with this decision. What say you? Do you wish to wed Conrad de Laval or not?" The forcefulness of Theo's words caused him to wince inside. The last thing he wanted was for her to pull up her defenses. He let out a heavy breath. "I truly wish to know how you feel about this," he said softly.

Her shoulders sagged as she dropped her gaze to her hands. "I-I think I love him."

Her voice was barely a whisper, and Theo had to lean forward to catch her words. "You think?"

"I love him." She looked Theo square in the eye, but the uncertainty within her eyes betrayed her words.

For a moment he just stared at her, hoping she would add a few more words of reason to defend her bold statement. But she did not. Theo dropped his head and rubbed his eyes, then his forehead. Conrad loved her lands and lusted after her. Rose might love Conrad, though her eyes said not. By all that was holy, Sir Walter was right, dealing fairly with a ward was not an easy business. Especially if you loved her to distraction.

Words from scripture flooded his mind. *Love suffereth long, and is kind; love envieth not; love vaunteth not itself, is not puffed up, doth not behave itself unseemly, seeketh not her own, is not easily provoked, thinketh no evil; Rejoiceth not in iniquity, but rejoiceth in truth; Beareth all things, believeth all things, hopeth all things, endureth all things.*

He dropped his hands and slowly raised his head. "All right, Rose. If you love him, then I will not stand in the way. You shall have my blessing."

Her eyes flooded with unshed tears, and her lips quaked. She stepped forward and knelt next to him. Gently placing her delicate warm hands on each side of his face, he relished in their tenderness. "Thank you," she whispered. Then, ever so softly, she kissed his forehead.

His heart exploded with love and joy, pain and suffering. He wanted to grab her hands as she pulled away, beg her to stay.

But he did not.

Instead, he let her swiftly turn away and run from the room.

And then Theo wept.

For never before in his entire life had he received such a loving kiss.

Twenty-five

He healeth the broken in heart, and bindeth up their wounds.
Psalm 147:3

OR THE NEXT WEEK, THEO HAD VERY LITTLE contact with Rose. Always, it seemed, she was with Conrad—walking the fields, whispering in the stables, laughing by the goat pen, kissing in the shadows. 'Twas enough to drive a man mad. As much as their actions tried his patience, at least Rose was here. On the morrow that would all change.

"Hopefully, I won't be gone long, my lord," Agatha said as she plopped her satchel on a trestle table. "I trust the servants can manage the kitchens without me."

"I'm sure all will be fine." Theo watched Conrad's men rush about the hall gathering their pallets and swords. He used to relish the silence of the hall before they had come. Tomorrow it would return, but this time the quiet would bring no joy. "All at Taine Manor are used to pitching in when another is indisposed."

"But I shall be gone a good month." She shook her head and rummaged through her sack. "But we can't have Lady Rose alone on the road with a bunch of bawdy knights. It just would not do." A few knights who heard Agatha's words raised their eyebrows in disagreement but were wise enough to say nothing.

"I am glad that you will be going to Crosswind first. Having Lady Catherine accompanying both of you will cause me to rest easier. No one would dare harm such a great lady or the ladies she travels with." Theo let out a painful sigh. "Aye, all will be fine here…just like before."

Agatha pulled her hands out of her bag and stared at Theo. "Why don't you tell Lady Rose how you feel?" she whispered.

Her blunt words stunned Theo. "What do you mean? I feel nothing."

"Right. Keep telling yourself that. You look at her like a lovesick goose. Mayhap if she knew how you felt, she might…"

Theo laughed sarcastically. "Truly, do you think she would give up a fine young knight like Sir Conrad for a broken-down sack of bones like me?"

The pity and defeat he saw in Agatha's eyes set Theo's teeth into a hard grind. "Then let us not discuss this further." Theo rose and stomped to his solar. Once inside, he latched the door and did not come out when the merriment in the hall began, nor did he answer Rose's pleas to join them.

He spent the eve and early morn trying to pray but often found his thoughts turning dark. Rose's happiness and well-being were his greatest concern, and he rejoiced that she had found both. Yet, in the deep recesses of his mind, he hoped she would think of him often and regret her decision to go away.

He crawled from his bed, stoked the fire, then dropped to his knees and folded his hands. "God, what is wrong with me?" he cried out. "Why are these demons always with me? Why do you let your servant live when he no purpose?"

A thud against the shuttered window disrupted Theo's prayer. First, he thought to rise and investigate, but his anguish held him to the floor.

"Lord, do you hear me? Come and take your servant to live with you."

Another, louder thud vibrated off the shutters. By the holy cross, what drunkard disturbed his prayers? Struggling to his feet, Theo made his way to the window and threw back the shutter, ready to give the intruder a severe tongue-lashing.

There, in the moonlight, stood Jude. "I was wondering when you would stop wallowing in your pity and open the window." The old man threw a leg over the window ledge and crawled into the room. He flapped open his cloak. "Whew, hot and stuffy in here."

"I have not seen you in days, months, and now in the middle of the night you appear? You disrupted my prayers," Theo said, rubbing the back of his neck.

Jude removed his cloak, revealing his quite skinny, almost emaciated body. It occurred to Theo he had never seen the man without his heavy, dark cloak. His clothes were a poor fit and hung loose about him. Grey and drab, something a slave or a servant would wear. However, the garments were surprisingly clean.

"Aye. They are pretty pathetic." He sat back in Theo's chair and placed his feet on Theo's stool, wiggling his toes by the fire. "Ah, that is better."

Theo lifted a brow. "Do make yourself at home."

Jude waved to the other chair in the room. "Sit."

Without argument, Theo dragged the chair toward the hearth and sat across from the old man. "Even though it is the middle of the night, I am glad you are here."

"I know." Jude closed his fathomless eyes, not offering up another word.

"She leaves in the morn."

"I know."

"I am not sure how I will survive without her."

Jude peeked open one eye. "I thought you said you were ready to die."

How the devil… "Were you listening outside my window?"

Jude opened both eyes but did not lean forward. "Do you truly believe I have to sneak about to hear what you are saying?"

Theo examined his thoughts and the man before him. "Nay. You have always seemed to know what I need or how I am feeling. Yet, I cannot imagine how you are able to do so."

Jude closed his eyes again. "I am just wiser than you. I have been around for a long time. It is truth, with age comes wisdom. Though, I have always been wise."

"Indeed. There is no protest there. So pray tell, what wisdom do you have to share with this worn-out, useless man?"

"Let us start by stopping the pity. There are many who have suffered more than you and are still able to hold their heads high, singing praises to God." Jude's eyes slowly opened and tightly held Theo's gaze.

"You are right. I should stop this melancholy. My mind knows you are right, but my heart cannot release its woe." Theo hunched his shoulders and dropped his head between his hands.

"Perhaps you need a change of scenery." Jude rose and grabbed his cloak. "Come. Dress. Let us leave this hot place for some fresh air."

With surprising quickness and fingers that had not been nimble in years, Theo rose and dressed. When finished, he followed Jude through the hall and out into the courtyard. They did not stop until they were standing in front of Theo's workshop. "You wish to go in here?"

"Why not? I wish to see how your heating system is coming along." Jude lifted the latch and stepped inside.

Theo followed, pondering Jude's words. "What is a system?" he asked.

Jude waved his hand as he stepped closer to the round iron brazier. "A useful word that will be overused in the future. Explain this to me."

"I am thinking instead of always using a hearth or a brazier to heat a room, one could use this round iron... I have no name for it as of yet."

"Try *stofa*."

"Aye, *stofa*. As this will heat a small space, but see, this long round pipe will lead the smoke from the room and—"

"Aggressive thinking for the times. Mayhap man is not ready for all this." Jude pointed to a drawing on the parchment. "And what is this?"

"Another thought of mine. A tower of sorts to hold fresh water, much like a well above ground." Theo pointed to one end of the tower. "This piping will run from the tower to the land below and spew out water into a larger trench, from there it will be forced into smaller trenches where it will hopefully flow to dry lands."

"Brilliant work. But you will need a lot of men to build these trenches and coin too."

Theo sat down on a stool by the table. "Aye, there is the problem. With Sir Walter gone and Rose no longer my ward, I cannot bring either idea to life. No one will see the profit."

Jude tapped his fingers on the drawing. "Then you should not have given consent to Lady Rose's marriage. You gave away your opportunity."

Of all people, Theo thought for sure Jude would understand. "How could I not? Her happiness is far beyond a few warm rooms or watered crops. Besides, Sir Conrad has promised to continue to be a benefactor in this."

"And you believe him?"

Theo's heart sank. "Nay, I do not. He has his sights on greater things. There was no enthusiasm when I showed him my work nor the land I wished to cultivate."

Jude nodded. "Aye, man cares more for building weapons to destroy each other than to care for God's creation." He lifted his clear eyes and then smiled. "However, there have always been a few faithful who are wise enough to see and listen." Jude turned and made his way to the door. "Fear not. All will be solved over time."

Time! Did he not realize all of Theo's efforts and coin would have to go back into caring for the people of Taine Manor? In the future, there would be no time to fiddle with these heating or watering *systems*. 'Twas just another dream that would never come to pass.

At the door, Jude stopped. "These things are not yours to

bring to the world. Your focus should be on the manor and Lady Rose."

Theo's heart fell. Not even Jude found value in his work, and his control over Rose would end the moment she left Taine. Truly his life did not have purpose.

"You are so thick." Jude tapped his forehead. "In the near future, your wisdom will be needed to maintain peace in the realm. Think on these words instead—Magna Carta. Here you and others will find their work successful." Jude waved his hand toward Theo's efforts. "This is not for you to discover."

His words of peace were strange to Theo but did start his mind thinking. The barons were always warring against themselves, and now against King John. If something could be put in place...a charter of sorts... Theo shook his head. Nay. Without Rose, he had no power to think about, let alone suggest, such an endeavor.

Jude turned toward the door. "You will not see me again."

A large hole opened up in Theo's gut and swallowed the last of his hope. "So you will desert me too?"

With a slow turn of the head, Jude looked at Theo. "I said you would not see me. I did not say I am leaving."

"You always speak in riddles. If you stay, surely I will see you." Even as Theo said the words he knew them to be false, for Jude came and went as he pleased. If he did not want to be seen, he wouldn't. Yet Theo always took comfort in knowing Jude was there.

"Aye. Now you have it." Jude nodded.

"Have what? I have not uttered a single word. What do you speak of?"

Jude tapped his temple. "Your thoughts are plain. Even if you do not see me, I am always here. Now then, worry not about your pride and vanity, they are not important."

Theo leaned his back against the table on which the drawings sat and gave a dejected laugh. "Do you truly believe I have pride and vanity with this face and this body? Nay, that has been buried long ago."

"You may have given up on your physical pride, but in your heart, you still search for the pride of self-worth."

Like a band of iron around his chest, Theo's breath came short. His shoulders sagged as he lowered his head. "You missed your calling in life. You should not be herding goats but sitting with the scholars and Cardinals in Rome."

Jude wrinkled his nose. "I'd rather not. You may not receive the respect you desire for all this"—he waved a hand at the table which held his life's work—"but take heart. What you did today will not go unnoticed."

Theo laughed and shook his head. He had done nothing but what a fool would do—he let Rose go. When he looked up, he was alone, but Theo was not surprised. Jude had a way of vanishing, leaving you to wonder if he was even there.

Twenty-six

*A new heart also will I give you,
and a new spirit will I put within you:
and I will take away the stony heart out of your flesh,
and I will give you a heart of flesh.
Ezekiel 36:26*

THOUGH ROSE CAME TO TAINE MANOR WITH LITTLE, she left with much. Besides two heavy trunks filled with clothing, she left with small gifts from peasants, servants, and the elderly knights. Her heart ached when she gazed up at the tower that had been her home for over half a year. She would miss the drafty, creaky ceiling and of course the cold wooden floors. Not to mention the odd brazier with its makeshift hood that Theo had designed and they had built together.

As much as she screamed about escaping these walls, when the time was here, her heart was filled with sadness and sorrow. The loud bleating drew her attention to the goat pen. There in a row were all the disciples, their small front hooves raised on the rail of the fence. Rose rushed over and gave each a scratch behind the ears. Oh, how she would miss them. Mayhap she should ask Theo if she could take Judas. After all, it was close to Easter and he would be given away. A loud bleat and a stamp of a hoof on the rail drew her to Judas.

Rose stooped and scratched his neck. A lone tear slipped down her cheek. "We are two of a kind, giving up on someone in great trial." When her attention drifted, Judas pawed her hand with his hoof. She smiled down at the goat and patted his head.

"He's always the greedy one."

Rose's heart kicked up its pace as she turned to see Theo standing slightly behind her with her father's parchments in hand. "Here." He held them out to her. "I forgot to give these to you last night. They are yours, and I know how much joy they bring to you."

An ache so great settled deep within her chest and stole her breath. "Nay, you keep them." Her hands covered his, and she relished in their warmth. "It will give you something else to read besides the scriptures."

He dropped his gaze to his boots. "I do not think I will have that much time to read anymore."

She squeezed his hands. "Do not say that. You must continue your studies. The weather is turning mild. Surely Lady Catherine will be happy to continue with you." A sick tug gripped Rose's stomach, and she wished she could call her words back. She had forgotten that Lady Catherine would be accompanying her to Rockbridge and would not return to these parts for at least a month or two.

The gracious man that he was, Theo did not give voice to her error. Instead, he nodded.

Tears pricked the back of her eyes. "Please," she said softly. "You would not accept Rockbridge's knights to stay and help with the keep and your other efforts, so you must keep my stories. Think of me when you read them."

His gaze mixed with hers. "I shall always think of you."

"There is one more thing I want you to have." Rose reached into a small sack tied at her waist and pulled out her worn childhood toy. "I want you to have this." She held out Bit with both hands.

Theo shook his head. "Rose, I can't take that. Your father brought it to you for comfort."

"I know, and now I am giving it to you for the same reason. I pray Bit will give you comfort when you are feeling low." A small smile tugged on her lips. "I also hope it reminds you of me often."

"I could never forget you," he said quietly.

She pushed Bit into his chest. "Nor I you, nonetheless, I want you to have him."

Theo's fingers brushed hers, sending a tender melancholy to her heart. His gaze locked with hers. "I shall cherish it always." He then quickly tucked the toy in his tunic.

Her lips quivered, and if she did not leave quickly, she would be in the throes of weeping and wailing as she was last eve. She let her hands drop to her sides. "When I am settled, I want you to come and visit me." How could she have said such a stupid thing? By that time it would be fall, and the roads would soon become treacherous again. Besides, he would never venture to Rockbridge, and in her heart, she knew Conrad would never allow her to come back here.

Yet, once again, he nodded.

Rose threw her arms around him, and he shuffled his feet to hold his balance. "I shall miss you."

Theo folded his left arm around her and managed to do the same with his right. "And I you," he said, his warm breath against her neck.

"Oh la, what a tender scene."

Rose pulled away from Theo's protection and shielded her eyes from the morning sun. There sitting on his horse and holding the reins of another sat Conrad with a haughty smile on his face. "Come, my dear. I do want to reach Crosswind before dark. Surely Sir Theodore understands the situation?"

For the third time, Theo nodded. And Rose wanted to throttle him.

Instead, she stepped to the horse and allowed one of the groomsmen to assist her. Once astride, she looked upon Theo, pressing every beautiful and imperfect thing about him to her heart.

They had not gone far when Conrad's smug mood lifted to one of merriment while hers drooped to the glooms. "Why so glum, Rose? Truly this should be a day of celebration, for you have left your captor forever."

Was that true? Was any woman born free of male control? For if truth be told, Conrad was soon to be her husband and Lord of Rockbridge and would have control over her as well. A sourness settled in her gut and brought a frown to her face.

Conrad moved his horse close to hers. "Mayhap we should ask Lady Catherine if a priest is available to wed us this day, instead of waiting until after Lent. For I swear I will perish if I do not make you mine this eve."

With a pull of the reins, Rose put some distance between them. "What you speak of is sacrilegious and could put both our souls in danger of hell's fire."

Conrad laughed and inched his mount closer. "Since when do you care what God thinks? We are both free of the bonds that kept us apart. I no longer have to spill my seed in a moth of a woman. Though marriage to Jocelyn had some benefits—I have a fine son and her holdings. I guess you are right. We should praise God for our abundant fortunes."

The day's heat could not sweep away the chill that crept up Rose's spine. "Pray tell, you must have loved Jocelyn a little? Otherwise surely you would not have married her?"

"How could I, after you. Nay, she was a pale comparison, though she was meek and compliant, which are always good virtues in a wife." He flashed Rose a brilliant smile. "Of course, you have more spirit, but I am certain you will not let that get in the way of pleasing me."

A curl of caution creased her insides. Did he jest? Surely he did not mean what he just said? A guard called from the front of the line. Conrad made his apologies and moved forward. Rose fell back until her horse trotted next to the cart where Agatha sat. The older woman chatted on and on while Rose tried to sort out her jumbled thoughts.

They arrived at Crosswind as the sun, giving off a pink and indigo glow, sunk in the western sky. Tired and out of sorts, Rose wanted nothing more than to take a nice warm bath and lie upon a soft pallet.

In the bailey, Lady Catherine waved a hand in greeting. "Welcome, welcome, Lady Rosemond and Sir Conrad. Come, I am sure you are tired and wish to freshen up."

After dismounting and handing her mare to a monk, Rose did not wait for Conrad but made her way to the gracious woman who stood at the entry of the great hall.

Immediately, Lady Catherine looped her arm through Rose's. "Tell me," she said in a low voice, "how fares Sir Theo?"

Not a question about the journey or about her betrothal. The first thing out of this great lady's mouth was a query about Theo. "He is doing well, my lady. All at Taine Manor are doing well."

"So I have been told by my son Hugh. He said that Sir Theo has almost purchased the manor outright and has been slowly fixing it up. I am so happy, for he was in a deep state of melancholy last summer. What a difference a year makes, or perhaps a woman makes." She winked as they crossed the threshold, and a servant handed Rose a cool drink.

"I am hoping it remains so."

"So do I, my dear. So do I." Lady Catherine patted Rose's arm. "I have given you Julian's room. You do remember it from the last time you were here, don't you?"

How could she not? Theo and she had fought over who should stay in the chamber. Rose nodded. "If it would not be too much trouble, I would like to bathe before we sup."

"But of course. I shall send up a tub and water. Now follow my servant and I shall attend Sir Conrad and his men." Lady Catherine hugged Rose. "We shall talk later."

Rose quickly followed the servant to the stairs when she heard Conrad enter the hall. Why she wished to flee him after years of wishing to be with him, she did not know. But nonetheless, she could not get up the stairs fast enough and into the safety of her room.

After her bath, Rose lay on the bed, thankful that the

monks would be at vespers before having a light meal, or mayhap they would have no meal at all since this was Lent. In either case, Rose did not rise until she heard a faint knock on her door.

"Who is it?" she asked.

"'Tis Lady Catherine. Come to help you dress."

Only in a castle full of monks would the lady of the keep offer to help a guest to dress. Rose opened the door, and Lady Catherine swept into the room. Her smile quickly turned to a frown. "You have not laid out a gown to wear?"

Rose took a heavy breath. "I am quite tired. Perhaps I should forgo this evening's meal."

With a laugh, Lady Catherine folded her arms. "A wise choice. I had to fight with the cook to slaughter a few chickens for Sir Conrad and his men, for usually during Lent our supper is nothing but watered-down pottage and tough bread. Still, I cannot shake the feeling that something else is bothering you."

With a shrug, Rose made her way back to the bed and gazed up at the tapestry of the praying boy. "If only it were that simple," she whispered.

"Did you say something?" Lady Catherine walked over to the bed and sat down next to Rose. "You know that is Julian when he was a little boy. Even then I knew he would serve God above all others. He found great solace in prayer."

"I am sure he did." Rose let her fingers glide over the tiny silver cross around her neck before she swiveled her gaze to Lady Catherine. "But if one hasn't prayed in a long time, it is hard. And I am not sure God wants to hear what that person has to say."

"You may not know this, but the scriptures say we should pray without ceasing. God wants us to bring our petitions to him. Look at you. Did you not pray over and over to be wed to Sir Conrad? And here, it has come true." Lady Catherine grabbed one of Rose's hands. "Is that not wonderful!"

Rose bit her lower lip and dropped her gaze to the coverlet. A long pause ensued.

"Or am I wrong in my thinking?" Lady Catherine asked softly.

A heaviness filled Rose's heart, and she felt the sting of tears within her eyes. "I did not pray at all. I was angry at God when my mother died, but I gave up on God because I thought he had denied me of my true love. I begged him to allow Conrad and me to be together. God answered that prayer by sending me away to a convent. I thought God didn't care about me and wished for me to be unhappy."

"But He did not deny you forever. For here you are, ready to wed the very man. For some reason, God wanted you to wait. Perhaps to see and learn something you did not know before."

Theo's rugged and twisted face flashed in Rose's mind. Had it not been for that man's patience, she would still be a bitter selfish woman. Aye, God may have rewarded Theo by giving him Taine Manor, but his dreams of gaining respect for his mind through his heating contraption were lost. Her heart lurched. He had given up much for her. Forever he would be known as the cripple who lived on the edge of the wetlands.

"Aye, I have learned much," Rose whispered. A lone tear slipped down her cheek, and she quickly brushed it away.

Lady Catherine wrapped her arms around Rose. "I know not why you cry when you should be joyous, but God does. Perhaps you should spend this eve alone in prayer." Lady Catherine rose from the bed. "I will have one of the servants bring you some pottage and bread. Fear not, for I am certain by the morn God will make all things clear to you." The door latch clicked shut, and Rose was left with her thoughts. Once again her fingers touched her mother's necklace. Mayhap she had been wrong about God. Mayhap she had been wrong about many things.

Neither prayers nor sleep would come. Rose stared out the narrow window and watched the full moon slip from one side of the sky to the other. Soon it would be gone from the heavens altogether and would not return until another day had passed.

Trying desperately to find the peace she needed, Rose threw a cloak over her shift and slipped out of her chamber, through the hall, to the battlements. The crisp early morning air brought goosebumps to her skin and cleared her mind. The stars twinkled in the cloudless night. No doubt, Theo was out there trying to raise his infernal sword. The thought sobered her. Was this how it would be? Every little thing would point back to Theo?

A bold arm circled her waist. "Do you not know it is dangerous to flee through the hall in the middle of the night?" he whispered in her ear, his breath rank with stale wine. "Good fortune that I could not make it to my chamber, for if I had, we would not be here—alone." His hand slipped upward as he tried to cup her breast.

Rose struggled and tried to pull away from him. "Cease this. It is unseemly and wrong."

Through her cloak, he gave her breast a painful squeeze. "Nay, this is not wrong. In a fortnight, we will be husband and wife. Who is to know if we indulge in the pleasurable fruits a little beforehand? Come, Rose. Let us find a quiet place, for I am heavy with need for you." He pushed her hand to the bulge in his breeches.

Fear clogged a scream in her throat. With all her might, she pushed him away. "God will know," she shouted.

Conrad put a finger to his lips. "Shh, Rose. You will wake the whole keep up. Is that what you want?"

Aye, she did. Anything to help stay Conrad's lude advances. A memory came roaring back to her, to another time when she had been fondled thusly, without her consent. Her mother had died… She backed away slowly.

"What is the matter with you? You used to enjoy my kisses. Now you act like a coy virgin, or mayhap you have become a shrew." He stepped closer and let his fingers wrap around one of her long dark curls. "Your hair is magnificent. It is what attracted me to you the first time I laid eyes on you." He lifted the curl to his nose. "It smells sweet like a wave of scented flowers being blown through the fresh air, and yet it is so womanly. I only need to rekindle the desire that used to burn bright within you." He stepped forward, and the moonlight caught the lecherous glow in his eyes. A glow that had always been there but that she had refused to see. She had been blinded by his outward appearance, never looking deep within. His heart was dark and black.

Her legs became weak with fright, and she held up a shaking hand. "Conrad, please. I can't, not here, not now."

He pulled her into his arms again. "I should have taken you the first night at Taine. I wanted to, you know. But that lump, Sir Theodore, caught me near the tower steps. The fool dragged me to look at his fool work in his shop. Babbled on about getting the idea from you. I should have struck him down there and taken you. Then you would not be so skittish now."

He captured her lips in a fierce kiss, not meant to offer love but to control. She squirmed, and he pulled up her cloak, searching for the hem of her shift. Rose pushed back. "Please, Conrad. Stop."

His hand drifted up her thigh. "You are so soft. I am a fortunate man. A lush wife and Rockbridge. This time I will get both prizes instead of only one."

His words gave her strength. Rose pushed against his chest and then slapped him in the face.

Instantaneously, he released her and cupped his cheek. "Is this any way to treat your future husband?" he roared.

Rose's whole body shook as she adjusted her cloak. "Tell me, Conrad, what do mean *only one?*"

He did not answer but stood with his smug smile. Voices could be heard down below.

"All those years ago, we could have been married. Couldn't we?" she shouted back.

An easy-natured mask fell over his lustful face. He held up both hands and stepped forward. "Be reasonable, Rose. How was I to know your father would truly disown you if we married? I thought he jested until he showed me the completed will. It said I could have you, but not Rockbridge. He even melted the wax and dipped his seal, ready to lay us penniless. Can you imagine? The man was mad."

"We could have been together," she whispered. "But you didn't love me enough to give up what you wanted the most." And then in the early morning light her eyes shone with the truth. This is not where she should be.

Rose hurried to the battlement steps just as a few knights and monks were ascending the stairs. She scurried through the hall and into her chamber. Quickly she donned a woolen brown bliaut.

"What's going on?" a sleepy Lady Catherine said from the doorway.

Rose jammed her feet into a pair of leather boots. "Quick. I need your help."

Twenty-seven

*When thou goest out to battle against thine enemies,
and seest horses, and chariots, and a people more than thou,
be not afraid of them: for the Lord thy God is with thee,
which brought thee up out of the land of Egypt.*
Deuteronomy 20:1

WEAT POURED FROM THEO'S BROW AS HE TRIED TO help Sir Rupert and Sir Gregory mop out the stable. They had all become lazy while some of Rockbridge's strong knights resided at Taine. Now that the knights were gone, all who were left had to add to their duties.

Sir Rupert plopped down on a bale of hay and wiped his forehead with a dirty rag. "Mayhap you should get Daniel back. With his help, we would have had this done in no time."

"Nay. The lad will stay with Sir Hugh where he can have a future." Spasms shook Theo's bad leg as pain flooded the appendage. He leaned against a stall and slowly massaged his thigh.

"You should not be doing this type of work," Sir Gregory said.

"Aye, I should. For it was my decision to let Lady Rose and Daniel leave. I'll not have you suffer alone for my choices." He did not add that Sir Gregory's duties in the workshop were finished as there were other more important duties to do—keeping Taine Manor afloat.

Sir Rupert rose and stretched his weary back. "Nay, it is our choice to stay. Therefore, any burdens this keep gives are ours to bear."

The spasms ceased, and Theo straightened as best he could. "And I am grateful."

Before further comment could be made, a shout came from the courtyard drawing their attention. With haste, they left the stable. "A lone rider approaches," called a guard.

"Any colors?" Theo asked.

The guard shielded his eyes from the afternoon sun. "I-I believe it is a woman. Methinks it is Lady Rose!"

By the holy saints, the man must have it wrong. Rose would not be traipsing through the countryside alone. Nonetheless, Theo ordered the gate to be opened, and sure as Christ died for mankind's sins, Rose did indeed ride into the courtyard on a lathered up destrier. Sir Conrad's destrier to be exact.

"Shut the gate and bring me a rope," she cried before quickly dismounting, throwing the reins to Sir Rupert.

An odd sensation rolled through Theo's chest, but he could not discern if it was pain or pleasure. Why would she return? A sickness entered his gut. Had Conrad harmed her? Though her hair lay matted against her face and dirt and dust smudged her cheeks, her limbs looked strong and nary could a scratch be seen. Yet that did not mean she was not hurt in other ways. Even though he was covered in sweat, his blood ran cold.

She came toward him and grabbed his upper arms. "We must get ready. Lady Catherine and Agatha are not far behind me, but they shall approach from the back of the manor, for I fear Conrad is not far behind them."

As if she had not left and was allowed to give command, Sir Gregory brought her a rope. "My lady, what shall we do with this?"

She turned slightly. "Take it to the back wall and watch for a cart to approach. It will carry Lady Catherine and Agatha. If Sir Conrad is hot on their heels, we will have to use the rope to pull them up." Sir Gregory nodded and took off to the rear of the manor.

Theo finally found his tongue. "What is all this, Rose? Why would Lady Catherine flee her home? Has Sir Conrad caused you harm?"

She waved him off and started heading to the weaponry. "Yea and nay. He did try to make me a true wife before the vow was given, but he did not succeed."

A kick of anger twisted Theo's gut as he tried to keep pace with her. "Then he did try to harm you. I shall have his hide for this. He promised he would be a good and kind husband."

"Oh, please do not get noble on me now. He may have been full of lust, but I do not think he would have been a bad husband."

Theo paused his steps. If she still had feelings for the man, then why did she run away? Why was she always so complex? "Rose. What is going on?"

"We cannot tarry. We have to keep watch for Lady Catherine," Rose said as she began ordering knights and servants to the walls. "She helped me escape. Her and Agatha too."

This was more than Theo could take in. "Why the change of heart? I thought you loved the man." Theo winced as the last remark came out in a low roar.

"I have finally seen the truth, which you knew all along but did not tell me." She entered the weaponry, and he followed. "Now what do we have here? A spear and a few very old bows." Rose held up a bow and wrinkled her nose. "Ack. This will not do." Quickly she tossed the bow aside and began rummaging through a pile of dull daggers. "We only need to hold off Conrad until Sir Hugh arrives with his men."

"Rose! Stop! What truth do you speak of? Why have you suddenly rejected the man you have desired for most of your life?"

A rusty mace slipped from her fingers and landed on the floor with a thud. "You knew, as did my father, that Conrad wanted to be Lord of Rockbridge someday more than he wanted me. Why would you consent to give me to such a man? I thought you cared about me."

Her eyes flashed with fury, and he could not look away. "I-I thought you loved him. I said I would not stand in the way of your choice. I only wanted you to be happy. That is all I have ever wanted."

"Aye. I know that now." Her lower lip trembled, and she turned back to the old weapons on a table. "You should have been more selfish. We can talk more on this later; right now we must get ready, for I am certain Conrad will not let me go without a fight." She picked up the spear and brushed past him.

With quick action, he caught her upper arm with his left hand. "What does this mean? Are you staying?"

She paused but would not look at him. "Not now, Theo. Later. We must hurry." With that, she quit the weaponry with Theo staring at her back.

Later, when the golden sun's rays began to slip away, another shout rang out in the courtyard. As expected, a cart was spotted at the back wall and did, indeed, carry Lady Catherine and Agatha, but no others were spotted behind them. Theo took a chance and told them to enter through the front gate. Once inside, Rose hugged the pair and they made their way to the great hall. Theo followed, ordering Sir Rupert and the other knights to keep a vigilant watch.

Theo did not sit as the three women found their way to a trestle table, clucking like a bunch of hens in a coop. "Ladies," he said politely. They did not cease their chatter. "Ladies," he added more forcefully. They brattled on. "Ladies!" His loud voice echoed off the rafters and brought the silence he desired.

All three looked upon him as if he were mad.

He cleared his throat and straightened as best he could. "Now then. I need a full account as to what has happened."

Rose folded her arms across her chest and tipped her head to the side. "I told you. Lady Catherine and Agatha helped me to escape."

Lady Catherine's blue eyes shined bright with anger and excitement. "I told Conrad that Rose was upset and needed a long rest after what he tried to do."

"I gave him and the guards a mug of nice, laced mead so they would sleep like babes," Agatha added.

"I then snuck out, taking the fastest horse I could find." Rose smiled.

No doubt adding more salt to Sir Conrad's already wounded pride. The man would be full of vengeance when he arrived. There would be no telling what he might do to Rose if he got his hands on her.

"I knew Conrad would blame Lady Catherine and Agatha when he found out I was missing. He would hold both for ransom for my return. Therefore, they had to flee too." Rose and Lady Catherine exchanged a warm glance.

"Fear not," Lady Catherine said. "I sent word to Hugh for help. All will be fine once he arrives with his men."

All three ladies gave a satisfactory nod. Theo was not as convinced. Hugh's place lay more than a half-day's ride past Crosswind. Sir Conrad would be at the gate long before Sir Hugh's arrival. And one thing was certain, Conrad de Laval would rip down every log of timber to get at his bride.

"My lord, my lord." Sir Gregory ran into the hall. "An army of torches has been spotted. They are coming this way."

Twenty-eight

Greater love hath no man than this,
that a man lay down his life for his friends.
John 15:13

ALL NIGHT LONG THEO WATCHED THE FLICKERING torches fill in the fields in front of Taine Manor. The tactic was done for intimidation, to show strength and power, but it also showed Sir Conrad's full lot. A smart tactician would have held some back, circling the keep. However, being young, he did not think like a seasoned warrior. There was the only advantage Theo had.

"I wager there is at least a hundred of them. Rockbridge knights are with him also." Sir Rupert spat on the ground. "Pack of traitors."

"Do not be so hard on them," Theo said, never taking his eyes off the threat in front of them. "Who knows what tale Sir Conrad may have told? More than likely they think we have kidnapped Lady Rose."

"I knew that man could not be trusted from the moment I set my eyes on him...sweet like a drop of honey in a bee's hive."

"Aye, and the worker bees are in front of us right now. We don't have the manpower to hold them off."

"Too bad we don't have a priest. For then you could marry her. That may not stop Sir Conrad's men, but it would give Rockbridge's knights pause." Sir Rupert shook his head. "I should have taken a knife to him when I had the chance."

The thought of forcing Rose into marriage curled Theo's gut. Doing so would make him as disgusting as Sir Conrad. "You would have been hung. Nay, that would have solved nothing but would have caused Rose much anguish. However, I have an idea. Follow me." Theo turned and left the gate wall, making his way to the great hall with Sir Rupert at his side.

There he found the ladies still huddled by the hearth. Rose stood. "We have a plan." Lady Catherine and Agatha nodded.

"Do you now," Theo said, more to be polite than interested in what they had to say.

"Aye. We may not have pitch to heat, but we have some water. We'll boil it and send it over the wall." Rose nodded her head; the ladies did the same.

Theo glanced at Sir Rupert who just shook his. "There are Rockbridge men fighting with Conrad. Some of the finest knights in England."

Rose beamed with a proud smile before thinking through what that meant.

"They will know we may attempt such a trick. Taine is made mostly of timber, it will not take much to burn us out or pull the walls down."

"We only have to hold them off until Hugh gets here," Lady Catherine offered.

"My lady, I mean no disrespect, but this keep will fall long before Sir Hugh arrives. I wager Sir Conrad will hold you for a fine ransom. And I do not doubt that he has one of Crosswind's priests with him. He'll force Lady Rose to wed before the sun sets. By nightfall, Sir Conrad de Laval will become one of the most powerful barons in England. He'll set the de Maury's against him and possibly the king."

Lady Catherine put a hand to her chest. "He'll start a civil war."

"Aye, and not knowing the ramifications until it is too late." Theo turned to Rose. "What we need is to get you and Lady Catherine as far away from here as possible."

"He'll be expecting something like that. I doubt I can sneak away from him twice." Rose tapped a finger to her chin. "There must be something else we can try."

"There is." Theo filled his lungs with a breath of air, then let it whoosh out. "At first light I will challenge Sir Conrad—winner take all. Lady Catherine and you will slip out the back with Sir Rupert. He knows the wetlands. You will hide there until Sir Hugh arrives."

Rose paled. "You'll be killed." She folded her arms over her chest. "I will not do it."

Theo reached out and gently touched her cheek. "You must. There is more at stake here than my life. Many will suffer if a war breaks out. Surely you do not want that?"

Her blue-grey eyes clouded with a rain of tears. She bit her lip and looked away. "This is all my fault."

Lady Catherine rose and took her into her arms. "Nay. These are the games men play for power. We are but pawns." She looked over Rose's shoulder at Theo. "We will all do what is necessary."

Theo nodded, not taking his gaze off Rose's shaking shoulders. He wanted to take her in his arms and console her. He wanted to tell her that he loved her more than he had ever cared for anyone else. But what would any of that do? Make her feel worse. Better to state the plan and then carry it out.

Theo turned to Agatha and Sir Rupert. "Once Lady Catherine and Lady Rose are away, make sure everyone here is cordial to Sir Conrad. Make him think you have all been waiting for a strong powerful lord. In secret, tell the servants and our knights to spread the word what really happened to Lady Rose and why she fled Sir Conrad. Many of Rockbridge's knights are honorable men. They may be swayed to change their allegiance to Sir Hugh."

"Would be easier if you just killed the whelp," Sir Rupert choked.

Theo took the man in his arms and patted him on the back. "Always, keep her safe," Theo whispered. He then let his gaze drift to Rose. Her long lashes were soaked with tears, and her lips a lush red. Small hiccups left her throat as her chest rose and fell. He longed to cup her cheek and tell her all would be well. Instead, he turned to his solar to find his sword.

Of course, she could not let their last meeting be sweet. Rose screamed and yelled outside his solar until Theo couldn't take anymore. He opened the door. "Get out of here, woman. Haven't you done enough?" His heart all but shattered when he saw the pain his words caused her.

She fell to her knees and clutched her chest. Her eyes brimming with sorrow. "I-I'm sorry," she cried. "I never wanted to hurt you."

If she did not leave, Theo knew he would crush her to him, and then he would never be able to let her go. "Lady Catherine," he barked into the hall. "Take her away from here. She disturbs the rest I need."

With a sympathetic look, Lady Catherine gently lifted Rose off the floor. "Come, my dear. Sir Theo needs his time, and we must get ready to leave."

This time, Rose fell into Lady Catherine's arms like a slop cloth. Rose looked over her shoulder at Theo with pleading eyes. He answered the only way he knew how, by slamming the door. Then he wept and prayed for most of the night.

As dawn approached, he gave up one more prayer. *Dear Heavenly Father, forgive your unworthy servant of all the injustices I have ever committed. Guard and protect Lady Rose. Allow her to have a long and happy life with a man that she loves and with a man that loves her. I ask all this in your Son's name who died for our sins. Amen.* When finished, he grabbed his sword in his left hand and thumped out of the hall to the gate wall.

As expected, in the early morning light, Sir Conrad rode forward and called for a full surrender. But naturally Theo, being the older, smarter man, couldn't help but goad the young knight. "I see you have returned Lady Rosemond's knights. How kind of you, Sir Conrad. You can send them along at any time and then be on your way. I thank thee."

Conrad strutted a borrowed horse in front of the gate, his sword glistening in his hand. "I do not have time for your impudence, cripple. Return Lady Rosemond and you may live."

Oh, the lad was sporting for a fight. Did he truly believe he could gain honor in fighting a few elderly knights and, what did he call him? A cripple. Well then, this broken-down hull had better teach the boy a lesson.

"De Laval, Lady Rosemond told me you kiss like a sloppy sow, and she would rather return to Godstow than to be wed to a pig like you." Guffaws could be heard from those inside Taine's walls as well in the ranks behind Sir Conrad.

"Come down here and say those words, you grotesque bundle of worm food." When not a soul chuckled at that remark, Sir Conrad's face twisted up like a mangled tree root.

Theo did nothing.

"Do you hear me, you sack of rot? Come and fight me!" Conrad's horse pranced and rose on its hind legs.

Again, Theo did nothing.

Conrad dismounted and walked close to the gate wall. "Will you let all within perish because you are a coward? Fight me."

"I could put an arrow in his neck, and we could be done with his prattle," Sir Gregory said with a pointed bow.

"That would just lead to useless bloodshed. I have no intentions of making Sir Conrad a fallen hero this day by starting a war. Nay. I think the whelp has stewed long enough. Remember what I ordered—when I am gone, sway the Rockbridge knights to our thinking."

Sir Gregory grabbed Theo's shoulder. "It has been a pleasure to have you as lord. I have had none greater."

Theo nodded as his throat clogged with emotion. He slapped Sir Gregory on the back, then stood and made his way to the gate.

Twenty-nine

Delight thyself also in the Lord;
and he shall give thee the desires of thine heart.
Psalm 37:4

AS THE GATE SLOWLY CREAKED OPEN, THEO LOOKED up at the blue morning sky. It was going to be a glorious spring day. A wonderful day to meet his Lord and Savior. But before he would see God, Theo had to make sure Rose was safe and out of danger. Therefore, he would have to keep Sir Conrad busy for a considerable amount of time.

Heavenly Father, be with your servant this day. Theo gripped his sword with as much strength his left hand would give him and marched out of the gate. Beyond stood Sir Conrad, his chain mail hood glittering in the sunlight like a crown of glory. Aye, that probably would be the tale the barbs would sing. The golden Sir Conrad slayed the ugly beast to save his lady love. That may be what others saw, but Theo's vision showed a different picture; he felt like David before Goliath.

"Well, well. So the monster wishes to fight after all. Conrad gripped his broadsword in both hands. "Then come, let us finish this quickly. For I have much to do this day."

A wing of gold caught Theo's attention as he noticed a small goldfinch make its way to where a wren perched. The birds sat side by side and sung their sweet songs. How odd for a beautiful finch to sit in peace next to a round brown wren. Perhaps it was just a brief coincidence, but Theo wanted to believe the beautiful bird flew to the wren on purpose.

"Come, now! Why do you tarry? I shall make your death swift. Lift your sword."

Death. Aye. Swift. Not if he could help it. Theo lifted his sword and growled. The whelp turned almost white. Good. If Conrad feared but a little, then Theo would have a small advantage…for the moment.

Even with his twisted right leg, Theo charged forward, screaming like a madman. Conrad held his sword frozen in front of him. The muscles in Theo's back shrieked with pain as he raised his sword with his left hand and struck the blade against Conrad's. Stunned by the onslaught, the younger knight stumbled back. There would only be a moment before Conrad's wits returned. Again, Theo used all his might to raise his sword and again struck the full blade of Conrad's weapon. The younger knight stumbled back and fell to one knee.

All present cheered. Sir Conrad quickly rose and gripped his sword, swaying side to side clearly assessing his opponent in a different light. The lad clenched his teeth. "So the monster has claws after all."

Theo clumped left as Conrad swiftly switched right and struck Theo's sword hard on the blade. With lightning speed, Conrad swung around; at the last moment, Theo raised his weapon. The blade caught on the edge of Conrad's sword.

The younger knight's eyes flared with the triumph. Yet, Theo wasn't about to give in, not yet. He took a deep breath and again raised his sword over and over against Conrad's. Twist left and right. Strike at the midsection and twist up. Theo's mind had all the moves…but the body did not.

Conrad deflected each blow and finished by cutting Theo's left forearm. The wound was minor, but the sight drove Conrad into a bloodlust. The young knight's blade slammed against Theo's. A slick trail of blood traveled to the hilt of Theo's sword. Another hard strike brought Theo to his knees. It would not be long now. Theo raised the sword once more and caught Conrad's shin.

Blood spotted the younger knight's breeches and caused a fury. "Why, you insufferable beast. This shall end now!"

Theo dropped his head, waiting for the blade to strike. *Father, accept your servant.*

Whoosh, thump. "Aww."

Instead of feeling Conrad's blade against his neck, the lad lay next to him, blood oozing from the middle of his forehead. As quickly as possible, Theo made it to his feet.

There, with slingshot in hand, stood Rose. Rupert stood with his hands on his knees, panting.

"I told you to get her away," Theo growled.

"Aye, but she's as stubborn as a mule and runs like a rabbit," Rupert replied.

Lady Catherine showed up, equally winded.

"I thought you could use my help," Rose said softly, her gaze steady on Theo's.

Conrad groaned and pushed up on one elbow, touching the middle of his forehead. Theo put the tip of his blade against the young knight's neck. "Yield, de Laval. You have lost."

"Nay, 'tis unfair," he cried.

One of Rockbridge's knights dismounted and came to stand over Sir Conrad. "Aye. It was unfair to begin with. You have lost, Sir Conrad. We serve Lady Rosemond, and it is clear to us she does not wish to wed you." He then turned to Rose. "What is your will, my lady?"

Rose lifted her chin. "Sir Conrad's men will surrender their swords."

A low moan escaped Conrad's throat as blood continued to seep from his forehead.

"And get Sir Conrad some help," she said.

Immediately all the knights complied. Two came and hefted Conrad under the arms and carried him into the keep while Lady Catherine followed, giving orders on how to care for him. The other knights followed along with few mumblings.

Rose rushed to Theo's side. "You're hurt. You need help too. Let me call for a few more knights."

Theo jammed the tip of his sword into the dirt and rested on the hilt. "Nay. A small wound that will heal quick enough. I need to stay here and give thanks to my Lord."

Rose blinked and scowled. "Can that not wait until later?"

He shook his head. "Nay. I must thank God for sending David."

Her scowl turned into perplexity. "David? Who is he?"

"Not he, but she. For before me stands David who slayed Goliath."

Theo knew the moment understanding penetrated her mind. For her frown turned into a smile that even the angels could not rival.

Weary, but satisfied, Theo made his way to his solar. It had been a long day. Soon after the fight, Sir Rupert and Sir Gregory wanted to know what they should do with Sir Conrad. Theo wanted to return him to his ever-shrinking group of loyal knights, but doing so right off might prove to be a folly. Conrad was still stinging from his defeat and might retaliate immediately if set free. So they changed Theo's workshop into a makeshift jail. There they housed him and his captain, plus any of his men who would not willingly give up their arms. Conrad howled at the audacity of housing him with his men. If he kept up his prattle, his loyal men might turn on him as well.

What was truly amazing was how quickly all of Rockbridge's knights rallied around Rose once the true story was known. They returned to their old duties at the manor as if they had never left. One even offered to off Sir Conrad's head, which Rose quickly rejected. While Theo and some worked on ordering the manor, Agatha the cook slaughter a few more chickens, and a grand feast ensued.

Rose was hailed as a champion and was carried around the keep like a queen.

Indeed, Theo had not seen Rose so happy in a long time. But as the day turned into night, so the merriment into slumber. Only a few still laughed and told stories in the hall when Theo entered. His gaze flipped in every direction, to every corner, but Rose was not present. No doubt she too had retired for the evening, for it had been an exhausting day.

He made his way to his solar where a fiery blaze burned in the hearth, and the small table was laden with cheese, bread, and cold chicken. What stilled Theo's steps was Rose, standing behind his straight-back chair, her black hair fanned out around her shoulders.

"I have been waiting for you," she said softly.

His heart squeezed. In the deep recesses of his mind he wished she would have stayed with Sir Conrad; for now, Theo was not sure he would ever be able to let her go again. "I thought you had gone to bed. You had a long day."

"You did as well. Come, sit and eat. You must be famished." She held out the chair, and Theo winced as he thumped loudly to it.

Folding her hands, she stood like a dutiful wife behind him. *Wife!* The thought unsettled him; he reached for the pitcher of mead, but she was quicker and poured him a cup. "Here now, I can do that," he said. "Come join me."

"I have already eaten," she said.

Her voice so timid put Theo on his guard. He took a gulp of mead and then ripped a piece of dried bread in half. "Nonetheless, I do not want you standing behind me like a servant. Sit."

She hesitated and then complied, but she remained unusually quiet. He popped a hunk of bread in his mouth; it tasted like sand.

A tight smile crossed her lips. "So how is your heating works coming along?"

What was this? He slammed his fists on the table. "With all that happened this day, you ask about that? I would think we should be talking about what to do with your past love who sits in my workshop as we speak." She cringed a little but did not rally to a fight, which Theo sorely needed.

"I would think he will keep for a while," she said calmly, dropping her gaze to her lap.

Theo pulled a hand through his long hair. "All right, Rose. Out with it. Why are you here and not in your chamber? What do you wish to speak of that cannot wait until the morrow?"

At first she said not a word, and Theo believed she would rise to leave. Then slowly, she raised her chin and stared at him. "I wish to know what your plans are for my future?"

So that was it then; he still held guardianship over her, and she feared he would not be as generous as he had been in the past. He sat back in his chair. "You have nothing to fear. I'll not stand in your way. Rockbridge is yours, and I will only guide you when you ask for my help."

"Nay. That is not the problem." She dropped her long lashes, covering her smoky eyes.

Problem? What other problems did she see? Sir Conrad would be dealt with. Her future was secured unless she put herself in the hands of another fool. Was that what she feared—her judgment or that he would deny her true love? How could he deny her anything?

He shifted forward and placed his hands on the table, his good hand over his twisted one. "There are no problems. If you meet another man and you love him and he loves you, I'll not stand in your way. However, the next time, I will openly tell you what I think before you make your final decision. Your father believed I would keep you safe. I failed when I did not tell you the truth about Conrad—I believed he loved you, but—"

"But only if I came with my lands."

She said it so plainly his heart ached for her. "Your father would have let you leave that night if Sir Conrad would have taken you without your lands. But what you don't know is that it was a test. Your father would have accepted Sir

Conrad with open arms if he would have accepted you, first and foremost."

"My father…" Pain flickered across her face. "I did hurt him. Didn't I?"

"I think the hurt was on both sides. Neither of you spoke what was in your hearts. So the truth was never heard. Rest assured, he may not have known how you felt while he walked this earth, but he does now, for he is in God's kingdom."

Tears slipped down her face. "I pray that you are right. And I pray that God will forgive me too. I have been so vile to Him and to you."

Theo reached over and wiped the tears away. "Fear not. I was not harmed by your words or your actions. But I am thankful you have made it back to our Savior's side. Now then, let us not speak of this again until you have found another man to marry."

"Oh, but I have," she said brightly, a wide smile chasing away her tears.

Theo's gut rolled, and his chest ached as his heart all but crumpled. So quickly she found another? Where? At Crosswind or along the way? One of Sir Conrad's knights? How fickle was she to give her heart to another so easily? Theo shook inwardly. And how foolish was he to still desire her.

He cleared his dry throat. "Rose. Let us not jump into something right off. A lot has happened. Let us give this time."

She rolled her eyes. "We have had enough time. This time I am sure."

"You can't keep throwing yourself at every pretty face. I want to meet this man." Theo winced once more at the sharpness of his words.

Her lips quivered and then broke out into a huge smile. "I wouldn't say he has a pretty face, and we have given this a lot of time. And you do know him."

God's teeth. It could not be. Had she fallen in love with one of his elder knights? Sir Rupert or Sir Gregory? "An old man would not be a good husband. Think on that before you boldly choose again."

She rose from her chair and circled the table until she stood next to him. "He is not that old, and I think he would be the perfect husband." She leaned over and placed a long, glorious, tender kiss on Theo's lips.

He closed his eyes and took in the dream of her sweet, soft lips caressing his like lovers do. When she broke the kiss, he opened his eyes. "Rose? What does this mean?"

She brushed the hair off his face and gently let her fingers trace every line and every scar. "It means I love you. And I want to be your wife. If you will have me."

Theo stilled her hand on his face and placed it in his. "How can you love a beast, a monster, a cripple?"

She took his hand and hers and placed them on his heart. "Nay, I do not love a beast, but the most beautiful man that God has ever created. So then, do you approve of my choice?"

All he could do was nod, for his face was wet with tears, but his heart sang with the words—I love you.

Epilogue

I will praise thee, O Lord, with my whole heart;
I will shew forth all thy marvelous works.
Psalm 9:1

ITHIN A FEW DAYS, SIR HUGH ARRIVED WITH HIS army of knights only to find an orderly keep and his mother flirting with Sir Rupert. Rose couldn't be sure if the frown Sir Hugh wore was because he had been led on a merry chase or because Lady Catherine had a suitor. However, it did not take long for the frown to disappear when he learned about Rose and Theo's wedding.

In fact, the man became insufferable. Constantly teasing Theo, saying cruel things, such as Theo being a crusty mangy mutt or a sneaky fox. When Rose tried to reprimand Sir Hugh, he laughed all the more and so did Theo. Theirs was an odd friendship that she couldn't begin to comprehend.

Rose sighed as she saw the pair stride off to the stables. She did hope that Sir Hugh would not goad Theo into taking Triumph out for a gallop. Trying to take her mind off the mischievous pair, she headed for the goat pen, hoping to find Daniel who had returned home with Sir Hugh. But he was not within when she entered the shed. Instead, she found Jude sitting next to the goat Saint Peter.

"How wonderful to see you. Theo told me you had left for good." She went over, knelt, and gave Saint Peter a good scratch on the neck.

"I said he would not see me again, but I did not say I was

going anyplace. So, Lady Rosemond, I see you have seen with your heart and not just with your eyes."

She laughed loudly. "Aye, and I could not be happier. I think I always knew but could not give up on a dream a young girl had weaved."

Jude nodded. "It is the folly of many to look for something they think will make them happy when the joy is right before them."

"As usual, you are right. I am indeed full of joy." She sighed and playfully rolled her eyes. "Though I am getting slightly tired of Theo telling me he loves me constantly."

"You are not tired. It is written plainly on your face."

Again, she giggled. "I am sure it is. Things could not be better. Theo smiles all the time, and his mood is quite light."

"Mayhap that is because he is to be wed to the most beautiful maiden in the realm."

Rose blushed. "I would not say that."

Jude cocked his head to the side. "I would, and I should know. Come, let us take the goats out to the field."

Rose stood as more goats came to her side. "All right, I could use a walk."

Jude slowly rose, and all the goats dutifully crowded around him. "So I see Sir Conrad has left with not so much as a mutter."

"Aye, and with very few men. Theo did not think Conrad needed additional punishment since it has spread through the kingdom that he was bested by a woman and a cripple." Rose paused. "Though I don't see what is wrong with that."

Jude stopped at the shed entrance as the goats filled the pen. "Neither do I."

Just then Theo emerged from the stable with Sir Hugh, and sure enough, a groomsman followed holding Triumph's reins.

"Oh no. Theo won't be prudent with Sir Hugh watching. Look see, I can tell his leg is really bothering him this day. Sometimes his pride still gets the better of him."

Jude nodded. "But his heart beats with love."

"Aye. I am happy with the way he is, but since our betrothal has been announced, he is trying so hard to act like, as he says it, a whole man." She shrugged and sighed again. "I just don't know what to do with him."

"Mayhap you should pray for him." Jude opened the gate, and the goats walked orderly out of the pen.

"I do pray for him all the time," she said.

"Nay. Pray for healing."

Rose looked at the man she had always considered wise. "He cannot be healed. He pleases me fine this way."

Jude closed the pen gate behind them but did not move. "This is not about you but about him. Pray for him to be healed, for he will not pray for himself. You must remember, with God all things are possible according to His purpose."

Rose gazed into Jude's translucent eyes but realized she had never truly made out his face. "All right. I will pray every day that God will heal my future husband, for I am completely devoted to him and am eternally blessed."

"Rose. Come and ride with us." Theo hefted himself on Triumph's back without help. "Did you see that?" she said, but when she turned, Jude was already through the gate with the goats waddling behind him. Surely he would not mind taking the goats out alone.

"All right," she called to Theo. "Do not leave without me."

"Never, my love. I will never go anywhere without you," Theo called while Sir Hugh chuckled.

Rose ran to the stable praising God for giving her the desires of her heart.

If you enjoyed this book,
please consider reviewing it where you purchased it.

Excerpt from

A LIFE NOT TAKEN

Secrets of the Queens, Book 1

OLIVIA RAE

Prologue

❦

February 12, 1554
Tower of London

$\mathscr{J}$OHN FECKENHAM, CHAPLAIN TO QUEEN MARY donned his heavy black cloak before clasping his sweaty palms together. He dropped to his knees and offered up one last prayer for the poor soul whose death this day would ease many minds. All this could have been avoided had Lady Jane Grey returned to the true faith. Yet, she had not. He would miss their lively doctrinal conversations for she did have a quick mind. The pity they could not continue in this fashion for another month or so. But he had failed to make Jane see the errors of her faith and she would not give up the church of her great-uncle, Henry the VIII for the true Catholic religion.

John placed his cap upon his head and slowly made his way to Gentleman Gaoler's quarters where Jane had been staying since she had been deposed. Though a satisfactory place within the Tower, it still held an unfortunate view of the Tower Green where her scaffold had been constructed.

Sir John Brydges, Lieutenant of the Tower was waiting by Lady Jane's door. A grim line creased his lips. From within the house, the weeping and wailing of Mrs. Ellen and

Mrs. Tilney twisted Feckenham's heart. All knew their parts to play. The question was did the fair Lady Jane?

John Feckenham followed Sir Bridges into the room. "It is time, my lady," Brydges said kindly.

The woman flinched as if Brydges words were a hard lash. Dressed in the black gown and dark French hood Lady Jane wore at her trial, the dried-eyed woman finally nods. In her hands she held a prayer book and a crumpled piece of parchment, no doubt her final words. As she departed the home and walked to the scaffold her lips moved slowly, though no words could be discerned—almost as if she were rehearsing the lines to a tragedy.

Few were present to watch this spectacle unfold, after all, Lady Jane did have royal blood coursing through her veins and her death was not subject for public display. We walked on in silence until we came to the steps of the scaffold. She turned, our gazes locked briefly. "God grant you all your desires and accept my own hearty thanks for all your attention to me. Although indeed, those attentions have tried me more than death can now terrify me."

Her words swirled through Feckenham's head and tied his tongue. Before his voice returned, she had ascended the scaffold stairs. With quick steps he followed.

She stood, her back ramrod straight as she fumbled with the parchment in her shaking hands. Slowly she began to address the small assembly. "Good people, I am come hither to die, and by a law I am condemned to the same. The fact against the queen's Highness was unlawful, and the consenting thereunto by me: but, touching the procurement and desire thereof by me, or on my behalf, I do wash my hands thereof in innocency before God, and the face of you, good Christian people, this day.

"I pray you all, good Christian people, to bear me witness that I die a true Christian woman, and that I do look to be saved by no other mean, but only by the mercy of God, in the blood of his only Son Jesus Christ: and I confess, that when I did know the word of God, I neglected the same, loved myself and the world; and therefore this plague and punishment is happily and worthily happened unto me for my sins; and yet I thank God, that of his goodness he hath thus given me a time and respite to repent.

"And now, good people, while I am alive, I pray you assist me with your prayers."

Here then she knelt and turned once again. "Shall I say this Psalm?"

"Yea," Feckenham said and hoped the woman could read the words as practice. She turned back to her prayer book and began to recite the fifty-first Psalm. He followed her English words with his Latin. When done, she rose and gave a timid smile. "God I beseech Him abundantly reward you for your kindness to me."

Feckenham could feel a heat creep up the back of his neck though the day was brisk. How had he been kind? Oh if only there had been another way.

As instructed, the woman handed her gloves and handkerchief to her attendants and her prayer book to Thomas Brydges, the lieutenant's brother. She removed her hood and began to untie her gown when the executioner stepped forward.

Startled, she stepped back. "I desire you to leave me alone."

Had she forgotten that her clothing would become the executioner's property?

Quickly her attendants came to her aid and helped with the unlacing. At least this small disaster had been avoided.

Feckenham looked around the green, but none seemed to think the behavior odd. Perhaps they had written it off to nerves instead of a queen forgetting her duty before her executioner. He breathed a sigh of relief. All would continue has planned.

A cloth was given to the woman to fasten about her eyes. The executioner came forward and knelt down. "My lady, I beg your forgiveness."

"You are forgiven," she said in a soft voice.

There was nothing else to be done. "My lady," the executioner said, "Please stand upon the straw."

She hesitated and her eyes grew wide as she stared at the block. Feckenham thought for sure she would bolt. But she did not.

"I pray you dispatch me quickly," she whispered before kneeling. Again she paused. "Will you take it off before I lay me down?"

"No, Madame," he answered just as quiet.

With shaking fingers she tied the kerchief across her eyes and began to fumble about with her hands, looking for the block. "What shall I do? Where is it?" she cried.

All about looked on in horror, if this did not conclude swiftly who knows what mischief would be had. Without further thought, Feckenham guided her to the block.

She lowered her head and uttered her last words, "Lord into thy hands I commend my spirit."

With a swift swing of the axe, by all accounts, Lady Jane Grey was dead.

Dear Reader,

The Sword and The Cross Chronicles has come to an end and I want to thank my fans for all your support and encouragement over the years; without you this series would have ended long ago. I feel truly blessed to be able to write romantic Christian stories for such a wonderful audience.

If you enjoy contemporary fiction, consider checking out *Joshua's Prayer*. It's an inspirational story that is sure to warm your heart without too many tears. You can find it via my website www.oliviaraebooks.com

To those of you who love historical novels, have no fear, a new series will be coming out very soon. I hope you are looking forward to taking a trip to Tudor England. It looks to be quite an exciting ride.

Finally, the future of an author's success relies on the approval of her fans. If you have enjoyed any or all of my books, please consider leaving a review where you have purchased them. A few kind words, even a word or two, can go a long way. Thanks so much.

Until next time...abundant blessings,

Olivia Rae

OLIVIA RAE is an award-winning author of historical and contemporary inspirational romance. She spent her school days dreaming of knights, princesses and far away kingdoms; it made those long, boring days in the classroom go by much faster. Nobody was more shocked than her when she decided to become a teacher. Besides getting her Master's degree, marrying her own prince, and raising a couple of kids, Olivia decided to breathe a little more life into her childhood stories by adding in what she's learned as an adult living in a small town on the edge of a big city. When not writing, she loves to travel, dragging her family to old castles and forts all across the world.

Olivia is the winner of the Golden Quill Award, New England Readers' Choice Award, and the American Fiction Awards. She is an Illumination Award Bronze medalist and she is a finalist in many other contest such as the National Readers' Choice Awards and the National Excellence in Romance Fiction Awards. She is currently hard at work on her next novel.

Contact Olivia at Oliviarae.books@gmail.com
For news and sneak peeks of upcoming novels visit:
Oliviaraebooks.com

Made in the USA
Middletown, DE
03 March 2020

85566481R00149